Maddie stiffened her chin. She was prepared to continue their argument. "You want to talk to me?"

"Mandisa," he started. He remembered what she'd told him about talking to her while wearing his hat, and pulled it from his head. "Have you heard the rumors about me?" He stepped up to her desk.

"I have," she answered quietly, eyeing him suspiciously.

"Most of them are true." He waited for her response, thinking she might fear him and demand he leave.

Her expression didn't change. After a minute, she said, "Is there anything else?"

He rolled the brim of his Stetson between his fingers. This wasn't as easy as he thought it would be. "I'm thirty-two years old, and I've never been married. I haven't dated seriously since right after college. That didn't go too well, and no woman has interested me since." He dropped his eyes. "Well, not until you." He wasn't expressing his thoughts adequately. He should have practiced what he would say. "I'm not dangerous," he said to persuade her. He planted his feet and waited for her response, then realized he hadn't asked a question.

"I'm not afraid of you."

"Good."

"I'm glad we cleared everything up." She stood and took her coat off the back of the door.

He cleared his throat to get her attention.

She turned to him, buttoning her coat. "Is there something else, Chevy?"

"Would you like to go to the movies with me?"

Her fingers froze on the top button of her coat. "Are you asking me out on a date?"

He widened his stance. "Yes."

KIMBERLEY WHITE

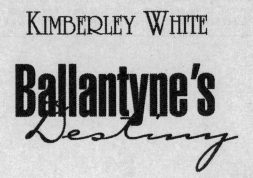

Ballantyne's *Destiny*

ARABESQUE®

BALLANTYNE'S DESTINY

An Arabesque novel

ISBN 1-58314-667-9

© 2006 by Kimberley White

www.kimanipress.com

Printed in U.S.A.

Chapter 1

"We have a problem."

"What kind of problem?" Chevy Ballantyne asked as he made himself comfortable in his older brother Greyson's den. "This family seems to have nothing but problems anymore."

Greyson ignored his observation. Chevy had been told his attitude wasn't the greatest lately.

"It's Pop." Greyson took a seat next to him on the sofa. "Kirkland told me something . . . I can't let it go." Greyson was the cerebral oldest brother, always cool and in charge. For him to be worried, it had to be something serious. As the youngest brother, Kirkland was often the source of trouble.

"What's going on?"

Greyson's eyes narrowed. "Kirkland told me about a rumor. Pop and Eileen Putnam."

"Pop and Eileen Putnam, what? What kind of rumor?"

"Kirkland said he saw it himself." Greyson's words were tight, spoken through clenched teeth. "Pop and Eileen after her husband died. Kirkland says Mama knew. Said he was going to kill Pop until Alex stopped him."

Chevy ran a callused hand over a two-days-thick chin stubble. He cursed. The action was so uncharacteristic of him, Greyson shrank back in surprise.

"Pop doesn't know Mama knows," Greyson said. "I want to confront him."

"Confront Pop?"

Confronting their father was something people didn't do. Not strangers, and not his three sons. Pop Ballantyne could be mean when he needed to be. He believed in hard discipline for his three rowdy boys, even though they were all grown and living their own lives. Challenging Pop never turned out good for anyone involved.

"Mama was too ashamed to do anything about it. I think we should stand up for our mother."

"It was a long time ago. Eileen's husband died, what? Three years ago?"

"Four," Greyson corrected.

"You were still in Chicago. Kirkland was spending more time in the capital than he was here. I didn't see any signs of Pop messing around. And you have to consider the source. Kirkland has always been a tattler. Throw Alex Galloway into the mix, and it gets even more convoluted." Chevy shook his head. "I don't believe it."

"I want to know the truth. If Pop was seeing Eileen behind Mama's back, we have to do something about it."

"What are we going to do?"

Greyson paused. Obviously he hadn't thought so far ahead. "He shouldn't get away with it."

"So we're going to interfere in Mama and Pop's marriage? It's not a good idea. Whatever happened, they're over it now. Remember the big anniversary celebration last summer?"

"Whatever Alex did, he made Eileen move out of Hannaford," Greyson replied as if he hadn't heard a word Chevy had said. Greyson was intelligent, ambitious, and usually very levelheaded. When it came to matters of the heart, all reason left him and he reacted impulsively, without fully analyzing the situation. Greyson's going off half-cocked—and dragging Chevy along—had been the source of most of their trouble as kids. It had also gotten them into big trouble most of their adult lives.

"I don't like it. We should stay out of it."

"You could know Pop had an affair and not do anything about it?" Greyson was going to pursue this. He wasn't hearing anything Chevy was telling him. Already he was condemning Pop.

"We don't know he had an affair, Grey."

"Exactly my point. We need to find out what went on between Pop and Eileen. And how Alex fits into it."

"Alex has been dead for years but he's still causing trouble in this family."

"Are you in or not?" Greyson asked, annoyed.

Chevy gave a curt nod, still not completely convinced they should interfere, but knowing a voice of reason would be needed to keep it under control.

"Good. I'll give Stacy Taro a call."

"I hope she gives you a discount for all the business she gets out of this family."

Just then, Greyson's wife, Sutton, breezed into the room. "What are you guys up to in here?" She kissed Chevy's cheek before sitting on Greyson's lap. They shared whispered words. "What are you doing home so early?"

Greyson answered, his voice noticeably softer when talking to Sutton. "We knocked off early to take a look at the progress with the Ballantyne Wilderness Lodge."

"How's it going?"

The Ballantyne Wilderness Lodge had been their youngest brother Kirkland's brainchild—his coming-to-maturity epiphany. The twenty-seven-acre vacation resort backed up to the forest where Chevy made his home. Chevy cut back on his workload at the paper mill in order to oversee the development of the vacation resort. He wanted to closely monitor the project, ensuring that they didn't destroy the wildlife. He worked with a firm to design the rustic homes where the guests would stay. Each home had five private suites with wet bar, balcony, fireplace, and Jacuzzi tub. The cabins would have their own library, TV room with satellite and videos, a great room with a large river-rock fireplace, and an outdoor hot tub. Activities for guests included snowmobiling, skiing, hiking, fishing, eagle watching, golfing, tennis, boating, and bicycling.

With Greyson running the paper mill, and Kirkland more of a businessman who managed the bottom line, his brothers hadn't balked at Chevy controlling the project. He was a card-carrying tree hugger. His life's mission was to preserve forests and save wildlife. He lived deep in the woods—the forest was his backyard—in a cabin he'd built with his bare hands. He'd suffered much teasing by the folks in town because of his chosen lifestyle, but he was more comfortable with wild animals than civilized humans.

Chevy watched Greyson and Sutton interact as Greyson updated her on the lodge, and his insides came to a slow burn. Lately, his emotions were all over the map, but the most re-occurring theme seemed to be jealousy. Greyson had Sutton and his stepdaughter Sierra. Kirkland was a newlywed, and he was the only father his stepdaughter Courtney had ever known. Chevy had no one. He hadn't had a woman in his life since college …and he was lonely.

"Are you coming to the Purple Party?" Sutton asked.

"Purple Party?" Greyson chuckled, tightening his grip on her waist. She leaned into him, mixing their chemistry until Chevy choked on it. He didn't begrudge their marriage. He had stepped in to help Greyson win her, but observing their perfect life magnified his loneliness.

"Kirkland and Cassidy are having a party to celebrate Prince's final tour. Next week. After they return from the concert in Charleston."

"Those two are crazy," Chevy mumbled.

"They're having a ball," Greyson countered with a smile. "Any occasion to have a party, and they're all over it. As long as Kirkland keeps his mind on business, I can't criticize. I'm glad they're getting along so well."

Sutton giggled. "They are cute."

Chevy cocked a brow. "Are you two getting along better?"

She made a gesture with her hand, indicating so-so. "We're getting there."

Greyson pulled her down for a quick kiss. "They're both trying to forget the past."

Good news for the entire Ballantyne family. The grudge between Sutton and Kirkland had recently threatened to tear the family apart.

"So, you'll be at this party, right?" Sutton pressed. "You've missed the last two."

"I'm really not a party person."

"An understatement," Greyson mumbled.

"You have to come, Chevy," Sutton persisted. "I don't like knowing you're locked up in your cabin alone while we're all having a good time. Getting out will do you good."

"I do get out. I went hiking last week."

"Hiking? In November? You could have been snowed in."

"I can handle myself. I've been hiking for years."

Sutton narrowed her eyes in steely resolve. "Then handle yourself at Kirkland and Cassidy's Purple Party."

He knew when he was beat. Sutton had grown to be as stubborn as her husband when it came to certain things, and his nonexistent love life was one of the things. "All right, I'll come."

Sutton smiled in triumph.

"But I'm not dressing up like Prince—or wearing any shade of purple."

Her smile faded. "We're all wearing purple."

"Greyson won't." Chevy knew his brother's masculinity wouldn't allow it. He wasn't being a good sport, but he'd told her he wasn't a party person.

"I already have our costumes picked out."

Greyson's face dropped. "I'm not wearing a costume, and I'm definitely not wearing *purple*."

Sutton wiggled around in his lap until she faced him. "Of course you are."

"No, I'm not."

The front door opened with a slam that reverberated throughout the grand home.

"*Mommeee!*" Sierra's shrill cry signaled trouble.

Sutton shot off with Greyson and Chevy closely behind her. They found Sierra standing in the foyer, crying. Her bright red hair was a mess, and her clothing was dirty and torn. The strap on her book bag was broken and she dragged it along behind her.

"What the hell?" Greyson asked as Sutton scooped her daughter into her arms.

Alarm, quickly followed by anger, moved through Chevy. He loved both his nieces, but Sierra was special, because he was special to her. They had a bond that surpassed the normal niece-uncle relationship. She shared his love of wildlife. She enjoyed hiking in the woods behind his home. He taught her everything he knew about plants and vegetation, but still she wanted to learn more. She often spent the weekend at his cabin, and he enjoyed their time immensely. If he ever had the opportunity to have a child, he prayed she would be as lovable as Sierra.

"What happened to you?" Sutton asked, releasing her so she could answer.

Sierra sniffled, hiccupping until she could put a sentence together. "The kids in my class were making fun of Uncle Chevy."

All eyes turned on him. He shifted uneasily.

Sierra walked over, bending her neck back until she could look at him with brave resolve. "I couldn't let them make fun of you, Uncle Chevy. They were being mean."

Chevy didn't need to ask what the children were teasing her about. For years, he'd been the town hermit. The kids even made up a song, taunting him whenever he went into town— which was why he rarely went. The rhyme had changed over the years, but it always had something to do with the hermit in the woods.

He shoved his hands in his pockets and shifted uneasily. A woman had started rumors about his sexuality—or sexual depravity, depending on who told the story. In a small town like Hannaford, juicy gossip often outweighed the truth.

"You wouldn't have let them make fun of me, right, Uncle Chevy?" Sierra looked up at him with innocent eyes. Second graders could be cruel, he knew that, but he didn't want a child fighting his battles.

Sutton took her hand, ending an uncomfortable situation for Chevy. "Let's go upstairs and get you cleaned up."

Greyson watched them climb the staircase.

"I'm sorry," Chevy offered.

"It's not your fault." Greyson shook his head wearily and led Chevy back into his study.

"Sutton won't punish her, will she?"

"I wouldn't doubt it, but I'll talk to her. I'll remind her of some of the trouble we used to get into as kids." Greyson moved behind his desk. "You have to do something about this. Aren't you sick of the judgmental people in this town taking shots at you?"

"Of course I am, but what do I do about it? People form their own opinions."

"I don't think you should change to please anyone, but, Chevy, you're a good guy. What they're saying about you isn't true …is it?"

"Greyson!"

He held up his hands. "You don't want to talk about it. You've never wanted to talk about it."

"Right."

"All I'm saying is, if people got to know you, they'd find out the truth for themselves. You aren't helping your cause by holing up in that cabin in the woods and avoiding civilization."

Chevy didn't care what the gossips of Hannaford said about him. He knew what kind of man he was. He was bothered that Sierra was now being forced to handle his problem. "I want to talk to Sierra before I go."

Greyson nodded.

Chevy waited for Sierra to change out of her torn clothing before taking her for a walk. He adored her, and would never scold her. He spoiled her, and didn't deny it. As they walked, he discouraged her fighting on his behalf, pointing out it was his job to look after her. The matter settled, they ventured into the woods and he showed her how the animals were preparing for the first winter's snow. When Sutton called for dinner, he walked her back before jumping in his truck and heading home.

He was welcomed to stay for dinner with Greyson and his family, but he needed to be alone. He didn't want to share Greyson's family anymore. He didn't want to be the crazy hermit uncle everyone pitied.

During the drive, he reflected on his life, taking an honest look at his part in his loneliness. He'd had a limited number of experiences with women, and all had gone badly. Whether the issue was sexual or his conventional attitude, it never worked out. The failures had been public, escalating the rumors. He never let on to how hurtful the rumors were. Instead he secluded himself—physically and emotionally.

Knowing his actions were now affecting his family, he had to change. Guilt saddened him when he imagined Sierra being accosted by her classmates. Like those women on talk shows, he thought, he had trust issues. He only allowed a small group of close friends inside his inner circle. He had perfected the art of being aloof until he convinced himself he didn't need anyone. He had to find a way to defrost his heart, and live life before it passed him by.

The only woman he had any interest in would never think twice about him. She was kind and beautiful. She lived by the old-fashioned values he cherished. They'd met in high school— she was a few grades behind him, so their schedules didn't cross often. Besides, she'd never really shown him any interest. Years later she'd become best friends with his sisters-in-law. She'd given Sutton a job at the library when she was financially and emotionally needy—another example of her kindness. Now he was forced to watch her from afar, to want her without being able to have her. If he were ever going to love a woman, it would be her.

Chapter 2

The idea was spontaneously conceived when Maddie showed up at the Purple Party wearing a frumpy dress and chunky shoes. "This isn't a good idea," Maddie said as her friends pulled her best church dress over her head.

"It'll be fun," Sutton said. "Richard and Kevin are setting up a stage and everything."

"But I don't dress like *this*." Maddie pointed to the Vanity 6 album cover lying on the bed.

"So you think we dress like *this*?" Cassidy stood next to Sutton and both held their arms out from their body.

"Can't we be someone other than Vanity 6?" Maddie asked as Sutton pulled her slip over her head.

"Who? Wendy or Lisa? The Doctor?" Cassidy teased. Since marrying Kirkland Ballantyne—a man eight years younger—she'd become a vixen waiting to explode. Tonight would be her big chance. She went to the vanity and started applying a thick coat of black eyeliner.

Sutton propped her hands on her hips. "You're going to have to lose the bra and panties, Maddie."

"Bra and p-p-panties?" Maddie stuttered. They'd gone too far now.

"You can't wear this with a bra and panties," Sutton said matter-of-factly. She held up a sheer black lace teddy.

"I can't wear *that*!"

"Cover the mirror, Cassidy," Sutton instructed. "We'll never get her into this if she sees herself. Trust us, Maddie. You have a gorgeous shape. You'll be beautiful. Why do you think we're letting you be Vanity?"

She had wondered herself. Before she could answer, Sutton continued. "You do know the words to 'Nasty Girl,' don't you?"

"Yes, but—"

"Good, because I don't want to look foolish." Cassidy shared a look with Sutton and burst into laughter.

"What?" Maddie missed the joke.

"Nothing," Cassidy assured her. "Let's finish up and run through our routine once before we go on."

Sutton laughed. "I like working with a real professional."

A few minutes later, they had transformed into Vanity 6, Prince's most successful girl group. Maddie surveyed Sutton's and Cassidy's outfits and clearly understood why the group had originally been named the Hookers. Cassidy was playing Susan, the cute innocent. Except Susan, like Cassidy this evening, always wore a white lace teddy with white stockings and garters. Sutton—the cement for their friendship—was all made up as Brenda, the take-no-mess, chain-smoking lesbian personality who wore too much blue eye shadow. Sutton donned a short-cropped blond wig to hide her natural reddish brown hair.

Somehow they'd roped Maddie into performing as the lead singer, Vanity. They confiscated her bra and panties and dressed her in a black teddy trimmed with dainty lace—Cassidy's bureau was full of nighties. Black stockings, a garter, and three-inch black heels completed her costume. Her jewelry consisted of a black choker with a huge jewel centered in the front. Cassidy painted her face with black eyeliner, mascara, a dusting of pink blush, and neutral lip-gloss. Sutton released the tight bun at the nape of her neck and fluffed her long curls around her face.

"Whoa," Sutton said. She and Cassidy stood a close distance, staring at Maddie.

"What? I want to see a mirror," Maddie insisted.

Cassidy shook her head in disbelief. "I knew you were pretty underneath all the granny clothes, but *whoa*."

"She kinda looks like Vanity. Give me more makeup," Sutton said, sitting at the vanity. "Make me look that good."

Maddie practiced walking across the room on the tall heels. She did feel attractive and feminine. "I'm not going onstage half naked."

"Didn't Vanity wear a black blazer sometimes?" Cassidy asked. "Check the closet. You can wear one of Kirkland's jackets."

"Ladies?" Richard knocked at Cassidy's bedroom door. "Are you decent?"

"We're dressed," Cassidy called. "Come in."

"We are *not* decent," Maddie muttered as she leafed through Cassidy's closet for a jacket.

Richard stepped into the room. "The stage is all…set…" His words trailed off.

Maddie turned from the closet to see what was the matter. Richard stood, staring at her with his mouth hanging wide open. "Whoa."

Sutton laughed at his reaction. "That's what we said."

"I'm Richard." The Morris Day look-alike pimped up to her with his hand extended.

"Maddie," she answered, dropping her eyes to avoid his hungry stare.

"Hi, Maddie. The pleasure is mine." He took her hand and placed a kiss on the back of it. He had managed to capture the Morris Day sleaziness portrayed in *Purple Rain*.

Cassidy cleared her throat. "Richard, you wanted something?"

"Ah, yeah. The stage is ready." His eyes roamed Maddie's face.

"Give us five minutes."

He dropped Maddie's hand, but did not look away when he answered Cassidy, "Five minutes." He backed out of the room, never taking his eyes off Maddie.

"Still think you look silly?" Sutton asked her.

Five minutes later Richard returned with his "Jerome" sidekick, Kevin. They ushered the women downstairs, shielding them from the partygoers' curious eyes. Cassidy lived in her husband's childhood home. He'd used his connections in the construction business to secure the best crew available to renovate the home. They'd busted down walls, added new windows and lighting fixtures, making it bright and friendly. New carpet and drapes made the home plush and warm. The kitchen had been completely remodeled—appliances, tile flooring, sink, and cabinets. An addition was added to the back, providing an office and great room. The tiny two-bedroom house had been transformed into a spacious three-bedroom dream.

Downstairs, the latest Prince song was thumping, shaking the floor beneath their feet. The house was crowded with men sporting huge Afros, deep waves, or long presses—any one of Prince's vintage hairstyles. The women imitated Apollonia in a safe, subtle way. Everyone wore some shade of purple.

Richard took extra care with Maddie, making sure she was comfortable with her part. He rubbed tiny circles in the small of her back. "Do you need anything?" he asked. "Are you ready?" he wanted to know. "Have fun with this. You look great."

Cassidy whispered to Maddie, "Someone has a crush on you."

"Back off, Richard," Sutton said. "We're just lip-syncing."

Maddie wasn't used to getting the attention of men. She was the spinster librarian for Hannaford Valley's only library. Her romantic life consisted of the stories she read in the romance novels Cassidy illustrated covers for. With her father's illness, she hadn't been to a party since high school. If not for her aunt volunteering to stay with her father for a few hours, she wouldn't be at the Purple Party, dressed to shame, right now. She had to admit she felt sexy, and playing the lead singer was sort of fun. Only recently had she become friends with Sutton and Cassidy, and she liked having girlfriends to clown around with.

They lined up onstage behind the red bedsheets Richard and Kevin had hung for curtains. Brenda, Vanity, and Susan—or Sutton, Maddie, and Cassidy—in the order dictated by the album covers, struck a pose. Maddie thought it was more *Charlie's Angels* than Vanity 6, but they fell into character easily, taking the performance seriously.

The music ended, and the crowd's attention was called to the makeshift stage. Kevin gathered everyone around. Murmurs and whispers made their way behind the stage. Cassidy and Kirkland threw the best parties in Hannaford and everyone was braced to see what they'd come up with this time.

Maddie's heart thumped when Richard introduced them. The funky-sexy beat for "Nasty Girl" began to thump. The

men grew restless with anticipation and started shouting for
the curtain to come up. It sent an adrenaline rush to Maddie.
Cassidy and Sutton grinned, and the curtain was ripped away.

Catcalls and whistles greeted them. Maddie moved front,
center stage. She gyrated her hips as she mouthed the provocative words of the song. Cassidy and Sutton sashayed up next
to her on either side. They worked their routine, using their
body language to accentuate the lewd lyrics. They turned in
unison and wiggled their hips down to the floor. Men started
throwing dollar bills onto the stage when they reached the part
about having sex on the limousine floor.

When they whipped back around, one at a time, the men
muscled the women at the party out of the way to get near the
stage. The audacious attention helped Maddie feel more comfortable taking the lead and mouthing the raunchy lines about
taking something out, doing it good, and coming with the
nasty girls. She truly was living in a fantasy, just like the song
said. Men were ogling her. It might not be politically correct,
but the attention felt good.

They were wiggling and crooning, "Please, please,
please," when Maddie noticed the men watching from the
back of the room.

The three Ballantyne brothers were standing with their
mouths agape. Sutton's husband, Greyson, looked as if he
were getting ready to commit murder. Kirkland—Cassidy's
husband—watched the routine with narrowed eyes and a
steamy red complexion. Chevy watched Maddie from beneath the brim of a black Stetson with sensual fascination—
and unconcealed suspicion.

Just when Maddie was becoming too embarrassed to
mouth the seven-inch remark, Greyson and Kirkland burst
through the crowd and rushed the stage, grabbing Cassidy and

Sutton by the waists and carrying them off. Sutton's feet flailed, but Greyson swatted her behind and she settled down. Cassidy was limp underneath Kirkland's arm while he demanded to know whose idea it was to have his wife put on a strip show.

After the women had been removed, Maddie stood in the middle of the stage, feeling naked and abandoned. The laughter and catcalls ended, leaving the room in silent disbelief. The women turned angry glares on her. The men's rambunctious attention didn't seem so flattering anymore. Someone cued the music and a slow, smooth Prince classic began to play. The crowd slowly disbursed into sets of two, swaying to the music.

Richard appeared onstage. "You were—"

"Come with me." Chevy took one long step up onto the stage. His deep, commanding voice left no room for argument. As he took Maddie's hand and led her away, she remembered the scene in *Purple Rain* where Prince shows up on his motorcycle to whisk Apollonia away.

"Hey," Richard called after them, "I was talking to her."

Chevy stopped, and slowly turned to Richard. He did not release her hand. "I'm talking to Mandisa now."

Richard threw up his hands and walked off the stage in the opposite direction.

No one called her Mandisa. Not even her parents after they'd come up with the exotic name. Not many people knew her real name was Mandisa Marie Ingram. Mandisa, meaning "sweet," originated in South Africa with the Xhosa. Her parents found it adorable: Sweet Marie Ingram. Adults found it cute, teachers mangled it, and her classmates teased her mercilessly, so she shed Mandisa and asked everyone to call her Maddie. Once she entered middle school, no one remembered her real name.

But Chevy had always called her Mandisa. Two years ago when he'd come to the library to deliver a message to Sutton from Greyson, he'd taken one look at her and said, "This can't be Mandisa Ingram from the booster club." She'd smiled to be polite, but she never knew exactly how to take his comment. Over the years, she'd pondered his meaning many times, finding it was impossible to read him.

Maddie remembered Chevy from high school, too. Everyone in Hannaford Valley knew the Ballantyne brothers, Alex Galloway, and Sutton Hill. The men were walking fantasies. No girl was immune to them. They were inseparable, which often caused them to get into mischief. As adults, their lives reminded tangled, but childhood fun had turned into adult drama.

Maddie's brief encounter with Chevy in school came when he'd been forced to assist the booster club in setting up the gym for a pep rally. He was being punished for something or other, and had not been happy to spend his free time after school swinging a hammer to build props.

That day she'd seen the same heated determination he was showing now as he pulled her along behind him, oblivious of the fact she was wearing tall heels. Being over six feet, he covered a lot of ground with his long, determined strides. The muscles in his back flexed as he climbed the stairs. He had disregarded the Purple Party admission rules and made his appearance in his usual attire of overalls, Timberland boots, and tight tee. His grip was strong, not allowing her to slip away.

Upstairs, Maddie heard Kirkland and Greyson shouting behind closed doors. Chevy took her to an empty bedroom—from the décor, Maddie knew it was Cassidy's little girl's room. He released her hand to close the door behind them. She sank down in a rocker in the corner of the room, pulling the lapel of the jacket together to hide her cleavage. Being in this close space with a man as large as Chevy was daunting.

"I don't know if you remember me," he said with a no-nonsense tone, "but I'm Chevy Ballantyne—Greyson and Kirkland's brother. I just want to ask you what the hell you think you were doing up on that stage."

"What? I-I— We were impersonating Vanity 6." Every argument Sutton and Cassidy had used to cajole her into performing seemed lame. Her first attempt at being flirtatious was turning into a disaster.

"I could see what you were doing." His head bobbed as if he were looking her up and down. "*Everyone* could see *everything*." He was watching her, but she couldn't read his expression because he tilted his head low to see her, hiding his face behind the brim of his hat. "The last time I saw you, you were dressed as a clown. This time…" His words trailed off with unmistakable, menacing disapproval.

The clown outfit had been Cassidy's idea—they were dressing for her daughter's first birthday party. *Who's responsible for coming up with this idea?* she asked herself, not willing to shoulder all the blame.

She pulled the jacket tight, hiding her cleavage. "Sutton and Cassidy thought—"

"My sisters-in-law have a knack for getting into trouble, and their trouble usually ends with my brothers running off doing some foolish thing in the name of love. You"—he took a menacing step closer—"should have known better."

"What do you mean by that?"

"You're a church girl."

He might as well have called her a *good girl*. She hated being the good girl all the time. She'd gone to college and majored in library science. When her mother became ill, she returned home—giving up her dream of living in a big city. She took a job in the small town's library and cared for her mother until she died. As soon as her mother passed, her father had a massive stroke, which made him an invalid. She'd taken over his care, putting in more hours than the home-care nurse because she couldn't afford to pay the exorbitant fees on a librarian's salary. Her only social activities involved the church, and she could only get out of the house one day a week for that. Meeting Sutton, and later Cassidy, had been what she needed to salvage a tiny piece of her own life. She'd always been a good girl. She enjoyed the taste she'd gotten of being a bad girl.

"What did you call me?" Maddie tossed back at Chevy, angry.

He hesitated a quick second. "You're a church girl. You shouldn't have been up onstage, dressed like that." He indicated her attire with the sweep of a massive hand.

"Just one minute, buster." She marched up to him and poked her finger in the middle of his chest. "Everyone else in this town might be afraid of you, but not me. Who do you think you are to reprimand me? We've never said more than three sentences to each other at any one time."

"Those skimpy outfits almost caused a riot! Sutton and Cassidy are married!"

"Sutton and Cassidy are grown women. They did what they wanted to do. Take it up with them, not me."

Surprised at her insolence, he narrowed his gaze. She'd always been quiet and submissive. This new attitude must have come with the Vanity getup, because she had never expressed herself so vigorously before. She was discovering quite a few things about herself tonight. She liked being sexy, and she had a backbone. The more she stood up for herself, the bolder she became.

"And take your hat off when you're talking to me." She reached up and knocked the Stetson off.

His hair fell in heavy black rivulets to the nape of his neck.

She was speechless. She couldn't remember ever seeing Chevy Ballantyne without his hat before. He was drop-dead gorgeous. All the Ballantyne men were handsome—Greyson had paid his way through college as an underwear model, and women caught the vapors when Kirkland walked down the street—but Chevy was well beyond their league. His eyes were too light to be brown, and too dark to be hazel. He had a square jaw covered by a hint of stubble. He'd shaved before the party and nicked himself on the chin. With his palpable masculinity, the cut looked natural. His eyebrows were dark and bushy. His expression was strong and determined with a hint of wickedness.

If Maddie could tear her eyes away from his captivating face, she could complete her inventory of the entire package. Chevy had a body solidly built by heavy lifting and hard work. His muscles were lean and brawny, rippling like those of the heroes Cassidy illustrated for the covers of romance novels. His grip had demonstrated he was physically powerful. His overalls fit tightly across the haunches of his bottom, and his legs went on for days, layered with power and strength.

Chevy stood stunned by her brazen tossing of his Stetson.

Maddie gathered her dignity and brushed past him out the door. She jogged down the stairs, holding the rail to keep from falling off the heels. She found her coat in the front closet.

"Vanity, you were rocking that lingerie." A man dressed as early-Prince with a big Afro wig, a purple-sequined jumpsuit, and purple suede boots draped himself on the closet door. "Where you going? The party is just getting started."

"Oh," she squeaked. "I have to go."

Another Prince dress-up joined them. "Let me talk to you for a minute, Apollonia."

"Can't you see I'm talking to the lady? And she's Vanity, not Apollonia. Apollonia was whack."

"Apollonia was just as fine as Vanity."

Another man joined them. "Can I have your phone number, whoever you are?"

Maddie let the men debate as she stuffed her arms in the coat and draped her scarf around her neck.

"How about another performance? I'll play the imaginary drums." This guy was supposed to be the Doctor.

"Where's your backup?" another guy asked.

Maddie's eyes widened. He was either Wendy or Lisa. The men surrounded her, firing questions and getting entirely too close for her comfort.

"Gentlemen," Richard said, pushing through the small gathering. "Give the lady some room." He gave the men a pointed look and they moved away. "How about a dance before you go?"

"I really need to get home."

"Just one dance." He moved closer with each word. She didn't see him move, but she felt him destroy her three feet of personal space.

"It's late." She looked over Richard's shoulder and saw Chevy coming down the stairs. He'd replaced the hat, and his angry gaze locked in on her like a guided missile. She felt her resolve melt. "I really have to leave."

She turned and bolted out the front door, racing for one of the cars idling in front of Cassidy's house. Kirkland always hired local jitneys to chauffer any party guests who might drink too much. Seeing as she hadn't driven in ages, the only car at her disposal was last driven by her father, and Sutton and Greyson were too busy to take her home, she darted to the nearest waiting car.

Chevy must be part cheetah, Maddie thought, because he reached the car at the same time she did. To her surprise, he pushed her hand away and opened her door. "I'll take you home."

Not a safe option, for many reasons, but mostly because she was too attracted to him, and he was too angry with her. "I prefer to use the jitney."

"It'll be better if I drive you."

"I haven't been drinking. I'm a designated driver," the jitney called to them.

"I haven't been drinking either." She could see where he might think she had been since she'd been onstage shaking her half-naked behind.

"I'm not worried about you." He nodded toward the porch. "I'm worried about those guys following you."

The men who had tried to accost her as she put on her coat were spilling out onto the porch. *They* had drunk too much.

She glanced up at Chevy. Steely resolve had set in around the hard planes of his mouth. "All right," she said as she climbed inside her car.

He tapped on the window. "Lock your doors."

She did. She watched out the back window as Chevy jogged to his truck and climbed inside. He pulled around and waited for the jitney to drive away. His headlights shone through the rear window all the way. She didn't know if she should be angry or flattered. She tried not to dwell on his rugged good looks and determined personality. She'd gotten over her crush on him a long time ago. *Right*. Her mind wandered, formulating a different reason for Chevy to be following her home.

The fantasy was shattered when the jitney pulled into her

driveway. She secretly hoped Chevy would follow her to the porch, wave the driver away, and take her in his arms. After a few heated words, he would end the argument by ravishing her mouth.

She crossed the lawn and put her key in the front door. Chevy honked twice and sped off.

Chapter 3

Greyson and Kirkland arrived at the Ballantyne Wilderness Lodge construction site together, still in their workday suits. The mid-November temperature was cold, and dropping rapidly. If the construction crew didn't work faster, early snow would cause a delay, putting the project behind schedule. The goal was to open the lodge by the next summer, but there was still a lot to be done. In their favor was the fact that the lodge relied on nature as its attraction, so they didn't have to build amusement-park-type rides. Completing the cabins was the most pressing part of the development. The other activities could be brought online as they were completed. Most were seasonal so the guests could still have the good time they expected without every part being up and running.

Chevy was in his element with this project. He enjoyed his role at the paper mill, but this was different. The mill was Greyson's baby. Chevy was the company's conscience, always advocating for replenishment of the trees they used to make their premium paper products.

Although the lodge was Kirkland's conception, it, like the

paper mill, was a family venture. Kirkland and Sutton owned the land along with another partner, so the decision-making process was smoother than if they had to deal with a board, or stockholders. Chevy and Greyson both invested venture capital, but Greyson remained a silent partner. He preferred to focus on the mill, and the consulting he did for the Chicago law firm where he used to be a partner. Chevy had been officially hired to run the day-to-day operations of the lodge until he felt comfortable turning the job over to someone else. He didn't need the salary, but he enjoyed being able to work outdoors.

Like his brothers, he wanted to conceive a business venture to contribute to the economic stability of Hannaford Valley. He hadn't figured out what the project should be. With his pariah status in the town, he had to be very careful not to select a venture that would fail because of his connection to it. He surely had enough money to invest. After graduating from college with a degree in forestry, he'd worked a series of low-paying do-good jobs until he was hired into a government position. He loathed traveling to the capital, and had been glad when Greyson came up with the idea for the mill. He invested the majority of his savings, and it had made him a wealthy man. In turn, he invested his new wealth in a solid portfolio and his net worth grew by leaps and bounds.

He lived a quiet, simple life that did not require much money to sustain. He owned the land where he'd built his home. He lived in a cabin he had designed and built with his own hands. He drove a 1996 Dodge Ram 1500, which he had paid off years ago. He didn't require a massive wardrobe of expensive clothing, and he had no family to support. He donated the maximum amount of his salary allowed to charities every year, and still had all the money he would ever need.

Chevy crossed the muddy grounds and joined Greyson's and Kirkland's conversation.

"Sutton is *so* on punishment," Greyson said. They were still talking about the Purple Party pandemonium.

"Yeah, right," Kirkland said. "How'd that go over?" he asked sarcastically.

"Oh, she squawked, but she didn't have a leg to stand on."

"What kind of punishment?" Kirkland asked as if he were considering the option for Cassidy.

"Straight to law school, work, and then home. I considered banning her from the library since Maddie is her boss." Greyson rolled his eyes at Chevy. "Did you see the way she was dressed up on that stage?" He stuffed his hands in his pockets. "*This* is why we need to have a baby."

Greyson found any excuse to insist on Sutton getting pregnant. He loved Sierra, but she was his stepdaughter. He wanted to have a child with his wife. Sutton wanted to finish law school and begin a career.

"Maybe if you get Sutton pregnant, you'll be able to handle her," Kirkland added.

"You just get your own wife under control," Greyson shot back.

"Believe me, I destroyed every Prince CD, album, tape, and eight-track I could get my hands on."

"What are you grinning about?" Greyson turned on Chevy.

"I don't *grin*."

"Your girlfriend is the troublemaker who got Sutton and Cassidy going. Vanity, ha!"

"She isn't my girlfriend." *And she isn't a troublemaker.* Mandisa was a good girl, a church girl.

Kirkland butted in. "Put those three together, and they always get into trouble."

Greyson's wheels started spinning. "You're right. We have to keep them apart." His harsh gaze turned on Chevy. "You have to keep your girlfriend away from our wives."

"She's not my girlfriend." *And they were in serious denial if they believed shy Mandisa Ingram was behind the Vanity 6 performance.*

Kirkland ignored him. "Did you see the way those hounds were whistling?"

They started walking away.

"And throwing dollars up on the stage," Greyson added.

"Those weren't dollars! They were tens, twenties, and fifties."

"Fifties! The fifty must have been for my wife. Sutton was working that camisole."

"If anyone was getting fifties thrown at them, it was Cassidy."

They forget about Chevy, leaving him standing as they walked off, arguing about whose wife was getting fifties tossed at her. Controlling Sutton and Cassidy would be near impossible. They were high-spirited and headstrong. They wouldn't sit still for their husbands telling them what they could and couldn't do. As soon as the party blew over, everything would be back to normal with Sutton and Cassidy running the show. Listening to Greyson and Kirkland making plans to control their wives was like a bad Abbott and Costello routine.

"Hey!" Chevy yelled. They stopped and turned around. "Mandisa is not my girlfriend."

"Who is Mandisa?" Kirkland asked.

Greyson rolled his eyes. "Just take care of her, Chevy. We don't care how you do it. Okay?"

Before he could answer, Greyson and Kirkland began walking, resuming their argument over the fifty-dollar tips.

"But she's not my girlfriend," Chevy shouted at their backs.

Greyson dismissively waved his hand over his head, not bothering to turn around.

"And the fifties were for her!" Chevy ran to catch up to them.

He gave up on convincing Greyson and Kirkland about his lack of relationship with Maddie. They ignored his pleas, and they started ranting whenever they thought about the party.

"I've never seen two more jealous men in my life." Chevy had been listening to them fuss the entire time they were surveying the construction.

Greyson laughed. "Just wait."

"If I had a woman, I'd trust her enough to know she wouldn't stray."

"Stray?" Kirkland turned his nose up. "Horses stray, not women. You've been living in the woods too long, big brother."

"Just wait." Greyson was still laughing.

"Quit saying that." Chevy had taken enough of his brothers' ribbing for one day.

"All right. I'll say this. We aren't jealous because we're worried about our wives straying. We're upset about other men hitting on them. No one wants to stand by and watch someone make a move on his woman. No matter how solid your relationship is you always wonder if another man can offer your woman more."

Kirkland jumped in. "It's even worse when you have a good woman, and you know men are just waiting for you to screw up so they can make their move. It messes with your head."

Chevy shook his head, tugging at his Stetson. "You two are pitiful. Those women have you wrapped around their little fingers." He walked off, leading his brothers to the first lodge, which had recently been completed.

"Just wait," Greyson called after him.

"Just do something about your girlfriend, and we won't have these problems," Kirkland added.

"For the last time, she is not my girlfriend!"

Chevy was driving to the hardware store when he came across Sutton's car in a ditch. As winter approached, he needed to complete minor repairs to the roof of his cabin, but waited until late in the day to shop. Since Sierra's mishap at school, he didn't go into town until the kids had gone home.

"What happened?" he asked, taking a look at the right front wheel.

"I swerved to avoid a rabbit, and ended up in this ditch. I was about to call Greyson to come and get me."

"I could try to push you out, but with all this mud, we'll both be stuck."

She checked her watch. "Can you just give me a ride into town? I'm supposed to be at the library before Maddie leaves."

"You're working this late?"

"End-of-the-year inventory. With school, working late fits my schedule. I'm going to get the keys from Maddie and close up. I can call Greyson from there to handle the car."

"Climb in."

Chevy and Sutton had always enjoyed a comfortable relationship. He loved her like the little sister he didn't have. When the rumors about his perverted sexuality started, she'd never turned her back on him. She included him in every family function, remembering he was alone in the cabin.

"The party was crazy, huh?" Sutton asked as they bumped along on the dirt road.

"I don't think Kirkland will be having another one any time soon." He glanced at her. "Greyson is still steaming."

"Yeah, but it'll do him some good. Wouldn't want him to take me for granted."

"Is that why you did it?"

"No," she answered sincerely. "We thought it would be fun." She shrugged. "Who knew?"

They should have known three pretty women wearing next to nothing and shaking their rumps would excite the men in the crowd. Chevy kept the thought to himself in the name of peace.

"Are you coming to Thanksgiving dinner?"

He tugged at his hat. "I might be busy."

"Busy? On Thanksgiving? Doing what?"

"We have to keep construction for the lodge on schedule." He didn't want to undergo the pain of watching Greyson and his family together on the holiday. No matter how welcome they tried to make him feel, he was still an outsider. He was the uncle everyone took pity on because he didn't have his own family to cozy up with. The saddest part for him came at the end of the night when he returned home to his empty cabin. When everyone else was tucked away in the arms of their lover, he was alone.

"Chevy?" Sutton prodded. "If you don't have dinner with us, spend the holiday with Kirkland or your parents. I don't want to think of you by yourself."

He gave a curt nod, not promising anything. "Here we are." He pulled up in front of the library so Sutton could jump out. "Don't worry so much about me."

"I can't help it." Sutton watched him with marked concern. She kissed his cheek. "I love you."

If any doubts remained about making his move on Maddie, they disappeared in the close confines of his truck cab. He had been playing and replaying their conversation at the Purple Party, and he validated the conclusion he'd come to eons ago—no woman made him feel the way Mandisa did. Watching Sutton moon over him and his sad state of loneliness was enough to push him to make a drastic move. If it didn't work out, at least everyone would get off his back.

"Just a minute," he said, parking the truck.

"What's wrong?"

"I want to go in."

Sutton raised a questioning brow, but her smile told him she knew his intentions. "The library is closed. I can pick up some books for you though. What do you need?"

"I need to talk to Mandisa."

He ignored his sister-in-law's smug grin and got out of the truck, following her into the library. He started to doubt his sanity as he walked behind her through the stacks to the office. The library was quiet, and he could hear his heart thumping in his ears. If nothing else, he wasn't a quitter. He was committed now. He'd have to go through with his plan, or Sutton would never let him hear the end of it. He stood at the threshold of Maddie's office, a delegate of one sent to save his brothers' marriages, hoping to grab some happiness in the process.

"Hey, Maddie. Chevy wants to talk to you."

Her head snapped up, and her golden brown eyes locked onto his soul. This was the Mandisa he knew. She was wearing a conservative dress with a high collar. Her hair was pulled back in a tight bun at the nape of her neck. She wore no makeup, yet her lips were plump and moist, begging to be kissed. She had a virginal quality about her that made him want to hold her gently, and teach her everything she needed to know to please him.

Sutton continued, "If you give me the keys, I'll get started."

"S—" She cleared her throat. "Sure." She handed Sutton the keys and said good night.

"Talk to you later, Chevy." Sutton left the office. She nudged him inside and closed the door.

Maddie stiffened her chin. She was prepared to continue their argument. "You want to talk to me?"

"Mandisa," he started. He remembered what she'd told him about talking to her while wearing his hat, and pulled it from his head. "Have you heard the rumors about me?" He stepped up to her desk.

"I have," she answered quietly, eyeing him suspiciously.

"Most of them are true." He waited for her response, thinking she might fear him and demand he leave.

Her expression didn't change. After a minute, she said, "Is there anything else?"

He rolled the brim of his Stetson between his fingers. This wasn't as easy as he thought it would be. "I'm thirty-two years old, and I've never been married. I haven't dated seriously since right after college. That didn't go too well, and no woman has interested me since." He dropped his eyes. "Well, not until you." He wasn't expressing his thoughts adequately. He should have practiced what he would say. "I'm not dangerous," he said to persuade her. He planted his feet and waited for her response, then realized he hadn't asked a question.

"I'm not afraid of you."

"Good."

"I'm glad we straightened everything out." She stood and took her coat off the back of the door.

He cleared his throat to get her attention.

She turned to him, buttoning her coat. "Is there something else, Chevy?"

"Would you like to go to the movies with me?"

Her fingers froze on the top button of her coat. "Are you asking me out on a date?"

He widened his stance. "Yes."

"I'd like to, but it might take me a couple of weeks to make arrangements."

"You could call me when you're ready."

"Okay."

He lurched forward to open the door for her. "I'll wait for you to call then."

"I will." She glanced up at him, but shyness did not allow her to meet his eyes. "Good night."

Chapter 4

Maddie lived in a modest home walking distance to the library. This was the only house her parents had ever owned. With her limited income, and her father's insurmountable medical bills, she'd come to realize it would be her home for many years. She pulled the collar of her coat up against her face, blocking the gusting winds. She enjoyed the freedom of walking, even on a brisk night.

Thinking of Chevy shielded her against the cold temperatures. She still couldn't believe that just moments ago she'd been sitting in the office while Chevy stood nervously asking her out on a date. He wasn't a man of many words, but his meaning had been clear. He didn't need to say a word for her to read him. She'd been admiring him from a distance for so many years she knew what each of his body gestures meant.

With his stalking presence and huge body, she should be afraid of him. His body mass was twice hers, and she felt small and vulnerable standing next to him. He dripped sensuality naturally, leaving him unaware of his affect on her. He spoke with a provocative country drawl. His gaze was intense, too serious, causing his forehead to bunch when he fought for the right words to express himself. He was shy, but simultaneously fearless.

He'd started his reverie by mentioning the rumors. She, like every resident in Hannaford, had heard the tall tales about the hermit who lived in the woods with the weird sexual perversions. The rumors had died down over the years as the Ballantynes single-handedly pumped new economic life into the flailing town, but occasionally someone would snicker when he visited town.

She'd earned her own place in the Hannaford gossip mill. She was the lonely librarian spinster destined to live out her days with a houseful of cats. She was met with piteous glances at church, and whenever she came into town.

People shook their heads and whispered, "Poor girl. You know, her mother died some years ago. She's taking care of her father. I heard he's very ill. Yes, she's a saint. Terrible, the way things turned out for her."

Maddie wasn't angry about their comments—how could she be? They were true. She had sacrificed her life to care for her parents. Her mother was in her forties when she gave birth to her. Her father, forty-nine. When she turned eighteen and left for college, her parents were well into their sixties. Now that she was thirty, her father was seventy-nine.

Her mother and father had been inseparable. They'd tried for children for many years, unsuccessfully. It rocked the small community when her mother turned up pregnant at forty-five. She'd survived the birth without any complications, and lived to give Maddie many fond memories. When her mother died, her father had withered quickly until a stroke left him debilitated. "If he had been a younger man who wasn't mourning his wife, he might have recovered better," Dr. Carter told her. "Grief is a powerful thing."

So Maddie had taken up the burden of caring for her father. At first he fluctuated, sometimes having very good days when he would work in his tomato garden. Over the past three years his health declined in proportion with his grief, and now he was confined to bed and needed care twenty-four hours a day. The family savings, Medicare, and his monthly Social Security checks were just enough to cover the cost of his medical bills—and the nurse's visits. Maddie's income covered the other essentials—food, utilities, and the like.

A horn startled her. Chevy pulled up alongside her in his truck. "It's cold. I'd be happy to give you a ride home."

"I like to walk." The walk to and from the library was *her time*.

"It gets dark by five this time of year. You probably shouldn't be walking alone."

"I live in town."

He turned off the engine and got out of the truck. He planted his broad shoulders and big body in front of her. "Just the same"—he snatched off his hat before continuing—"I'll walk with you."

She hid her smile. "You can put your hat back on." They were outside, and it was cold.

He nodded, a gesture of thanks, and plunked the hat back on his head.

She started walking and he fell into step beside her. He was as nervous as she. They had moved two of the short four blocks to her house when he finally spoke, breaking the heavy silence. "What movie would you like to see?"

"I don't know. It's been a while since I've been to the movies." Caring for her father didn't allow many occasions for recreation.

"When you call, I'll check the paper."

"Okay." There was only one theater in Hannaford, and

it had only one screen. If they wanted to know what was playing, Maddie only needed to look down the street at the marquee.

"Chevy?"

He looked down at her.

"How come you didn't ask me what arrangements I had to make before I could go out with you?"

"I didn't think it was my business." He made a low, strangling noise. "Is it a boyfriend?"

"No. My father is very sick. I have to look after him when the nurse isn't there."

He bobbed his head, but the brim of his hat blocked his eyes.

"Do you understand?" she asked.

"I do."

They stopped at her walkway. "Do you still want to go to the movies with me?"

"If you can make arrangements, I would."

She tilted her head back, trying to see his face in the shadows. "I better go in."

"Good night." He stood watching her until she was inside and closed the door. She peeked through the curtains and watched him turn and walk away, back in the direction where he'd left his truck.

There were many layers to Chevy Ballantyne. The rumors had pushed him to the fringes of town. He avoided most social interactions. When they were together, Maddie could sense a smoldering sexuality and good nature. She watched him walk away with rapid, vigorous steps that warned he was to be taken seriously—some should actually fear him. But the soft drawl of his few words was warm and cautious, but hopeful.

Maddie turned away from the window once Chevy disappeared from sight. The living room of her small home had been transformed into a sick ward for her father. A hospital bed consumed most of the room. Medical supply boxes were stacked high in every corner. Machines beeped and blinked and buzzed. When he'd first become ill, he'd been dependent on a respirator, but he'd made it over that hurdle. The only personal items in the room were photos of her mother. Tons of family photos were shoved in any space where there was no medical equipment.

The nurse was at her father's bedside, helping him eat. "He had a good day today," Todd told her.

She'd grown up with Todd, and always felt a little embarrassed when he was assigned to care for her father. He never showed anything but professionalism and caring, but Maddie couldn't help feeling ashamed of her plight. While everyone else from high school had gone on to live a full, independent life, she remained tied to her parents.

Todd stood and smiled, his light skin a contrast to the dark sable of his beard and mustache. "Time for me to go, Mr. Ingram, but Maddie's home."

"How are you, Dad?" She went to her father and gave him a kiss on the forehead. "He does look bright and alert today." His eyes actually fixed on her and followed as she stepped away to hang up her coat.

"You have a happy glow, too."

Maddie pressed her cheeks. It must have been Chevy's heady effect on her.

Todd updated her on the day's events, going over the medications and treatments he'd given. "I'm working the entire week, so I'll be back tomorrow—trying to make some extra money for Christmas."

"What about helping your uncle at the clinic?"

"I'm splitting my time since I started seeing people in the

evening. My uncle is trying to cut down on his hours. As soon as he finds someone to take over, he'll retire."

Despite her understandable embarrassment, she did feel a certain comfort in having someone she knew personally taking care of her father. "My father responds well to you," she told him.

"He seems to enjoy it when I read to him." He lifted a beat-up paperback from the foot of the bed. "We started a mystery today." He went on about cognitive therapy being as important as occupational or physical therapy. She didn't understand all the medical science behind it—God knew she'd learned enough while taking care of her father. She did notice how alert her father had been when she walked through the door, offering her some encouragement.

Todd slipped on his coat and gloves. "Anyway, he should be worn out, and you should have a quiet night. Get some rest."

Maddie saw Todd out, and then cooked herself a light dinner. By the time she settled down in the third bedroom, which had been remodeled to provide her with a small den, he had gone to sleep. The television monopolized the den, leaving room for only a love seat and small table. She needed more days like this. Quiet and restful. Normally, her evenings were consumed with trying to follow complicated medical directions and administer her father's treatments. Things had been better since he wasn't on the respirator and requiring suctioning to keep his airway open, but Maddie had found the quality of the nurses really made the difference. She understood caring for an incapacitated old man was daunting, but she had encountered professionals who did not provide adequate care. She detested coming home after working all day to find her father lying in bed wearing a diaper saturated with his own wastes. She would know immediately he had not been out of bed, or bathed, or properly fed.

The doctors told her to place him in a nursing home. She couldn't afford to pay for the reputable facilities in the capital where she knew he would get excellent care. She would have to use a small, privately owned facility plagued with overcrowding and understaffing. She'd actually gone to visit a few when he first became ill. She'd run out vowing never to place her father in such a place.

Hannaford Valley had a small retirement village just outside town. The nursing home was a separate building, but had been closed when it didn't meet code. There were twenty apartment residences for seniors who needed a little assistance in maintaining an independent lifestyle. The living was adequate and safe, but not suitable for her father. She couldn't give him *adequate*, when he'd devoted his life to making a good home for his family.

As she watched the Travel Channel on the thirty-six-inch television she'd purchased after saving for two years, she dreamed of seeing the world. Although caring for her father was exhausting, Maddie loved him, and would do anything for him, but her obligations didn't squelch her desire to have her own social life. Performing at the Purple Party had been shameful, but for a brief moment she felt invigorated. Going out with Chevy might be the beginning of something special—the building of a private life all her own. A place where her dreams of being held by a man would be well received.

Maddie switched to Lifetime and settled in for a steamy love story, and imagined having a whirlwind romance. Her dating experiences were limited to the high school prom, and a wild frat party. At thirty, she'd only had one sexual partner and he had been so inept she couldn't be certain she wasn't still a virgin. After college she'd returned home to care for her parents, and there weren't many prospects in town then—everyone her age was off at college or beginning their careers.

Chevy might be a little too much for her. He was wild, but tame. Dark and dangerous, but grounded and trustworthy. She smiled, remembering how well she'd handled him at the party. Every time he saw her the first thing he did was snatch the Stetson away. She'd learned from listening to Sutton and Cassidy that the Ballantyne brothers needed to be managed with a firm hand.

The phone rang, and Maddie jumped for it. Not many people called her home, and those few were usually connected with business.

"Maddie, it's Cassidy."

Maddie and Sutton were linked together when Sutton returned to Hannaford. She'd needed work, and Maddie had needed help at the library, so it was a natural fit. Working together, they soon became friends. Sutton had introduced Maddie to Cassidy, including her in their lunches and mall visits. They'd gotten along well, and were beginning to spend more and more time together—when Maddie could get away.

"What's going on, Cassidy?" Each being busy with her own life, they rarely found time to speak on the telephone.

"Can you run in the morning?"

"Sure." They'd started running a mile at the nearby high school whenever their schedules allowed. Cassidy was busy with her work, and Maddie was often too busy with her father to make it a regular routine, but since early morning runs, they'd been finding it easier to meet.

"I need a day with the girls, too," Cassidy said. "Courtney is more rambunctious than usual. Kirkland is still sulking about the Vanity 6 performance. My parents have invited us over to celebrate my mom's birthday. Honey, I am stressed."

Cassidy's parents hadn't been thrilled with her becoming a single parent, by less than conventional means. It had caused a rift between them that they were still working on closing. "Sutton said she's in. The final year of law school, Sierra fighting at school, Greyson pressing for a baby—she needs a day with the girls, too. What about you? How's your father?"

"He had a good day today."

"I don't mean to be insensitive, but you need a break, too."

Maddie wasn't offended. "You're right. I just don't know if I can get away right now."

Cassidy's was caring and understanding. "You need to take some time for yourself."

"I know, but it's…" She hesitated, and then couldn't contain her joy any longer. "I have a date, and I need to make arrangements for my father so I can go. My budget won't allow me to take too many breaks at one time."

"You have a date?"

Maddie could hear the smile in Cassidy's voice.

"It's Richard, right? You knocked him out at the party. He couldn't stop staring at you. He's called here about a million times trying to get your number from Kirkland, but he's so mad about the Vanity 6 thing, he won't take Richard's calls. How did he find you?"

"Richard?" There was nothing wrong with Richard, but he wasn't her type. He'd only noticed her post Vanity 6.

"You remember Richard," Cassidy was saying. She stopped abruptly. "If it's not Richard, who are you going out with?"

She spent the next few minutes gushing about her future date with Chevy. She'd wanted to go out with him since high school, but more recently when he reappeared at the library while playing matchmaker for Greyson. "I'm going to go for it," she announced.

Cassidy laughed. "Watch out, Chevy. What exactly are you going for?"

"A date. Are you listening to me?"

"Oh, a date. I thought you meant—never mind."

Maddie had the feeling she was missing the big picture, dating novice that she was. "What were you thinking?"

"Never mind. We'll talk in the morning. Six o'clock."

Chapter 5

As a member of the National Black Farmers Association, and Hannaford's head tree hugger, Chevy kept very busy in the valley. Besides working on the Ballantyne Wilderness Lodge, he looked into any complaints City Hall received about unlawful or unethical farming practices. The major agricultural commodities in Hannaford were poultry and eggs, dairy products, alfalfa hay, and apples. With winter quickly approaching, most farmers were preparing the land for the next season. Today he was visiting the Kent farm with his father to discuss the problems black farmers were having securing loans from the Department of Agriculture. A national lawsuit had been filed, but many farmers were still being denied access to the monetary settlement intended to remedy the initial discrimination.

"Thousands of black farmers across the country are having the same problem," Mr. Kent said.

The lawsuit resulted in a $2.3 billion settlement from the Department of Agriculture for loan discrimination. Eighty-five percent of the farmers seeking a settlement had been unfairly rejected.

"Before they pay out," Mr. Kent said, "the agriculture department says we have to find a white farmer in the area in the same situation who applied for a loan around the same time and was accepted."

Pop added, "Are there any white farmers left in Hannaford?"

Chevy readily supplied the names of the last three white farmers in the area. He knew this land as well as he knew his own body. "Those farms were inherited, and they aren't using them as their only source of income."

"How am I going to save my farm? The crops this season weren't what they should've been. Winter's coming." Mr. Kent shook his head in defeat.

"Don't give up yet," Pop told him.

Not long after moving into the home Greyson had purchased, Pop sold off his livestock and used his free time helping the struggling farmers in Hannaford. With his advancing age, and his sons off living their lives unable to work the land, he'd decided to become more active as an advocate for black farmers. This pleased Chevy's mother as it increased Hannaford's acceptance of the Ballantyne clan as a member of the town.

Pop continued, "My son will think of something. He knows the land, and he knows how the government works."

Chevy was proud to hear his father speak about him in this way. He only hoped to live up to everyone's expectations. The government was a slow-moving, stubborn machine. Obtaining the money owed to the Kents would be a daunting task, at best.

"I'm going to take a look around, Mr. Kent."

Mr. Kent nodded his approval, and Chevy left them inside while he surveyed the farmland. There wasn't much to see, but he found it hard to be stuck in the small confines of the

Kent house. He was an outdoorsman. He enjoyed observing nature and watching animals in their natural habitat more than sitting around the den smoking cigars with a bunch of the guys.

He'd had an ulterior motive for accompanying his father to see Mr. Kent. Somehow, he thought being around his father would give him a clue about the Eileen Putnam story. Anything Alex was mixed up in should be subject to scrutiny, but he knew his father.

Pop Ballantyne was a strict disciplinarian who worked hard to support his family. He didn't express his emotions openly, but there had never been a doubt about how much he loved his rowdy boys. Anyone who knew Pop couldn't dispute his undying love for his wife. This was why Greyson's insistence on investigating the Putnam situation puzzled him. No matter what Kirkland thought he saw, or Mama believed she knew, there was no way Pop had an affair. Chevy had gone along with Greyson's scheme not only to keep him in check, but to help prove Pop's innocence.

The Ballantyne men were faithful to their women. Pop had instilled in his boys at an early age the importance of honoring the woman you chose to love. Chevy couldn't deny that Greyson and Kirkland had encountered many obstacles to settling down with their wives, but those obstacles never had anything to do with infidelity.

As Chevy walked the grounds, he thought of the scene Maddie had caused at the Purple Party. He usually refused Kirkland's invitations, but he was glad Sutton had talked him into showing up to the Prince celebration. At first he only wanted to make a quick getaway from the purple-wearing look-alikes. He'd been trying to find an excuse to leave early when the Vanity 6 show began. Parts of his body still responded to the imagined vision. When he got home that night he couldn't sleep because he kept seeing Maddie dancing in the black camisole. Eventually he climbed out of bed, found an old copy of Vanity 6's first album, and put it on the vintage turntable he'd scored from his parents when they moved into the new house. He lay on his back underneath a sheet picturing Maddie on the makeshift stage. He found it convenient to sleep in the nude—he spent most of his time at home walking around in the buff—and when "Nasty Girl" filled the cabin his hand slipped beneath the sheet.

Maddie was beautiful. He'd always known it. What had surprised him was the hidden fire he ignited when he chastised her for enticing the men at the party. He never, ever expected quiet, shy Mandisa Ingram to swat away his hat and give it to him with both barrels. *No one* touched his hat. Now he was patiently—at least he wanted her to think so—waiting for her call. He was a little rusty when it came to dating, but somehow he'd muddled through asking her out.

"Chevy," Pop hollered across the field, "let's go." Pop waved to him, making his way to Chevy's truck.

He spoke to Mr. Kent before he climbed into the truck and started off.

Pop said, "It's a shame the way the government is doin' these po' farmers. It's not many of 'em left. The least we can do is help 'em any way we can."

"It'll work out," Chevy agreed. They had traveled a few miles before he spoke again. "Pop, do you remember Eileen Putnam?"

He hesitated as if he were trying to remember. "I recall her, yeah. Why?"

"Whatever happened to her?"

He scratched his head. "I don't know. Why?"

"So many people leave here and we never hear from them again."

"I guess they do." He didn't offer any more information.

Chevy didn't want to arouse suspicion so he shifted the conversation back to the plight of the black farmers. He'd always had a good relationship with his father. As the middle child, Chevy was quiet and a bit withdrawn when compared to his brothers. He was the peacemaker of their group, and it seemed he was always refereeing between Greyson and Alex. As an adult, he remained the voice of reason, struggling to keep his brothers out of trouble—their troubles always involved the women in their lives. He'd always been able to go to his father with his problems, and he was given frank, honest answers. He respected Pop and the way he'd sacrificed for his family. It was his father's devotion that made him want a family of his own.

Chevy was back at his cabin, eating dinner alone in the kitchen still dreaming of having a family, when the phone rang, stopping him from sinking into a foul mood of loneliness.

"I didn't mean to disturb you," Maddie replied to his harsh hello.

He sat up straighter, instinctively reaching for his hat. She had that affect on him—made him feel as if he were in kindergarten and she were his teacher. "You aren't disturbing me."

"Do you always sound so—so grizzly when you answer the phone?" She was scolding him, but he could hear a trace of laughter in her voice.

"Sorry," he mumbled.

"Apology accepted. I was hoping you still wanted to see a movie together."

He wanted more, but a movie was a good place to start. "I do."

"Next week Saturday works well for me."

"Next week Saturday it is," he answered, anxiously cutting her off.

Chevy's first mistake was taking Maddie to the neighborhood theater. His arrival caused such a stir the box office attendant punched the wrong keys and sent the automated ticket printer into spasms. The machine malfunctioned and everyone in line had to be ushered to the next window, upsetting those who were waiting in that line. His towering presence was so daunting the confession stand worker spilled most of their popcorn onto the floor. He scrambled around on hands and knees apologizing profusely as he collected the kernels (as if Chevy would have eaten the popcorn from the floor). The man bumped into another worker, tripping him and sending extra-large sodas into the air. Unruly teenagers started giggling and pointing once they realized the source of the commotion was the town hermit. When Chevy turned his menacing scowl on the teens they fled into the theater.

"This wasn't such a good idea," he said, looking down at Maddie's horrified face.

"We should go."

They did. When they reached his truck, the rear tire was flat. He usually carried a spare, but had removed it to haul the materials from the hardware store. He ended up calling Greyson to repay the favor he'd done when he found Sutton stranded on the side of the road. Too embarrassed to be in Maddie's immediate vicinity, he'd sent her home with Greyson while he waited with his truck for his brother to return.

Maddie lived in walking distance of the theater, but he would have died of shame if he'd had to walk her home, their date having failed miserably.

"What happened?" Greyson asked once they were on the way to Chevy's cabin.

"I shouldn't have listened to you and Kirkland, that's what happened."

Greyson blew out an exasperated breath, but his words reflected the sympathy he felt for his brother. "Maddie told me the people in the theater were …They're jackasses, Chevy. You can't be so passive when they start poking a stick at you. They'd never speak to me or Kirkland that way because they know we'd never take it."

His brothers would haul off with a right to the jaw. He turned and watched the countryside go by. "Was Maddie angry?" He wouldn't be able to bear it if he embarrassed her.

"No. She's worried about you. She said you didn't say much while you were waiting for me."

"I shouldn't have asked her out in the first place. Mandisa Ingram is way out of my league. Do you remember her in high school?"

Greyson shook his head. "I didn't spend much time with the underclassmen."

Different from Greyson's continuous fights with Alex Galloway, Chevy's only confrontation with Alex happened because of Maddie. He had always been able to tolerate Alex's arrogance, but when he turned his sights on Maddie, he'd jumped to protect her.

"There's a virgin I'd like to get my hands on."

Chevy turned away from the bleachers they were painting, as punishment for some antic or another, to see who Alex was referring to. Mandisa was standing with the pep squad hang-

ing ribbons and streamers for an upcoming game. Chevy had seen her many times in the hallway, but he was more shy then than now. She was pretty in a sweet and innocent way.

"Do you know how you can tell she's a virgin?" Alex was asking.

"Sutton's your girlfriend," Chevy reminded him.

"This isn't about Sutton."

"It should be. Leave Mandisa alone."

A slow opportunistic smile spread over Alex's face. "You like her?"

"Leave her alone," Chevy repeated.

Alex held his hands up in withdrawal. "Okay, man."

"You knew her in high school?" Greyson asked, dragging Chevy back into the present.

"I remember seeing her around."

"So, how are you going to make this right?"

Chevy shrugged one shoulder, stiffened by tension.

"You're not going to just let her go, are you?"

He didn't want to let Maddie walk away when he'd finally gotten up the nerve to ask her out. But he knew the best thing to do was not drag her into his life and cause her shame or embarrassment.

"Maddie's a good woman, and she likes you," Greyson went on.

"I don't want her to get caught in the cross fire again."

"*That's* chivalrous." Greyson did sarcasm well. "You're a Ballantyne, Chevy. We're natural seducers." His pride materialized in a grin. "We might play around a little bit, but once we meet the right woman we go after what we want. Women have no chance against our charm. Maddie isn't going to know how you feel if you don't show her. If she's the one you want, you better start fighting for her. You're strong enough to get her. You're the only one who doesn't realize you're a good catch. Forget the rumors and live your life."

Greyson had a point. Mandisa liked him well enough to go out with him once. There had to be a mutual attraction. He would never know what was possible if he didn't give it a try.

After a short pause, Greyson continued. "Let me ask you again, and this time tell me how you really feel. Are you going to give up on Maddie because of one bad date?"

"Hell no. She's my woman."

"I guess the rugged angry black cowboy *is* back in style." He laughed at his own joke. "Time to discuss your wardrobe."

Chapter 6

"We should work on endurance," Maddie told Cassidy as they stretched for their early morning run.

"Stretch out the miles, but don't worry about our speed," Cassidy agreed.

They finished their stretches and started out at a slow jog.

"How did the big date go?" Cassidy wanted to know.

"I was hoping to avoid this topic."

"That bad, huh?"

"Awful." She gave Cassidy the blow-by-blow of her date with Chevy. "My dream date turned out to be a nightmare."

"How'd you leave it?"

"He had Greyson drive me home. I haven't spoken to him since."

They jogged several paces before Maddie picked up the conversation. "I'm sure he has more dating experience than me"—*if you were to believe the rumors*—"but I'm more confident when we're together."

"Confidence is one problem Kirkland has never had." Cassidy grinned with secret memories. "Is it a turnoff having to be the dominant one?"

She laughed at the absurdity of Chevy being submissive to anyone. If the raw sensuality of his handsomeness wasn't enough to make a woman stammer and stutter, graphic appreciation of his massive size would. "No, I'm not the more dominant, just less shy than Chevy."

"You know what you want."

Exactly, and she wasn't sure if Chevy was asking her out because her attraction to him was so strong and he felt obligated to explore it, or if he had feelings for her of his own. "Is this awkward—talking about Chevy—since you used to date him?"

"Sutton fixed us up on a blind date. We went out a few times, but it didn't click for either of us."

"Why not?" She needed to know, but probably shouldn't have the picture of him with her friend dancing around in her head.

"Well…" Cassidy paused, gathering her thoughts. "To be honest, I found him very intimidating."

"Intimidating? Chevy?" He was gruff, and a little rough in a black cowboy sort of way, but she'd never be afraid of him. She knew how sweet and shy and nervous he could be around women.

"He's huge, Maddie!"

"He *is* tall, and very well built." Picturing him in his signature overalls and wide brim hat made her feel soft and feminine. "It's one of the things that's so great about him. He's big and strong and you know he'll protect you. He seems a little salty, but he's really very shy around women."

"And those are the reasons you're made for him, and not me. He's putty in your hands."

They rounded the track for the start of their last lap.

"You know," Cassidy said, "there aren't many women with enough chutzpah to challenge him the way you did at the party. It speaks volumes that he gave in so easily. And then he asked you out on a date. If he's the same Chevy I know, he doesn't travel far from his cabin, and he sure doesn't date."

"I wonder how much patience he'll have for the situation with my father." Maddie spoke openly to Cassidy about the trials of taking care of her father. She was the only person Maddie had ever invited to her home since her father fell ill. With the living room transformed into a hospital ward, bringing people home didn't bode well. After their openmouthed stares, they usually found an excuse to leave as quickly as possible. Besides, the cramped space wasn't conducive to entertaining. Other than the nurses, she and her father were always alone in the tiny house.

"Chevy is a very caring person. You can tell by the way he loves nature and animals. He'll be okay about your father."

She'd take it slow, see how things worked out between them before she introduced him to her situation with her father.

"Have you talked with Sutton?" Maddie asked.

"She's on board with the girls' day out, but she has to clear it with Greyson first," Cassidy answered between deep intakes of breath. "They have to make arrangements for Sierra. He's been really busy with a big project."

"Are the guys still mad about the Vanity 6 performance?"

A catlike smile spread across Cassidy's face. "It was a blast. I haven't done anything as outrageous as that since high school. It took a lot to get Kirkland over it. He stills grumbles about it now and then. Greyson was a little more upset."

She could imagine. The performance had ticked Chevy off, and he wasn't married to anyone up on the stage. "I'm going to call Chevy when I get off work today," she declared with sure conviction.

"You just do that," Cassidy encouraged by punctuating each word. "Go after what you want."

"He's my man." She tried on the words. "I'm going after what I want. As a matter of fact, that will be my resolution for the new year, and I'm going to start planning now. I'm going to accomplish some of the things I always said I wanted to do."

"You should."

"I am. Starting with seeing if my attraction for Chevy Ballantyne is real."

During the winter, Maddie closed the library early. Most residents of Hannaford bolted themselves indoors at dusk, sure to rise at dawn to work their lands. Unlike most city libraries that were extremely busy during the winter months because of college students, the Hannaford Library became a tomb when the weather turned cold. With the college annex the Ballantynes had lobbied for, the need picked up some, but not much as most chose to visit the annex library for their needs. Only a handful of people had ventured in today. She made the rounds, securing the library for the night.

Maddie had spent most of the workday formulating a plan to make her dreams come true in the new year. She'd always coveted the opportunity to travel and see the world. Why had she selected a monotonous job like small-town librarian as her life's work? A lot of it had to do with her parents' illness tying her down, but why hadn't she chosen to be the town's doctor, or a politician? She enjoyed the solitude and easy demands of the library, but she still wanted to see the world outside Hannaford Valley.

She locked the door behind her and started her walk home. The streets were quiet and only a few residents lingered. They waved as she passed, always a kind smile for the "poor spinster librarian who was forced to care for her parents and would never have a life of her own." Funny how they could spare her such charity, and be so harsh on Chevy, the town's designated "hermit." The kids at the theater had been cruel—some intentional, some genuinely shaken by their first encounter with the mysterious man who lived in the woods. Her heart ached for Chevy. He had hidden them well, but she could sense his hurt and embarrassment at their reaction.

Like a ghost out of the mist, Chevy pulled up next to her in his monstrous truck. He approached, his muscles flexing underneath snug denim overalls. When he reached her, he pulled off his hat and his hair fell softly around his ears, accentuating the stubble on his chin.

"Evening, Mandisa."

"Hi, Chevy."

"Can I walk with you?"

She nodded and he fell into step beside her. He wasn't a man of many words, but his heady presence spoke louder than a full set of encyclopedias.

After minimal small talk, he asked, "Can I have a chance to make up the other night? Maybe we could go into the capital tonight for a movie."

"I can't tonight, but I'd like to go out again."

"But not tonight." He turned sharply, something indescribable burning in his glare. "Do you have plans?"

Jealousy, she easily discerned—and she liked it. She liked knowing he had enough feelings for her to worry she might be seeing someone else. He had no idea how ridiculous the notion was. She hadn't dated since college. "My father—it's hard to get away on short notice."

"You have to make arrangements," he remembered.

"I'm responsible for my father. My aunt lives in the next town, but she isn't able to visit often."

"It must be hard for you."

With those kind words, she felt more at ease about his acceptance of her dating limitations.

"How is he? Your father, how is he? My parents are healthy, and getting along well. I can't imagine how it would be to see them sickly."

"It's very hard, but he's been improving."

As they walked, she talked with him about the burden of her father's illness. He listened intently, never judging her as ungrateful. She was sure to tell him how important family was to her, and how much she loved her father. He had strong ties to his family also, but he understood how hard it could be to forgo your dreams to do what was right. It felt good to share these intimacies with Chevy. True to his proven nature, he listened more than he spoke, allowing her uninterrupted expression of her dilemma.

"I've been going on," she said when they reached her house.

"Everyone needs someone to talk to."

"Who do you talk to, Chevy?" She knew she was pushing the boundaries, referring to his self-seclusion in his cabin.

He watched her for a long moment, then answered, "You, Mandisa. I talk to you about the things that are important to me."

His candid answer took her by surprise. She stood speechless, contemplating the gravity of his statement. Open communication was the foundation to build a relationship upon.

"You should go inside." Chevy shattered the silence. "It's cold."

"Thank you for walking with me." She had reached the porch before he called after her.

"If I heard you right, you're open to having another date with me."

She smiled. "You heard me right."

* * *

The following Saturday he made the date happen. Maddie had just finished feeding her father and was preparing to read to him from the book Todd had left behind when the doorbell rang. Not expecting any company, she hurried to look out the window. She smoothed her hair and pulled the front door open.

"Mrs. Ballantyne," she said with question.

Chevy's mother assessed her for a brief moment. "You're my son's girlfriend."

"Girlfriend? I wouldn't say—"

"Chevy brought it to my attention that as God-fearing, community-serving church folk, we've been lacking in our duty to you. We all knew you were here, alone, caring for your father and none of us stepped up to help."

Another woman Maddie recognized from church was exiting a compact car parked out front. She retrieved a bag from the backseat and started up the walk.

Mrs. Ballantyne continued. "Mrs. Kent and I are going to sit with your father tonight to give you a—a—"

"Respite."

"Yes, a respite."

"I appreciate what you're offering to do, but I usually spend weekends with my father."

Mrs. Kent joined them, nodding. "Except for the occasional Sunday you make it to service."

Maddie stared at the women, at a loss.

"Can we come inside, child?" Mrs. Kent asked.

Maddie apologized, helping the women inside with their bags. As she hung their coats, Mrs. Ballantyne explained how someone from the church would be giving her weekend respites. "Sutton's mother will be coming next weekend."

Maddie was overwhelmed with emotion. "I don't know what to say."

Mrs. Kent draped an arm over her shoulders. "We should've been doing this a long time ago. Hannaford takes care of its own. We should be apologizing for leaving you alone to shoulder this burden."

"Tell us what we need to know."

Maddie took the women into her father's "bedroom" and reintroduced them. Her parents had been very active in the church before illness struck, and Maddie was sure she saw a gleam of recognition in her father's eyes. She pulled out a picture board she'd spent many hours making with snippets from colorful magazines. "He's had all his medications for the evening. He's been very alert the past few weeks, so if you hold up this board, he can point out his needs."

Mrs. Ballantyne took the seat next to her father's bed. "You're reading to him?" she asked, examining the paperback. "I think we can handle it from here."

"Yes, we can," Mrs. Kent added, bringing a chair up to the other side of the bed.

Maddie stood at the foot of her father's bed.

"What's the problem?" Mrs. Kent asked.

"I don't know what to do with myself. I haven't had a free evening in…" She couldn't remember how long it had been—years? Surely not years.

"Why don't you get dressed and go into town?" Mrs. Kent offered. "Have you eaten?"

"No." She always settled her father before she had her dinner in front of the television.

"Why don't you go into town and have dinner?"

"Maybe." She felt unsure, almost uncomfortable with going to dinner alone. "I guess I could grab something to eat."

Mrs. Ballantyne nodded. "Don't feel obligated to leave your own house. We're going to come around every weekend. Let us look after your father while you catch up on your rest—do some of the things you've been putting off."

Hadn't she been talking about that very thing with Cassidy? Doing some of the things she'd always wanted to do in life. "I will go for dinner."

The women watched her, a little confused about her hesitation.

"I'll go change."

Cassidy discarded the old jogging pants for fresh jeans and a thick sweater. She tugged on a pair of warm boots and switched her essentials into a matching purse. She worked up her courage for having dinner alone, under the watchful eyes of the residents of Hannaford. She deserved this break. She could trust her father's care to Mrs. Ballantyne and Mrs. Kent. As she brushed her hair back into a neat bun, she made plans for future weekends. She could have her ladies' day out with Cassidy and Sutton. She might even go into the capital and spend the day at the mall. She could do the normal things women her age did without worrying about her father.

She would have to thank Chevy for making it happen. He'd found a way to give her a slice of her freedom back. How considerate of him to speak to the church on her behalf. She had never thought of approaching the church to give her a break from her responsibilities. She would never have had the nerve to ask, afraid they would've seen her as an ungrateful daughter not willing to live up to her commitments.

Maddie was pulling on her coat when the phone rang.

"My mother tells me you're free for dinner tonight."

A warm feeling spread through her chest. "Is she matchmaking?"

"My mother is the queen of matchmakers. Would you like to have dinner with me?"

"I'd like that a lot."

Chevy arrived at her door fifteen minutes later, giving her enough time to sit and talk with Mrs. Ballantyne. She told Maddie the story of her romance with her husband, up to their marriage and the birth of her three sons. Her pride was palpable. She had a special place in her heart for Chevy, her sensitive son who required a mother's undying love and protection.

"Good night." Cassidy kissed her father and raced for the door. "I'll be back by ten."

"Hold on a second," Mrs. Ballantyne called after her. "My son knows better than to pull up in front of a young lady's house and honk the horn for her. He can't possibly expect you to come out. He's been raised with more manners."

"And respect," Mrs. Kent added, folding her arms over her chest. "I don't think your father is liking what he's hearing." She peered down into Maddie's father's face.

Maddie hesitated, more embarrassed than ever. She wasn't quite prepared to introduce him to her father yet. She'd been having a good conversation with Mrs. Ballantyne and believed she had glimpsed the source of Chevy's compassion, so she pulled her into the den for a candid discussion.

"I asked Chevy not to come in," she admitted with downcast eyes.

"Why in the world would you—" Instant understanding.

"I'm not ashamed of my father." She slipped her hands into the pockets of her coat. "This situation I'm living in is a lot to ask someone to accept. I don't want to spring it on Chevy during our first date." She met Mrs. Ballantyne's eyes. "Do you understand?"

She watched Maddie for a long moment. "I do."

Relief removed the tension stiffening her shoulders. She was excited about starting a relationship with Chevy. A huge part of them being a successful couple would be embedded in their families. She didn't want to get off on the wrong foot with his mother.

"Like it or not, Maddie, you and your father come as a package. Whoever you're dating—whether it's my son or another man—has to accept your ties to your father. It's better to test his staying power early on." She offered the advice with the confidence of a mother who raised an honorable son. "Do you understand?"

She nodded. "This is good advice."

Mrs. Ballantyne smiled, and pulled her into her plump body for a hug. It had been too long since Maddie felt the loving embrace of a mother. She indulged, satisfying the need by holding Mrs. Ballantyne for a long time. She had mourned her mother, and gone on to accept her purpose in life, but every now and then she missed tender moments like these.

"Go on now." Mrs. Ballantyne gently released her, straightening her coat collar. "Don't keep my son waiting."

"You built this?" Maddie asked, disbelievingly. She'd heard about his famous cabin—and about the things that went on inside with the town's hermit—but she never could have imagined the grandeur of a home made of logs. Perimeter lighting illuminated Chevy's cabin. The roof was made with driftwood shingles, and white cedar framed large windows at the front of the cabin. With the light dusting of snow covering the grounds, it was a picture of tranquility.

Chevy climbed out of the truck and rounded the back, and helped her out.

"Can we take a look around?"

He answered with a tug on his hat and gave her a walking tour of the outside of the cabin. Pride in his craftsmanship was evident as he detailed constructing the house.

She was fascinated with details—a hazard of her job—and exhausted Chevy with questions. "Why did you choose wood? If you were going to build a house, why not something more modern? Or commercial?"

"Wood is stronger than steel." He went on to explain the physics behind his claim, giving Maddie insight to his level of intelligence. He wasn't just a simple cowboy. "With good care, this house will last for centuries," he said.

"You can pass it down generations. To your children."

He took her elbow, helping her over uneven ground. "Wood is nature's insulator," he said, avoiding a touchy topic. "Wood insulates six times better than brick. It gets cold out here in the winter. The lake on the other side of the woods really drops the temperature."

"You're building the Ballantyne Wilderness Lodge on the other side of the woods."

He nodded, continuing her tour. She noted his inability to boast about the good he did for the town.

"All the logs lock together." He demonstrated by locking his fingers. "I used logs with a double joint and groove, and secured it with advanced insulation and sealant."

"The fireplace is made of stone?" Maddie noted as they rounded the side of the house.

"I used to hunt until Kirkland reminded me a tree hugger should also be an animal lover. Sierra said it was 'creepy.' I took down the trophy heads over the mantel and donated them to a museum he had worked with."

"Are you a vegetarian?"

"No. I have nothing against hunting what you need to eat. I don't support animal research, or cosmetic testing."

"I've never understood why someone would want to kill an animal to make a coat." She smiled. "Of course it could be because I don't have the money to buy a fur coat."

A faint smile crossed his lips. "No alligator pumps either?"

"Never." She crossed her heart.

"Are you afraid of dogs?" Chevy asked as he unlocked the front door.

"I love dogs." Owning a pet would be too much work with her father.

"I have two chocolate Labs. They're skulking around inside. I rescued them from the animal shelter." The captivating hint of his smile again. "They have an attitude about being abandoned."

Inside, Chevy's home was even more spectacular. It was cozy, decorated with oversized furniture in dark burgundy, forest green, and golden browns. Much attention had been given to every aspect, including the layered drapes and soft lighting. He made a blazing fire in the huge fireplace, and the cabin warmed to a toasty temperature. She was wrapped in warmth and man-décor, and it felt good—inviting. She grilled Chevy with questions as she wandered room to room inspecting the details of his work.

The chocolate Labs were huddled together in a pile on the kitchen floor. They lifted their heads and scented the air, but didn't move. "Maddie, meet Porter and Placido."

"Latin." She smiled in recognition. Another indication of his hidden intelligence. "Porter is Latin for 'gatekeeper,' and Placido means 'to quiet.'"

"I'm impressed. They live up to their names when the mood suits them," Chevy said with some humor.

Porter disentangled himself and lazily strolled over to Maddie for inspection. She knelt down and stroked his shiny coat.

Chevy's gaze moved over her, warming her in places that hadn't been touched in a long time. "Mandisa originated in South Africa. It means 'sweet.'"

She stood, taking in the masculine features of his face. "Now I'm impressed."

Her body leaned slightly forward, inviting him to advance the moment of intimacy, but he was too much of a gentleman. "I should get started on dinner."

"Can I help?"

"No." His eyes slid away. "I want you to have a good time. Here. With me."

"I'm already there."

The pensive shimmer in his eyes disappeared. "Make yourself at home."

She left him in the kitchen to cook dinner while she freshened up in the guest bath. When she emerged from the bathroom to complete her inspection of his cabin, Chevy had added music to the mellow atmosphere. Toby Keith floated through the air from the vertical CD player mounted on the living room wall. She liked that Chevy let her roam his house alone, becoming familiar with every detail. He meant her to spend a lot of time there.

The master bedroom was breathtaking. Situated in the rear of the cabin, the room ran the length of the cabin. A large triple-pane glass window overlooked a cluster of trees. On the opposite side of the room was a sliding glass door leading to a back porch surrounded with rosebushes, which had been pruned for the winter. Maddie could almost smell the fragrance wafting into the room on a warm, sunny day.

This room was decorated in shades of browns and tans. The

sleigh bed was huge and inviting with a thick down comforter and a pile of fluffy pillows. On each side of the bed was a matching, sturdy oak table. They were identically decorated with brass lamps, and photos of Chevy with his brothers and Alex. The bottom shelf of each was stacked with books. Maddie made herself comfortable on the thick area rug, checking the spine of each book for its title. Forestry and animal subjects dominated his small collection.

She found a photo album and sat on the chaise next to the fireplace to leaf through it. The second fireplace was much more intricately designed than the one gracing the living room. Vintage photos of his parents crowded the mantel. Wedding pictures of Greyson and Sutton, and Kirkland and Cassidy, stood as pillars to the family monument. The babies, Sierra and Courtney, were sprinkled throughout.

Chevy's shadow heated her space. "I thought you might like something while you were waiting for dinner." He stood over her, Placido and Porter flanking him, holding a small platter, a bottle of wine, and a longneck bottle of beer.

She took the platter from him while he retrieved a folding tray and set it up next to her. He'd taken the time to slice fresh fruit. She dipped an apple wedge in caramel. "This is great."

"Beer or red wine?"

She offered him a lopsided grin. "Beer." *Tonight*, she decided, *will be a night of indulgence.*

He liked her choice and gave her a beaming smile as a reward. "I would have picked the beer, too." He took the platter and arranged the tray just so, stepping back to double-check his work.

She had learned he was a stickler for detail.

"Are you comfortable?"

"Very." She felt like Cleopatra all stretched out on the chaise with a handsome manservant waiting on her.

"You're not bored?"

She gestured to the photo album.

"Dinner won't be long."

"I'll be right here."

He watched her for a long, nervous moment before he excused himself to finish dinner. Placido and Porter stayed behind, draping themselves at the foot of the chaise, amplifying her queenly feelings. *A night of indulgence,* she thought as she watched the rear view of Chevy walking away.

Chapter 7

Chevy entered his bedroom and almost dropped the tray of fresh fruit onto the floor. Maddie was stretched out on his chaise, looking like an Egyptian queen. As his eyes roamed the deep curves and lush swells of her body, he immediately declared her the queen of his cabin. She made a simple pair of jeans and a thick sweater look like designer fashion. She was the first woman—other than family—to visit his home, and he was happy to see her so comfortable in his bedroom. He hoped she would be spending much more time there.

Clint Black was crooning about the joy of being in love when he approached her. She looked up at him, satisfaction shining bright in her eyes. Her natural beauty was blinding, striking him mute whenever she looked at him so intently. He managed a few intelligible phrases, left the snack he'd prepared, and returned to the kitchen to finish dinner. Placido and Porter fell under her spell, staying behind to sit with her until dinner was ready.

The timer bell rang, reminding Chevy the beef sirloins had been marinating in Italian dressing, freshly chopped cilantro, and chili powder for an hour. He placed the steaks on the center grill of the stove to cook for thirteen minutes. The glazed fall vegetables baking in the oven had been plucked directly from his garden, including the salad greens he was mixing dressing for at that very moment. He used extra-virgin olive oil, sherry vinegar, finely chopped shallots, minced garlic, and ground pepper to make the complementary vinaigrette. He arranged their steaks on china with eye-appealing detail, and topped them with fresh cilantro, chopped tomato, sliced avocado, and sour cream.

Dessert came courtesy of his mother. She was always giving him a sweet potato or apple pie, along with an interesting cookbook she picked up while on a shopping trip with Sierra in the capital. She was responsible for his interest in cooking. She'd advised him early on to know how to take care of himself. She was still providing the occasional dinner to Greyson and Kirkland, but he enjoyed being in the kitchen experimenting with new foods.

For the first time in a long time, he set two places at his table. The base of the glass tabletop was made from a hundred-year-old tree he'd hauled from the capital years ago while performing contract work there. The tree had been removed in the name of economic progress, but Chevy had found a way to salvage a small part of it's history.

Happy with the presentation of dinner, he escorted Maddie to the kitchen table. He pulled out her chair and shooed Placido and Porter out of the kitchen.

"This steak is wonderful." She raised an eyebrow playfully. "You cook, too?"

"I know my way around the kitchen."

"Better than that. It looks like a professional chef's workspace in here. What is this called?" She indicated the steak with her fork.

"Carne Asada." He dropped his eyes to his plate. Nothing seemed good enough for her. He needed to do better, to give her more. "Next time we'll go out to a real restaurant. On a real date."

"Couldn't get any more real than this. I was hoping you would make *this* a habit."

For a smile as radiant as she offered, he would gladly make it a regular occurrence. Anything to encourage her addiction to him.

"I would change only one thing."

"What?" He wanted her comfortable in his space, and he wanted her happy.

She stood, moving her place setting from the opposite end of the table. She sat at his left elbow. "This is much better."

"Much," he agreed.

They ate, sharing easy conversation. She had a nice way of relaxing him, and soon he no longer worried about tripping over his words. Working at the library, she read a lot and had vast knowledge on a variety of subjects. She discussed the topics that were important to him, asking questions to increase her understanding of forestry. She promised to put aside some books for him about raising Labrador retrievers. After dinner and dessert, they moved into the living room.

"You don't have a television," she noticed as they sat together on the sofa.

"I rarely watch it. You?"

"I'm a cable junky. I read a lot at work, but I spend most of my evenings glued to the television."

He took note of what gave her enjoyment.

"Your mother told me what you did." She focused all her vibrant energy on him. "No one has ever done anything so considerate—so kind for me." Her voice caught as if she were overcome with emotion.

He placed his hand over hers, covering it protectively. Her skin was soft, her bone structure delicate. The hairs on the back of his neck tickled his skin. "Someone should have a long time ago. What you're doing is noble, but you deserve to have some fun."

"And what about you, Chevy? Why do you spend all your time here alone? Why haven't you left this town to find happiness of your own?"

"Leave Hannaford? This is my home."

"You've never considered leaving?"

"Once. In college. I decided to attend school in the capital. Hannaford Valley allows me to live in the middle of nature, but everything I need is a short drive to the capital. I've never seriously considered moving away permanently."

"I dream about it all the time."

This discovery made him bristle with concern. He was just getting to know her. He didn't want to think about her leaving one day. He asked, "Why have you stayed?"

"After I finished college, I had to come back because of my mother. Now my father's sickly. Hannaford Valley was a good place to grow up, but there's so much more of the world to see. I read every travel book that we get at the library. One day I'd like to travel around the world." She went on to describe exotic destinations she'd read about and wanted to visit. She dreamed of living in a large metropolitan city, and working in the hustle and bustle. "You've never thought of traveling?"

He shrugged one shoulder. "I'd like to see the rain forests before they're destroyed, but I'm not as passionate about it as you are."

"Well, traveling will have to remain a dream." Her mood turned melancholy.

"It upsets you."

"No. Not really." She tried to lighten her mood, but he could see she felt trapped in the tiny town by her familial obligations.

He tangled his fingers with hers. "I have to tell you, Mandisa. I'm glad you're here."

One side of her mouth lifted, and her eyes dropped to their hands. "It's nice being here with you, too."

The last woman Chevy dated had not been a good a choice. He picked a pretty face and mature body, instead of a woman with good moral fiber. Her beauty had blinded him, because he highly valued an honest, principled woman, and he forgot to look for these qualities in her. He let this woman entice him into sexual exploration, assuring him no sexual fantasy was off-limits. She encouraged him to drop his inhibitions and demand what he needed to make the things in his imagination reality.

His sexual explorations came with firm borders, and when she had asked him to do something outside his boundaries, the accusations started. "I do what I have to do to make you happy," and "Anything you ask me, I do." She always had freedom of choice. Besides, she had been the aggressor, encouraging him to play her games. Guilt wouldn't force him to engage in activities he didn't feel comfortable about.

And then there was the matter about his *size*. She called it thrilling when their relationship was going well. She would use terms like "mutant" to describe it later. He was a big guy—over six feet, and two hundred and thirty pounds of solid muscle. Big and tall, solid and muscular—the words described *every* part of his anatomy.

His refusal to go beyond his limits became a chasm they

couldn't cross. Their relationship began to deteriorate once they both realized it was based only on sexual attraction. She didn't like being denied when she had "gone the extra mile" to make his fantasies happen. She told Hannaford's biggest gossip about one of their more vigorous sessions on her way out of town.

The story spread like wildfire, growing more bizarre with each telling. His world had come to an abrupt halt. His mother almost died of shame. The town started avoiding the sexual deviant, pushing him to find peace by building a cabin deep in the woods, which only fueled the stories. The children in town picked up on their parents' unkindness and made up little rhymes about the hermit in the woods.

Eventually, the pressure became too much and he decided the nonjudgmental embrace of nature and the wild was all he needed to live a good life. He'd retreated to his cabin, carving out a good career and learning to avoid social situations. He stopped dating. He went into town just before everything closed down for the evening. He became the hermit in the woods. But he never stopped being lonely. Watching his brothers find love and marry had been extremely hard for him. He was happy for them, but it intensified his misery. By the time he decided to reenter the dating game, no woman who had heard the rumors would come near him.

Except Maddie. She didn't show one ounce of fear. She knew of the rumors, but she still accepted his invitation for a date. Attempting to go to the movies had been a disaster, but she'd given him another chance and allowed him to cook dinner for her.

"Are you always this quiet?" Maddie asked, forcing him to put away painful memories.

"Mostly."

"Do I frighten you?"

He chuckled heartily. "How could a tiny thing like you scare me?"

She laughed with him. "It does seem silly, doesn't it? Why would you be shy around me?"

He understood her point. "You want me to be more talkative."

"More of a conversationalist, yes. I spend a lot of time alone. When I'm with you I want us to get to know each other, and the only way we're going to do that is to talk to each other."

"You want me to carry my end of the conversation?"

"Yes, I do."

"Are you seeing anyone?"

"You," she shot back, not wilting from his bold question.

"Why'd you agree to go out with me?"

"I had to see what it was like."

He grinned. "Why aren't you scared of me like the other women in town?"

"Scared of *you*? You're a big softy."

"Softy?" he rumbled.

"I know. You're a big, scary cowboy. I'm shivering."

He didn't know whether to be offended or glad. She'd stood up to him when he thought to reprimand her about the Vanity 6 performance. Now that he thought about it, it was her moxie then that had encouraged him to explore his attraction for her.

"Why'd you ask me out?"

"I'm asking the questions here," he teased.

She was unfettered, and waited for him to ask his next question.

"You're not intimidated by me?" he asked, still somewhat puzzled by her reserve.

"Not at all."

"What *do* you think about me?"

She took a minute to consider her answer.

"And I'm not a softy," he warned. The fire crackled, pushing him to press for an answer. "You've had enough time to get your answer together, Mandisa. What *do* you think about me?"

"You have a larger-than-life, hawking presence, but inside you're very sensitive. You're very handsome, but go to great trouble to hide it. You're devoted, astute, and gentle." Her gaze warmed. "Sexy. You're very sexy in a rugged sort of way."

He felt his face heat with her uninhibited assessment.

She continued. "You use intimidation to hide your loneliness, but I'm lonely too so I can see it clearly."

He watched her, speechless. She'd successfully touched a part of his heart no one dared to approach. She openly discussed his weaknesses as if they were flaws to be redeemed. She admitted her attraction without qualms, not worried he might react negatively. She was tough with enough mettle to meet any challenge.

"Did I get it right, Chevy? Are you all of those things?"

Chapter 8

"I'm all those things," Chevy answered, "and much more."

Maddie had no doubt. He was a man made of many layers, and the better she got to know him, the more complicated she discovered he was. She could spend a lifetime with Chevy Ballantyne and only scratch the surface of his personality.

"You're lonely?" he questioned. "Restless, but you couldn't be lonely."

"Both," she admitted.

"How could you be lonely? You're so—"

"So what?"

"Everything." His eyes met hers. "You're everything."

It was her turn to be shy, overwhelmed by his presence.

"What do you need?" he asked.

"Need?" The space separating them on the sofa shrank, and he towered over her.

"To settle you down."

"I don't need to be 'settled down' like one of the creatures of the wild." She tried to add levity to the moment, decreasing the heaviness of emotions filling the air.

"Yes," he answered softly, "you do." He tightened his hold on her hand to emphasize his point.

She was going to challenge him, moving their conversation to familiar ground, when he reached out and touched her. He used two fingers to trace her hairline. He started at her temple, gently stroking along the grain of her hair. "You do." He touched her with the confidence needed to calm an angry filly.

If this minimal physical contact made her insides explode, what would happen if he really touched her?

He moved in, millimeter by millimeter, leisurely shadowing her body with his. Her stomach danced with anticipation as if she were free-falling from a tall building. She wanted to throw her arms around him, ending the suspense, but she froze, waiting. For the first time, she understood what everyone meant about him being intimidating. His emotions were so strong she could feel his energy caress her skin.

He cupped the back of her head, and tiny sparks raced through her body. His fingers began unwinding her hair, removing the pins holding her bun. The pins hit the table next to the sofa, one by one, reminding her she was nearing the moment of reckoning. The sound was deafening, throbbing in her ears.

He moved in closer, pushing her body back. Denim brushed her arms and pressed against her chest. He smelled good—a mixture of fresh rain and sunshine. The sound of the pins disappeared, replaced by his rapid breathing. Her eagerness to be kissed increased, and her breathing began to match his.

His hand skittered down her arm, barely touching her, yet she jerked with each brush of his fingers. He used a firm grip on her thigh, bending her knee until her foot rested on the sofa beside him. She inhaled sharply as he fit his body between her thighs. Her eyes drifted shut, and when she opened them, she was lying flat on the sofa with him looming over her, his weight pressed against her.

He maintained his grip on her thigh with his other hand in her hair. He massaged her scalp, reminding her to breathe.

"One more question?" he asked, his voice a faint whisper in the back of her mind.

Her insides were going crazy, her heart jumping and her nerves vibrating. He couldn't possibly want her to work through the scrambled mess he'd made of her brain and answer. It had been so long since she'd been kissed, but she remembered it was nothing like this. Chevy hovered over her, bathing her in nervous anticipation. Her desires were at war. She wanted to pull him into her, but was afraid she wouldn't be able to handle his intensity once it was fully unleashed.

He gave her a minute to gather her senses, combing her hair out with his fingertips. His eyes were locked on her lips as he spread her hair out around her. "One more question?" he asked again, his lips dangerously close to hers.

Her eyes roamed over his face, taking in the determined jaw with its five o'clock shadow. Her hands wanted to stroke his chin, but her arms refused to move, lying limp at her sides. Her lips parted, and she almost found the willpower to push away her emotions and answer him. He moved slightly, shifting his balance onto his elbow, and Maddie felt his hardness press urgently against her thigh.

"Mandisa, can I kiss you?"

Her mind screamed *yes*, but it took great effort to put the three letters together to form the word. "Y-y—"

Before she completed her utterance, Chevy pressed his lips to hers. His body dropped down on her, covering her like a comfy winter blanket. His hand moved to her ankle, and he deepened the bend in her knee, making room to fit snugly between her thighs. The hardness lying against her thigh shifted, pressing—demanding entrance. The barrier of their clothes was too much, but not enough. She struggled to manage the kiss and the sensations shooting through her body.

Chevy sensed her fight and eased the pressure between her legs, applying it more heavily to the joining of their mouths. Her eyes drifted closed and she gave herself over to his ministrations.

Chevy's kiss was everything a kiss should be. He kissed her tenderly, as if she were a treasured jewel, nibbling the corners of her mouth. At the same time his mouth preyed on hers, demonstrating how much he wanted her, thrusting his tongue inside and demanding she accept him. She felt cherished and desired at the same time. He gathered her in his arms, bringing her entire body into the kiss. His lips were soft, but firm. He tasted delicious, like sweet potato pie. He smelled scrumptious, rugged and outdoorsy. His kiss was delectable, making her body tremble.

Chevy pulled away when she couldn't take any more raw emotion. He pulled his hands through her locks. "Mandisa. Sweet."

Chapter 9

Chevy hadn't been to a honky-tonk bar with his brothers since the night Alex Galloway announced his engagement to Sutton. The Denim & Lace was located in a modernized shanty just outside Hannaford Valley, deep in the mountains. The bartender served beer and whiskey from above the bar. The owner served moonshine from underneath the counter. The crowd was as diverse as the residents of Hannaford: old, young, educated, and illiterate. Most of the patrons were men, so the bar was rowdy and overflowing with testosterone. The women frequenting the bar were not the type you took home to meet your family, although most would go as long as the hourly rate was paid. Too many of the women remembered Chevy, acknowledging his presence with finger waves and bold winks. Greyson didn't miss their flirtatious gestures but was wise enough not to mention it.

"Another round," Chevy called to the bartender over the music.

"Sutton and Cassidy are planning a 'ladies' day out' with Maddie," Greyson said. "I thought you were going to get a handle on your girlfriend."

"From what I hear," Kirkland said, smiling, turning on the boyish charm, "he's been handling Maddie just fine."

"What do you mean?" Greyson asked, annoyed at being out of the loop.

"Mama's all fired up about Chevy's new girlfriend. She's crazy about Maddie."

"You took her to meet Mama?"

Kirkland answered, "He went to Mama and shamed her about not helping Maddie out with her father." He shook his head. "You got Mama to help you pimp a woman."

"I did not, and you're not funny," he chastised.

Greyson ignored his rising anger. "You shamed your own mother so you could take Maddie out?"

"Kirkland's exaggerating."

"I don't know what happened on their date, but when Cassidy's on the phone with Maddie, there's a lot of oohing and aahing going on. She stops talking whenever I come into the room," Kirkland added. "*And* she stopped asking me to give Maddie Richard's messages."

Chevy sat forward, clamping down on this bit of information. "Richard has been leaving messages for Mandisa with you?"

Kirkland nodded, taking a long swig of his beer. "Almost every day since the Purple Party."

He could feel his anger flaring. Richard had no reason to be calling his woman. "What does he want?"

"Maddie." Kirkland rolled his eyes toward Greyson and they both watched for his reaction.

Richard was a dog in need of neutering. Kirkland had picked up the stray in the capital. He worked a construction site Kirkland was involved in and they'd become distant friends. He usually showed up at Kirkland and Cassidy's parties gawking at the prettiest woman in the room. This time it had been Maddie. Chevy hadn't given Richard much thought after the party, figuring he'd move on to the next pretty face. He'd been wrong.

He refused to give his meddling brothers the satisfaction of saying they were right about his newfound jealousy. They watched him, waiting for an explosion of temper. Maddie was his woman now. After the kisses they'd shared no other man would come near her. Richard was inconsequential. *No other man* would ever taste her lips. No other man would ever press his body into the softness of her plush curves.

He grumbled, "Why did you call us here, Greyson?" He brought his beer to his lips, hiding a sneer and stifling a growl.

The bartender brought three longneck bottles of beer to the table and hastily departed.

Greyson watched his brothers carefully. "Stacy Taro will be in town the Monday after Thanksgiving."

"Why is Stacy coming here?"

Chevy listened as Greyson explained to Kirkland his inability to let the Eileen Putnam thing go. He swore Kirkland to secrecy, threatening to beat him to a pulp if he breathed a word of what they were planning to do. Some things would never change. Kirkland had always been the tattletale, running to their parents and blowing the whistle on Greyson's and Chevy's mischief. Greyson's bullying never worked, but he reserved the right to try as the oldest.

"You're down with this?" Kirkland asked Chevy.

He tugged at his hat, torn between his two brothers—always in the middle. "You know how Grey gets," he answered simply.

"Exactly. What're we going to do with the information, Grey?"

Greyson twisted the cap from his beer with too much vigor.

"Listen, Pop has been preaching to us since we were teenagers about how to treat a woman. How can we let him get away with cheating on our mother?"

"I don't think he did," Chevy said.

"We'll soon know for sure."

The table fell quiet as the gravity of their actions became evident.

Kirkland wanted to know, "Why does Stacy have to come here?"

"She's the best PI in the business, and she knows our family dirt better than anyone," Greyson answered.

Kirkland agreed. He'd recently had to employ Stacy to help him get out of a sticky real estate deal. "I'm not dealing with her when she gets here. She's all yours, mountain man."

Greyson chugged his beer. "Sutton and Stacy *cannot* be in the same place at the same time."

Kirkland and Greyson turned collectively to Chevy, and he didn't like the way they looked at him. "What?"

As the middle child, Chevy was often overlooked by his parents. Greyson was the cerebral corporate attorney who gave up everything to return to Hannaford Valley to save his hometown and claim the woman he loved. Greyson was Pop's greatest pride.

Kirkland was the baby, Mama's boy. Spoiled to believe he could do no wrong, until he did the greatest wrong. Overflowing with his pretty-boy good looks, charm was his weapon of choice.

Greyson masterminded the trouble, Kirkland reported it to his parents, and somehow Chevy always ended up in the middle. During his teen years he'd felt somewhat invisible, but his relationship with Greyson and Alex pulled him through. He'd taken to protecting Sutton as she bloomed into adulthood while her future fiancé, Alex, was off at college.

He'd accepted his role in the Ballantyne family without too much rebellion. While Greyson was in Chicago making a name for himself, and Kirkland was in the capital finishing college, Chevy became an only child in his parents' eyes. He came around every day to help with the animals Pop then farmed. He performed minor repairs on their childhood home. He escorted his mother to church when the weather was too bad for her to drive. He stopped by every Saturday for dinner. Temporarily being an only child allowed him to grow closer to his parents. He wallowed in his mother's tenderness, and absorbed his father's mean disposition.

He knew his parents on a different level than his brothers ever would, which was why he'd never believe Pop had had an affair. His mother wouldn't stand for it. She'd never cover up her husband's wrongdoings. More likely, she would have called her three hulking sons home and demanded they help her dispose of his remains.

"Why don't you come in with me today?" Mama asked as Chevy pulled the car in up front of the town's only church. She'd insisted he drive Pop's car because she refused to climb up in his "beat-up old truck" in her Sunday dress and hat.

"I can't come in dressed like this, Mama."

"The Lord wants you to come as you are. Let me out, and go park the car." She angled her plump frame out of the car, shutting the door on any further discussion.

Chevy had not planned on attending service. He hadn't been to the church in years other than to drop off or pick up his mother. The last thing he needed after the movie fiasco was to go into church wearing jeans and cowboy boots. But his mother's wrath would bring Pop's scorn, and that combination was scarier than anything the uppity society people could dish out.

Chevy parked the car and reluctantly made his way through the crowd inside the church. Mama knew he didn't like to place himself on display, and it bothered him when she wasn't standing near the door waiting so they could find a seat together.

"Brother Ballantyne." The reverend beat a path over to him. He insisted on greeting his parishioners before and after service.

The reverend was a quiet soul who delivered an uplifting message about how to overcome the trials and tribulations of everyday living. No hellfire and brimstone from him. That message had been worn ragged by his father, from whom he inherited the church and a faithful congregation. A middle-aged man, he had a quiet nature that was reflected by his quiet lifestyle. Everything he did held a message of warm welcome. He toiled at the church doing good works. When he wasn't at church, he was at home with his wife and new baby.

"Today is surely a day of blessings." He gripped Chevy's shoulder and tightly embraced his hand in a firm shake.

Chevy pulled off his hat. "Reverend. You haven't seen my mother, have you?"

"She's probably sitting up front as always."

Great, now he'd have to walk the length of the church searching for her.

"I sure am glad to see you here, Brother Ballantyne. We need more men to attend church regularly. Nice to know you found your way here as easily as those who find their way to the honky-tonk outside town." The reverend knew everything about everybody.

Chevy was saved the chore of finding something humble

to say that wasn't an outright lie of denial when the reverend was called away. They shook hands again and the reverend was off, greeting other parishioners who looked as if they were hiding a world of sin.

"Check the front pews," the reverend called as Chevy stalked up the main aisle.

He avoided direct eye contact with anyone as he made his way through the malingering crowd. His mother saw him and waved from her seat nestled on the end of the third pew. If not for the two apple pies she had baked him the night before, he would be very upset with her for roping him into attending church. He excused his way up front while kneading his hat between his fingers.

"Mama, please don't wander off again," he said, fitting his bulk into the seat next to her at the end of the pew. "I don't want to have to look all over for you at the end of service."

"Will you listen to this?" Mama said, a distinct cheerfulness in her voice usually reserved for those she was trying to make a good impression on. "My *son* is trying to tell me what to do. Can you believe it, Maddie? I bet you don't speak like that to your father."

Chevy's ears perked up the way Placido's and Porter's did when he picked up their feeding dishes. He leaned forward slightly to see around his mother. Maddie was sitting next to her wearing a conservative black dress with a dainty collar. Her hair was pulled back into a tight bun, but he knew how soft and curly her locks were. His fingers itched to touch her again.

"Hi, Chevy," Maddie said with a small smile. Dark, thick lashes brushed her cheeks.

"Why don't you switch places with me? I want to talk to Sister Rhett about the upcoming breakfast."

Sure you do, Chevy thought as he watched his mother hustle to switch places with Maddie. This time her matchmaking was welcome. He didn't mind Maddie's thighs being pushed against his as more people joined them in the pew. He enjoyed listening to the choir sing as Maddie hummed along. He didn't want the reverend's message to ever end as he inhaled the soft flowery scent of Maddie's perfume. He stole subtle glances at her throughout the service, knowing his soul would be condemned to hell if he didn't stop imagining how far they might have gone on his sofa a week ago.

"Can you have dinner with us, Maddie," Mama asked after service.

"I have to get back to my father."

Mama enlightened him. "The sisters are sitting with him so Maddie could join us at church today. I'm going to say hello to a few people. I'll be right back. Unless you want to tag along so I don't wander off," she added with a huge grin.

"Your mother is sweet," Maddie said as his mother walked away.

He could no longer resist touching her. His fingertips cascaded over her wrist and gently took her hand in his. Her skin was cottony soft and beckoned to be stroked. "Sit with me for a minute."

She gracefully sat in the now empty pew and smoothed the skirt of her dress tightly over her legs. She had strong, shapely thighs. "How are you?" she asked.

"I've been thinking about you."

She smiled and boldly reached over and took his hand into her lap. She stroked the back of his hand with neatly polished nails. "Me too."

The simple words conjured up obscene thoughts. Chevy glanced around and was happy to find most of the congregation had gone to gather in the lower level for brunch and further socialization. He cleared his throat, forcefully pushing down his growing lust. "You're going to have a ladies' day with Sutton and Cassidy?"

"Yes. Thanks to you speaking to the women at church."

"No camisoles," he said as a joke, but a sudden fire flared in his belly.

Her eyes dropped in shy obedience. "My performing days are over. Just lunch and a movie."

"Be good." His fingers danced across the hairline over her ear, and he felt her shiver at his touch. "Would you like to go out with me again? Next week?"

She paused to mentally check her calendar. "Next week is bad with the ladies' day."

He didn't like not having immediate access to her.

"You could come by and have lunch with me at the library sometime," she quickly added. "If you can take the time from your day."

They were so polite with each other it unnerved him. He broke the cycle. "I want to kiss you."

Her lashes dropped, and a flash of red crept up her neck.

"Right now," he told her, a definite dare in his tone.

"Did you like my kisses?" she asked, joining in the daring game.

"I think about them every night. When I climb into bed. When I wake up in the morning. When I breathe."

Another small shiver moved over her body and escaped through her touch on his hand. He trapped her hand between his, clearly using it as a metaphor to represent what he really wanted to do. He couldn't resist the sensuous call of her lips. He leaned forward, preparing to taste her.

Maddie's eyes flipped upward over his shoulder. "Your mother is coming."

* * *

Thanksgiving was painful. Chevy sat quietly as his parents' dining room gushed with lively conversation. Sierra and Courtney were seated at their own table, although it had been hard keeping Sierra away from her uncle Chevy. Greyson sliced Sutton's turkey and seasoned her food while balancing banter with Pop about the inner workings of the paper mill. Kirkland was nestled between Cassidy and Mama, as attentive as ever to both.

Chevy watched the dynamics of his growing family and couldn't help but miss Maddie. He'd hinted about inviting her to the family dinner when he brought her lunch at the library, but she declined without an explanation. He supposed it had something to do with her father. He felt guilty as he wished she were with him. She had familial obligations and he respected that. But it didn't stop him from missing her.

He had tuned out the family chitchat, concentrating on his second helping of food, when his mother's words to his father woke him from his insulated bubble. "Chevy has the loveliest girlfriend, Jack."

The table fell silent.

His mother continued, oblivious of the silent raucous she had caused. "I wish she could have come for dinner tonight. Her father needs so much care. I'll pack up something. You'll take it to her tonight, Chevy."

"Chevy's got a girlfriend?" Pop asked in unmasked disbelief. "When did you come out of the cabin long enough for *that* to happen?"

Was he supposed to answer?

"Are you talking about Maddie?" Cassidy asked. Chevy could see a switch flip behind her eyes. She had started recording the conversation to ensure accuracy when she repeated it to Maddie.

"Beautiful girl," Mama replied, still unaware of the awe hovering over the table.

"I didn't know it had gotten so serious," Cassidy said, casting an accusing glare on Kirkland.

He shrugged.

"Why do you two look so guilty?" She looked between Kirkland and Greyson.

"This isn't about *me*," Kirkland countered.

Sutton elbowed her husband. "Yeah. Why do you look so guilty?"

Greyson chuckled. "I didn't say a word."

"You two are up to something," Sutton said, "and we want to know what it is."

Greyson and Kirkland tripped over themselves to settle their wives as Sutton and Cassidy demanded they share whatever they knew. The noise level swelled. Greyson found the whole thing funny, laughing as he fended off his wife's playful swats. Pop huddled over his plate, shaking his head as his sons' antics. After detonating the bomb, Mama innocently wandered over to check on Sierra and Courtney.

"You're awfully quiet, Chevy." Sutton's voice rose over the milieu, too keenly noting his absence from the squabble.

"I'm eating." He filled his mouth with a mound of mashed potatoes.

Everyone quieted down, turning their attention on him. His angry glance around the table challenged anyone to pry into his personal business with Maddie. Telling looks were passed around the table with more vigor than the basket of rolls. No one dared suffer his newfound burly wrath.

Except for one.

The unbridled bravado came from a four-foot half-pint. "Uncle Chevy has a girlfriend. Uncle Chevy has a girlfriend. Uncle Chevy has a girlfriend," Sierra sang, holding in her giggles behind her hands. "Uncle Chevy has a girlfriend."

He cast her a look clearly marked "traitor." Sierra stopped singing her little rhyme. She was so adorable, his shadow, he couldn't really get angry with her.

"Chevy and Maddie sittin' in a tree," Sutton started singing.

"K-i-s-s-i-n-g," Cassidy joined in.

"First comes love." Sierra knew the words to this song, too.

"Then comes marriage," all the women in the room chanted.

"Then comes Chevy pushing a baby carriage," the men barked, giving the finale.

Chevy doubled over his plate of food and withstood a second round of the family sing-along. For the first time in a long time, he felt like laughing.

Chapter 10

Maddie pored over a catalog researching upcoming titles to be ordered for the library. Through the open door of her office, she heard a vaguely familiar male voice.

"Hey, Sutton, I didn't know you worked here."

"Part-time after school," Sutton answered.

"How's the family?"

Their voices faded into the background as Maddie flipped through the section of the catalog displaying new releases of books on forestry and horticulture. She hastily marked a few, already picturing how she would deliver the books to Chevy personally. Her goodwill might earn her another round of his magical kisses. Her mind slipped into replaying her date with him—she often relived every detail of their first kiss, and each time her body responded as if she were thrust in the middle of the action. Her name mentioned on the other side of the doorway caught her attention.

"I heard Maddie works here," the man said, clearly fishing for information.

"She's the boss. Is she expecting you?"

"No." He chuckled, distinctively masculine and somewhat wolfish. "I've been trying to reach her, but haven't been very successful. When I found out she works here I thought I'd try to catch her."

There was a slight hesitation before Sutton said, "She's in the office. I'll show you." She added an out for Maddie. "She might be too busy to see you now."

Maddie looked up just as Sutton entered the office. She was making all kinds of crazy faces, but kept her voice calm and normal. "Maddie, Richard's here to see you."

Richard stepped around Sutton, all smiles. "You're a hard woman to get in touch with."

"Hi, Richard."

He turned to Sutton and she reluctantly excused herself. He closed the door behind her. "Vanity." His eyes roamed over the parts of her body the desk couldn't hide.

"Maddie, please. Vanity is my evil alter ego."

He threw his head back and laughed too heartily.

"You've been looking for me?" she asked, closing the catalog. Being linked to Chevy while talking with another man seemed indecent.

"I'm in town visiting the family until after the New Year. I'd like to take you out while I'm here."

She tried to sidestep his request. "Where are you in from?"

"San Diego, California."

"San Diego!" Maddie leaned forward, planting her elbows on the desk.

He smiled—much neater this time. Or it could have been Maddie's fascination with traveling to new places that made him look more handsome.

"You like San Diego?" he asked.

"Never been. I'd like to though."

"It's a beautiful place. If you're ever out my way, look me up and I'll take you on a personal tour."

Before Maddie realized, Richard had pulled a chair up to the opposite side of her desk. He told her what seemed like fairy tales about a land far, far, away called California. He explained how a promotion at work moved him from Charleston to San Diego. His family—aunts, uncles, a sister, and a brother—still lived in Hannaford Valley so he came to visit every holiday. He and Kirkland became acquainted in Charleston while working together, and he always tried to pay him a visit while in town.

"Going to the Purple Party had an added bonus," Richard said. "I met you."

Sutton cleared her throat. "Time to close up, Maddie."

Richard stood, hesitant to leave. "I could tell you more about California over dinner."

Maddie glanced in Sutton's direction where she met a harsh stare. "My evenings are usually tied up."

"Lunch then? Tomorrow?"

She didn't want to date Richard, but she did like hearing about California.

Seeing her waver, he pressed on. "A quick lunch. I'll bring pictures."

"All right," she answered, but she didn't look in Sutton's direction—even when she heard a faint gasp coming from the doorway.

Richard solidified the time, and left quickly as if he knew Sutton might try to persuade her to change her mind.

"Chevy *is not* going to like this," Sutton said the moment the bell over the door tinkled.

"It's only lunch."

"Uh-huh. If you think Richard only has lunch on his mind, *Vanity*, you've got another *think* coming."

"Since when does Chevy have the right to say who I eat with? We've only been out twice, and the first time doesn't really count because he ended the date early."

"Three times—counting church—and that's a holy place so it's worth more points."

"Church was a fluke." She didn't ask how Sutton knew about their meeting in church. She had a feeling Mrs. Ballantyne was playing matchmaker.

"He's *fed* you. More importantly, Chevy cooked for you."

Sutton said it with such drop-dead seriousness, Maddie began to fear the seriousness of the act. As a kindergartener, when she was bad, her mother used to threaten her by saying, "I'm going to write your name and put it on the refrigerator!" The declaration was said with such conviction, Maddie would burst into tears, promising to be the best little girl in the world if only her mother wouldn't write down her name and tape it to the refrigerator. The threat was harmless, and really made no sense, but tell that to an impressionable child. Sutton's assertion about Chevy feeding her made Maddie feel like a bad kindergartener again.

"Why are you getting so upset about Chevy cooking dinner for me?"

"You don't know what it means when one of the Ballantyne men feeds you. It's their weapon of choice for seduction. It's like a spider spinning a web. You're the unsuspecting beetle that climbs into the web. Then *bam*"—she clapped her hands together, causing Maddie to jump—"you're caught—all his for the taking. He claims possession, and it's all over—*finite*."

"Get out of here." Maddie tried to smile, but couldn't with Sutton's level of seriousness.

"Ask Cassidy. Kirkland did it to her."

Maddie began to rethink her luncheon date with Richard. Her

heart fluttered a little when she imagined Chevy getting angry, and directing all that raw, pulsating energy in her direction.

"They learn it from their mother."

Maddie locked eyes with Sutton. She'd been effectively shaken.

The corner of Sutton's mouth quirked, betraying her humor. "Relax. It's not like Chevy is going to tie you up with spaghetti noodles."

She giggled. "Quit messing with me."

"Don't say you weren't warned. Chevy is going to flip his lid when he hears his girlfriend went out on a date with another man."

"Chevy and I had two dates," she reminded Sutton. "That doesn't make us a couple. Besides, *no one* is going to tell Chevy about my date—lunch—with Richard."

Sutton feigned insult. "Chevy is my brother-in-law. I can't let his girlfriend run around dating other men and not tell him. He'd kill *me* if I hid it from him. And I don't know if you've looked at Chevy lately, but he's a *big* man—too big, and too mean, to have angry at me."

"Sutton, don't you dare." She came around the desk, following Sutton out of the office, shutting off the lights behind her.

"If he asks, I have to tell him."

"He won't ask."

"Maybe, maybe not." She leaned against the front door of the library. "See you tomorrow."

"Sutton!" Maddie called after her, but Sutton was out the door, laughing all the way to her car.

Chevy held Maddie's hand securely inside his as they strolled through the botanical garden in Charleston. She reveled in the possessive comfort of his size while enjoying the winding pebbled walkway. Seasonal vegetation remained beneath the light dusting of snow. They passed through an elaborately decorated iron gate into the main courtyard. Chevy led her to a bench in a secluded area. Not many people were visiting the gardens in late November, and Maddie enjoyed having Chevy to herself in a place where he was most comfortable. The fences surrounding the garden were an architectural mix of textures and statues, all meant to relax the weary soul.

"Climbing roses fill the fence in the summer," Chevy said, his deep voice fracturing the calm atmosphere. "Native plants provide the landscape." He pointed toward the hardy plants near the fountain and lining another pathway. "The shapes, textures, and colors are what make this a winter garden. There's a Zen garden inside I want you to see."

"You know so much about flowers and forestry and animals."

"My brothers say I spend too much time with the trees and animals, and not enough with people." He pulled the lapel of her coat tight and wrapped her scarf around her neck. He tugged her hat, covering her ears from the cold.

"How often do you come here?"

"As much as possible. It's relaxing here, don't you think?"

She nodded. "I like that you shared this with me."

He moved closer, placing his arm around her waist on the bench.

"What's over there?" Maddie pointed to an octagon-shaped atrium across the courtyard.

An easy smile spread across his face, enhancing his stunning features. "The butterfly atrium." He stood, taking her hand and pulling her along behind him like an excited child. She followed willingly, his enthusiasm infectious.

Standing inside the thirty-one-hundred-square-foot man-made atrium was overwhelming. Three hundred butterflies shared their habitat with rare flowers and shrubbery. The smell of lavender filled Maddie's nose and she would come to always associate the fragrance with her attraction to Chevy.

He took her on a tour along the winding pathway, pointing out the various species of butterflies in different stages of development. He pointed out the *Danus gilippus*, blue morpho, and Zebra swallowtail. His knowledge came not only from frequent visits, but independent research. Vibrant colors excited the senses—red and black, green and yellow.

Maddie had never fully appreciated nature's offering until Chevy helped her to slow down and observe all that was offered. The surly cowboy became a gentle giant as he spoke in hushed tones so as not to scare off the butterflies. His eyes danced with passion beneath the brim of his Stetson. He was transported into another world as he explored the atrium, and ushered her along with him, hoping to share the intimacy of his world.

The inscription on the large boulder outside the entrance to the botanical gardens read PATHWAYS LET YOU ENJOY THE JOURNEY AS MUCH AS THE DESTINATION. As Chevy helped Maddie into his truck for the drive back into Hannaford, she couldn't agree more. A simple visit to a garden not fully in bloom because of the season had escorted Maddie into the secret place housing Chevy's heart. She learned more about him by watching his interactions with the thing he loved—nature. She watched the gentle giant soothe the untamable, and spit fire when what he treasured was threatened. Their relationship had been progressing at a slow, safe pace, but she sensed there was danger ahead. Beneath the layers of controlled gentlemanly behavior was roaring passion.

He held her hand the entire drive home. By the time he

pulled up in front of her house, he had filled her up and she felt happy and contented. He walked her to the door, lingering on the porch beneath the light and finding excuses not to leave. He seemed reluctant to go, and she didn't want him to.

"I had a wonderful time," she told him, confidently placing her hands against his wool jacket. She wished she could climb inside and press herself against the heat of his chest, soaking up the warmth of his body.

He answered by brushing his fingers along the hairline over her ear. He pulled her into him, wrapping his arms tightly around her waist. She wallowed in the erotic tranquility he offered. He pressed a kiss to the top of her head, cupping her neck while he did it.

She giggled.

"What's funny?"

"Sutton was teasing me about you cooking for me."

"What did she say?"

Maddie gave him a brief summary of Sutton's claims. "Is it true? Is food your magic weapon?"

"Magic, no. You're the only magic in my life."

His candid compliment made her stagger mentally. She'd come to know him as a man who didn't say much, but when he did, it was powerful and sincerely meant.

His mouth twitched with sexy intent as the right corner moved upward in a wicked grin. "Food can be a very sexy instrument of seduction—when used the right way."

"Chevy!" The master of propriety was flirting with her? After the initial shock, a hot wave of desire shot from her toes to the bun tightly fastened at the nape of her neck.

"You are so beautiful." Chevy lowered his head, his lashes dipping. He pressed their lips together, bringing her into the kiss by his hold on the back of her neck. He transferred his desire through his kiss, startling Maddie with the raw sensuality of it. Her arms wound around his back, slipping beneath his jacket and over his cotton shirt to feel the mass of his muscles. He fed her, and she hungrily accepted. He transported her further away from Hannaford than she'd ever dreamt of going. This journey didn't involved planes. He flooded all recesses of her mind, invading her senses and claiming ownership of her thoughts, feelings, and actions.

An insane need came over Maddie, and she wanted to wrap her legs around his waist. When his hands dipped lower, cupping her bottom and dragging her closer until she didn't know where he stopped and she began, she delved into his mouth, using her tongue with an expertise she didn't recognize. She let her longing for him reach out, an attempt to match his desire. She failed miserably, unable to retain position of rational thoughts and allow him to consume her at the same time.

Overwhelmed, she attempted to save herself by pulling out of the kiss, but Chevy wouldn't allow it. His fingers massaged her scalp, holding firmly as he nipped at her mouth. The kisses they'd shared at the cabin had been magically memorable, but what he did to her mouth now—there were no words for the emotions he evoked.

He leisurely pulled away, and her body reluctantly released him. His eyes were hazy with want. His voice was hoarse and raspy when he spoke. "Good night, Mandisa."

Kirkland barricaded himself in the room he'd added to his childhood home, which served as the family room. Courtney had chosen to join him, leaving Maddie and Cassidy alone in the room Cassidy used as her studio. Harsh bass thumped behind the closed French doors of the family room, but the rap music would not be contained. At times, they could hear Kirkland rapping along with Courtney's soft giggles joining in the chorus. Maddie, having grown used to Chevy's preference for country R & B, couldn't understand how the two brothers could be so different.

Cassidy didn't seem to notice the bump and grind of the music as she sorted through photos of her models. "What about him?" She handed Maddie a picture of a hunky, shirtless man. "With her?"

She compared the two photos. "They look like the perfect couple."

Cassidy had a good eye. As an illustrator of romance novel covers, she'd painted hundreds of couples in various stages of undress. She'd also painted pictures on commission for those who could afford her fees. She was responsible for the artwork that would hang on the walls of the Ballantyne Wilderness Lodge.

"I'm glad you could drop by," Cassidy told her, putting away the mounds of photos they'd been looking at. "It's fun just hanging out together."

"I miss Sutton though."

Sutton was busy with law school and her family. She hadn't been able to join them on this impromptu visit. Chevy had taken Maddie to dinner after work and brought her along when he had to pick up some contracts from Kirkland. She'd stayed behind while he'd run some errands and was waiting for him to pick her up.

"Things with you and Chevy look like they're going well."

Thinking of him made her smile. "Very good."

"You mellow him out," Cassidy observed. The doorbell rang and she excused herself to let Chevy in.

"*What* is my brother listening to in there?" he wanted to know.

"Rap," Cassidy answered, "always rap. Go see him before you leave."

Chevy came into the room, removing his hat when he saw her. "Are you okay?" Concern filled his eyes.

"I'm fine." She avoided looking at Cassidy.

"I'm going to talk to Kirkland for a minute. Be right back?" He said it like a question.

"I'll be right here."

Chevy sauntered off toward the family room. The music escaped the room with a blast when he opened the door.

Cassidy wrapped her arms over her chest. "Well, well, well."

"Don't say anything." Maddie hid her grin.

"'Are you okay?' What did he think I was doing to you while he was gone? Is he always so protective of you?"

"I hadn't noticed."

"Hadn't noticed, my foot." Cassidy threw a rag soiled with paint at her, barely missing.

Chevy returned quickly, ushering Maddie out of his brother's home as if they were on a tight time schedule, which they were. It was difficult to steal moments together when she had to be available most hours to care for her father. Chevy was more than patient, becoming a master at etching out time for them to be alone. This night they ended up on Chevy's sofa sharing his kisses. He had been eager to get her there, constantly checking the clock on the dashboard of his truck. He drove faster than usual to his cabin, and put Placido and Porter out in the dog walk without their usual stroll into the woods. The fire had just caught when he helped her to the sofa and took her in his arms.

Chevy pulled away long enough to explain his urgency. "I

just saw you four days ago at church, but it seems like it's been weeks."

She felt it too—the need to be with him again, as if they'd been separated too long. She let her eyes drift closed, as he descended on her mouth again. No matter how much he missed her, his kisses were tender. The only sign she had of his longing came in the stroking of her cheeks. His thumbs moved over her face as he brought her deeper into his kiss.

"Mandisa," he whispered, converging on her neck.

She flinched with every nip of his lips. Desire jumped from nerve to nerve, directed by the skill of his touch. His tongue darted out, tickling her ear. He took the sensitive lobe between his teeth and nibbled, distracting her from the journey of his hands. His fingertips pushed her blouse upward, his nails gently scratching the skin of her belly. He covered her body with his, kissing the tip of her nose. "Do you have *experience* here?"

"I don't understand." She didn't understand the question, or why it had to be asked at this particular moment—when her hormones were rallying for action.

"Are you a virgin?"

"Chevy!" She felt her skin sizzle with embarrassment. "You can't ask me that question."

"Why not? I need to know."

"Why do you need to know?" He shifted and she felt the ironclad reasoning behind his asking. "Forget I said that."

"Fine. So, answer."

Her stomach danced. "No."

"I don't have much patience for deflowering. How much experience are we talking here?"

"You're being wicked." She moved to pull away, but his arms tightened, crushing her solidly to him.

"How much? I don't need details, but I want to know if you've done everything you've ever dreamt of doing. Has your past experience been everything you thought sex could ever be?"

"Why are we openly discussing my sex life?"

"You told me you'd heard the rumors. I told you most were true. Didn't you think I'd want to know about your—sexual history?"

"I guess."

"So answer."

Her experience had been limited to one man in college. It hadn't been enough to satisfy her. "No, it wasn't all I needed."

He digested the information while his fingers danced on her belly, tattooing her with indelible ink. He pecked her lips quickly, and followed that with a longer, more meaningful kiss.

His body pressed against her insistently. His fingers explored her rib cage while his thumbs traced the underwire of her bra. Her breaths were coming in quick puffs—in direct opposition of the laziness of his kiss. She tilted her head back to give him better access to the tender skin of her collarbone. His hands cupped her breasts. A thumb slipped inside her bra, next to her skin. Brazenly, he pinched her nipple between two fingers, stifling her squeal of delight with his mouth.

How could he be both aggressive and gentle simultaneously? Maddie didn't want to ask questions, because she didn't need any answers. The only important thing at that moment was the way he was making her body feel. Frenzy, longing, wanton abandon—he evoked them all with his skill of seduction. Both of his hands slid upward to cup her head while his mouth moved to taste her breasts. She hadn't felt him open her blouse and expose her shivering skin. He blazed a trail across her bosom with his kisses.

His tongue lashed out, blistering her puckered nipple with his heat. He jerked backward from the arcing electrical charge. He regained his composure quickly, diving between her breasts for more.

His hand cascaded down her neck, over her shoulder, along the hairs on her arm. She shivered when his fingers glided over her hip. He approached her thighs with caution, allowing her time to extinguish the fire. She softened beneath him, cradling the hardness of his body with the pliability of hers. His hand danced fearlessly over the zipper of her slacks, dipping between the juncture of her thighs. Her back arched with the first graze of his fingers.

The phone rang.

Chevy cursed.

She panted, trying to comprehend the intensity of her desire.

He held the phone against her ear.

"Hello?" Her voice was husky with unfulfilled need.

"I'm sorry to interrupt," Todd said, "but it's getting late. I would have made arrangements if I had known you'd be late…"

Maddie reached for Chevy's arm, bringing his hand away from her breast to read his watch. She bolted upright. "I'm sorry. The time got away from me. I'll be right there."

Chevy cursed again.

"I have to go." She pulled him to her mouth for a kiss.

"But you'll be back. And we'll finish what we started."

"What is wrong with you today?" Sutton asked, taking the pushcart away from Maddie. "You haven't shelved one book in the right place."

Maddie accepted her scolding. Her brain had been mush since Chevy's incredible kiss the night before.

"It's a good thing I came in today." Sutton shooed her away. "Why don't you take lunch?"

"I'll be in the office."

Sutton tossed her a questioning glance before moving down the stacks with the cart of books.

Maddie was floating on clouds. Chevy's blazing kiss had released something in her—unblocked a door—opened a lock—lifted a spell—absolved her sins—she sighed heavily. She couldn't stop dreaming about him.

"Maddie?"

When she came out of her dream state, Richard was leaning over her desk, waving his hand in front of her face.

"Are you okay, Maddie?"

She waved off his concern. "Deep in thought."

"In a trance." He laughed. "Did you forget about our date?"

She was so hung up on the word "date" she couldn't process his question. Sutton's warning had been right—Richard thought they were going out on a date when all Maddie wanted was to hear more about life in California.

"Lunch," he reminded her. "I have pictures. I also have travel books and brochures about different tourist sights. You being a librarian, I thought you'd enjoy the reading material." He smiled innocently. "They're in the front seat of my car."

"Lunch," Maddie repeated lamely, her brain still lagging behind. She couldn't let Chevy's sexy, domineering, sensual, gentle presence in her life distract her.

"So, are you ready?"

"Sure." She pushed her chair back from her desk. "Let me grab my coat and purse."

Richard started prattling on about how happy he was she hadn't canceled their lunch. "I was really hoping to spend some time with you before I left."

"What's going on here?"

Maddie stepped from behind the door where her coat was hanging to find Chevy filling the doorway. He looked like some bizarre version of Little Red Riding Hood, gripping a wicker picnic basket lined with a red cloth.

"Hi, Chevy," Maddie said, still not fully realizing he was playing the part of the very angry Big Bad Wolf. "I wasn't expecting you."

"I see," he answered tightly. His eyes swung to Richard. "What are you doing here? And what did you mean by 'wanting to spend more time' with you, Maddie?"

"Richard invited me to have—" Her words faded quickly with the angry glare Chevy shot her way. "—lunch with him to discuss…" It even seemed lame to her with the unbelieving Big Bad Wolf breathing curls of white smoke from his nostrils.

"I'm taking Maddie out to lunch," Richard answered much more coherently.

Her head snapped in his direction. Couldn't he see this wasn't the time to be foolishly brave?

"You're not taking her anywhere," Chevy said matter-of-factly. "Maddie's my girlfriend, and my woman doesn't go out to lunch with other men."

"Are you with him?" Richard asked her.

"Well—we—ah—we—" Maddie didn't know how to answer. They had never officially defined their relationship—not that she wouldn't want to wear the title—but if Chevy was only using the label as leverage… Besides, he couldn't make such an assumption and demand it be true without giving her the chance to agree, or disagree. While she was debating the finer points of relationship etiquette in her head, Richard pushed on, escalating the situation.

He pulled his eyes slowly away from Chevy to look at her. "Maddie, get your coat."

Was he giving her an order? Maddie's mouth dropped in silence.

"You don't tell my woman what to do." Chevy gripped the handle of the basket so tightly his knuckles turned red. Maddie thought the handle would snap seconds before it actually did. He opened his hand, releasing the basket without regard to how it landed on the floor.

"Wait a minute—" she started, but the men had excluded her from the conversation as if she were a trophy to be won.

"You interrupted me the last time I tried to talk to her," Richard said, referring to Chevy's behavior at the Purple Party.

"*This* will be the last time you try to talk to her."

"Do you think I'm afraid of you?" Richard took a step forward. Despite him being at least two inches shorter than Chevy, he initiated a physical challenge.

"Stay away from Maddie."

"No."

Chevy's head twisted to the side as if Richard had just spoken in a foreign language. "I said"—he stepped forward, grabbing Richard around the neck—"stay away from Maddie."

Richard's legs flailed as Chevy backed him up against the nearest wall, pinning him to it. His hands came up, trying to pry Chevy's grip off his neck. Chevy leaned into him, his mouth close to Richard's ear as he spoke through gritted teeth. Maddie couldn't hear what they were saying, but the words were flying fast and furious as they struggled for dominance.

Sutton raced into the room, and Maddie realized her screams had sounded an alarm. She hadn't even known she was shouting.

"Greyson!" Sutton shouted. "Greyson! Chevy's trying to

kill Richard!" She huddled next to Maddie as they both yelled at the men to stop fighting.

Before Greyson arrived, Richard twisted his body and landed an elbow to Chevy's ribs. The move loosened Chevy's grip and Richard charged him. Sutton grabbed Maddie's shoulders and pulled her back out of the way of falling bodies. Chevy and Richard ended up on the floor continuing their fight for superiority. They wrestled, their heated words directed to each other so Maddie couldn't make out anything they were saying.

"What the hell?" Greyson ran through the doorway and jumped into the middle of the fight.

Was he helping Chevy, or attempting to break it up? Maddie couldn't be sure. Her heart was racing so fast—with fear for Chevy's safety—her brain was deprived of blood and oxygen. She didn't want Richard hurt either. Especially when the whole fight had started over an innocent lunch. Sutton had been *so* right.

Greyson managed to untangle Chevy and Richard. He shoved Chevy behind Maddie's desk before pushing Richard out the door. Richard said something about being anxious to see Chevy again when they could finish what they started before he huffed out of the library. The bell over the door tinkled, breaking the stunned silence in Maddie's office.

"I told you," Sutton whispered.

Maddie raced to Chevy. "Are you all right?"

"You didn't get hurt breaking it up, did you?" Sutton went to Greyson and wrapped her arms around him, clearly shaken by what had happened.

Greyson instinctively pulled her close. "I'm fine. You?"

Sutton nodded.

Chevy was breathing hard.

"Are you okay?" Maddie asked again, her hands moving over his chest. "You look okay. Are you?"

Sutton retrieved his hat and handed it over.

"What the hell was that all about, Chevy?" Greyson asked.

Chevy's breathing changed from angry grunts to the animalistic snort of a wild stallion. His eyes moved from Greyson to Maddie, and she shivered with the possessive madness shining bright behind his brown orbs.

His arms shot out and he pulled her against him—hard.

"Jealousy," he ground out before kissing her—hard. "Leave," he growled above her head.

"But—" Sutton began, but her protest was sharply cut.

Maddie tried to balance herself on legs that felt like noodles after Chevy's fierce kiss. Her mind had turned to cotton, and she pictured herself fighting to wade out of a room filled with the fluffy stuff. She heard the office door close behind her, and a sudden urgency made her heart pound.

She was her mother's child, and she could not let Chevy get away with making decisions for her. This wasn't about her wanting to be his woman, as much as he demanded it. This was about her independence and his respecting her right to choose. She was formulating her argument, still fighting her way out of the cotton room, when Chevy grasped her by the arms, his hold firm. Before she could protest, he converged on her mouth, staking his claim. Her eyes floated closed under his ministrations and when she *came to* she was draped over the top of her desk and everything that had been covering it was shoved to the side.

"What did you think you were doing? Going out with Richard?" he asked. Despite the expenditure of his anger through their kiss, his voice still sounded menacing. His body pressed hers into the desk, a very hard bulge resting on her belly. "You're *my* woman."

"I'm—"

"You're. My. Woman," he repeated, emphasizing each word. "I understand you're a modern-day woman with a career and a life of her own. I know you have to be strong and always in charge in order to earn your respect from the world. You have a lot on your shoulders taking care of your father and working too. I get all that, Maddie. But you need to get me. I like that you're feisty and confident, I do, but let there be no doubt. I—am—the—dominant—one—in—this—relationship. When it comes to you seeing other men, I'm putting my foot down and telling you it's not going to happen."

Maddie opened her mouth to protest his me-Tarzan-you-Jane routine—although she had to admit his take-charge attitude was a carnal turn-on—but he stopped her with his firm words.

"The best thing for *you* to do," he ground out, "is to remain very, very quiet and kiss me again."

Her glaze flickered over the hard, set lines of his face. She didn't dare challenge him as she had done at the Purple Party. This fight he would win. Beyond the jealousy was a level of desire he'd never directed at her before. He waited for her to protest, and when she didn't he lowered his head and gave her another heart-stopping kiss.

Chapter 11

Stacy Taro breezed into town the day Mama and Pop Ballantyne left for the ten-day Alaskan cruise their sons had purchased for their last anniversary. If all went as planned, she would answer all of Greyson's questions while they were cruising. Stacy was a dynamo crammed into a tiny package. Chevy found her wandering the front lobby of the paper mill, chattering away on her cell phone in Japanese. According to Greyson, her father was Japanese and her mother African. Not beautiful, but wildly exotic, she encompassed both cultures' features with her milk chocolate skin and eyes that slanted upward. She appeared disheveled and disorganized, but with an underlying lethalness.

A full five feet tall, Stacy managed to make a skyscraper-sized raucous in the lobby. She paced while holding army-green file folders beneath one arm and a briefcase slung over the other.

"Ms. Taro?" Chevy asked, coming up behind her.

She whipped around ready to wail on whoever had interrupted her phone call. "Holy cow!" she exclaimed. She spoke to the person on the other end of the phone, ending her call. She flipped the phone closed and shoved it into her pocket. "You're a big one. Any more like you at home? I have to know now, because if Greyson sends one more p-h-y-n-e brother to see me I'm going to pull my gun out and start shooting people wildly in the streets."

"I'm Chevy. I'm the last."

"Where's the mountain man?"

"He's finishing up a meeting. He asked me to bring you up." He reached for her briefcase.

Stacy jerked away. "No. I carry my own bags." She patted it for emphasis. "There are toys in here." She lowered her voice, speaking conspiratorially. "If I were to show them to you, I'd have to kill you." She smiled, a lethal, dangerous smile. "However, there are toys in my suitcase I'd *love* to share with you." In case he didn't understand her meaning she added, "At night. With the lights out. Or on, if you prefer."

Chevy gritted his teeth and showed Stacy to the elevator. He endured her shameless flirting all the way to Greyson's office. Kirkland stepped out of his office as they were making their way down the hallway. He looked up, saw Stacy, and ducked back inside before she saw him.

"Mountain man!" Stacy dropped the files and the oh-so-important briefcase on the floor and ran across Greyson's office to jump into his arms.

He grabbed her and spun her in a wide circle before setting her on her feet. They talked about old times and old adventures while Chevy looked on, gaining insight into what Greyson's life had been like when he lived in Chicago.

"And this one." Stacy hiked her thumb in Chevy's direction as they sat at Greyson's conference table. "Is he for me?"

Greyson scratched at his mustache. "I'm afraid he's taken."

Stacy muttered an unladylike word. "You mean to tell me I missed out on all three?"

"Afraid so," Greyson informed her with a smile.

Another unladylike word.

"There are plenty of eligible bachelors here in Hannaford Valley."

Stacy's brows rose at the possibility. "Let's get down to business so I can go sightseeing."

Chevy got into the habit of meeting Maddie after she finished at the library and walking her home. Even when the snow fell, covering the town in eight inches, she insisted on walking home. She ran faithfully every morning with Cassidy at the high school track. She didn't even own a car. Her father's jalopy was parked at her house, but she never used it and spoke often about selling it.

Chevy decreased his involvement at the paper mill and limited his time at the lodge to normal work hours. He wanted to spend every possible moment with Maddie. Working around her schedule and trying to find someone to sit with her father while they were out limited the time they had together. He wasn't complaining—he was happy to have her in his life any way he could get her. Stealing time walking together, or going to lunch, was adding up to a real relationship.

"Has the detective found out anything?" Maddie asked as they walked. She knew he was still uneasy about hiring Stacy to dig up his father's past.

"I don't know if she's working or chasing men. Greyson guarantees she's the best, so we'll wait and see."

"I got a postcard from your mother."

"Really?"

She dug into her purse, producing the colorful card. "Sounds like they're having the time of their life on the cruise."

Chevy read his mother's message to Maddie. Mama adored her and was not shy about making her wishes for their future known. Maddie had begun to spend more time with his mother during church functions. Mama had also done more than her fair share of visits with Maddie's father. They were building a friendship separate from their relationships with Chevy, and he liked knowing how well Maddie fit into his family.

"Oh—why is Dr. Carter at my house?"

Chevy recognized the town doctor's car by the medical license plates. "Don't get upset. It could be noth—"

Maddie sprinted off at a nice clip through the snow, leaving Chevy behind. Her running every day was paying off. He raced behind her, knowing how upset she would be if something had happened to her father. He burst through her front door moments after she'd made it inside.

"Calm down." Todd, Dr. Carter's nephew and nurse, reached out to hug Maddie.

Chevy placed himself between them, wrapping his arms around her shoulders.

"Hi, Chevy," Todd said.

He responded with a grunt. This jealousy thing was worse than Greyson and Chevy had warned.

Dr. Carter was next to Maddie's father's bed finishing his examination. The old man leisurely completed his work while Todd explained what was going on. "It's good news, Maddie. I was reading to your father—we finished the mystery and you'll never guess whodunit—and I asked him if he enjoyed it. He turned his head toward my voice and made eye contact with me. I wasn't sure if it was purposeful so I started asking him more questions. He couldn't answer any—except his daughter's name. He looked right at me and said, 'Maddie.'"

"What?" Maddie shrugged off her coat as she sat on the bed next to her father. She took his hand in hers, holding him with a tender touch. "Dad? I'm here."

Mr. Ingram had once been a vibrant man. Now he was fragile and his left side didn't move as well as his right. As Chevy watched Maddie interact with her sickly father, he realized two things. One, her father would always be her favorite hero. And two, Chevy was in love with her.

Maddie looked up at him with a tearful gaze, and then swung her eyes to Todd. "He's not saying anything now."

Todd joined her, speaking to her father with a strong voice. "Mr. Ingram, do you know who this is?" He placed his hand on Maddie's shoulder, but considering the occasion, Chevy decided he wouldn't break his fingers.

Mr. Ingram's eyes focused on Maddie. He looked at her as if he had never seen her before, studying every detail of her fretful face.

"Who is this?" Todd prodded.

"Maadee," he drawled. "Maadee."

Maddie sucked in a huge breath, dropped her head in her father's lap, and began sobbing.

Chevy signaled for the doctor and nurse to leave Maddie alone with her father. They crowded into the small den to give her a measure of privacy. After exhausting all small talk about the weather, Dr. Carter's practice, and the latest Ballantyne construction projects, Chevy joined Maddie at her father's bedside.

She grabbed his hand, hauling him right up to the bed. "Dad, this is Chevy Ballantyne." She looked up at him, full of smiles. She looked lighter, happier than he'd ever seen her. "I've been telling Dad about you."

Remembering his manners, Chevy pulled off his hat. "Nice to meet you, Mr. Ingram."

There was no sign of recognition from her father.

"The doctor wants to talk to you," Chevy told her. "Can I have him come back in?"

Maddie nodded, still focused on her father.

Dr. Carter returned to the makeshift bedroom along with Todd to give his assessment. "These things are hard to predict with any certainty, Maddie. We've talked about this before. His level of dysfunction always seemed too severe for the level of injury." He looked at Chevy. "We thought it had more to do with grief than a true estimate of what he was capable of doing."

Maddie nodded. "But this means he's getting better, right?"

"He's made a tremendous stride in his recovery. Since he's showing improvement, we can build on it."

Todd jumped in. "Medicare will cover the physical and occupational therapies if we can demonstrate the possibility of improvement."

Until that moment, Chevy hadn't realized finances might be a problem for Maddie. It had been insensitive of him not to. His own financial picture was made better by his investments in the family business and his need for only the simple things in life. He hadn't thought about how draining it might be for Maddie working in a small-town library, trying to meet her father's medical needs.

"Do we have any idea how this happened?" Maddie asked. "My father hasn't spoken in almost a year—since he came off the respirator."

"It's hard to say," Dr. Carter answered.

"What do I do from here?"

"I'll work on finding therapists who can come out and work with your father," Todd said.

"It would be best if we could work something out so Todd here is the primary nurse for your father. Obviously, he had a big part in breaking through to him. Patients are like that. They connect to one caregiver better than another."

"No problem," Todd said enthusiastically.

Why did this make Chevy jealous? He had serious work to do on managing his possessiveness.

"How far do you think he'll progress?"

Chevy dared the men to squash the hope in Maddie's eyes.

"It's hard to say," Dr. Carter answered honestly, "but we're going to work toward full recovery and accept the best we can get."

After the men left, Chevy sat with Maddie alone in the den, holding her close. She was bubbling with happiness as she showed him photo albums of her with her parents before their illnesses had consumed her life.

"I never believed my father would talk again. I always hoped—and did a lot of praying, but it had been so long… This is the best news."

Chevy kissed her cheek. "I'm happy for you."

"Todd is great. My father has always responded to him better than the other nurses. I trust him. He'll do everything he can for my father—"

He quietly interrupted her reverie. "Maddie."

"Yes?"

He took the photo album from her lap, closed it, and placed it on the coffee table. "Can I pry into your personal life a bit?"

"Yes," she answered cautiously. "You look so serious."

"I hadn't realized until tonight—"

She attempted to finish his thought. "How sick my father is?" Her lashes dropped and her happiness suddenly disappeared. "I wasn't trying to keep it from you. I thought it was best to wait awhile before I introduced you. I'll understand if you don't want to see me anymore. It's a lot to handle."

"Stop seeing you? I don't want to stop seeing you. I want to see more of you."

"You do?"

"Yes," he answered firmly, without hesitation.

"Then what do you want to talk about?"

"I hadn't realized how much of a financial burden taking care of your father is." He fully understood the emotional toll. "Are you doing…okay?" He broached the touchy subject with delicacy.

"We get by."

A woman like Maddie shouldn't just "get by." She should have everything she dreamed of.

"If there's a way I can help—"

"Do you think I'd ask you for money? I'm not going to ask you for money, Chevy."

"I didn't mean to wound your pride. Health care is expensive, and I have—"

She placed her fingers on his mouth. "I cherish the things you do for me because they come from your heart. Taking me out, spending time together—those are the things I need from you. They're special because you do them to make me feel special. I would never ask you for anything."

As Chevy leaned in to kiss her, he noted this new reason for how strong his feelings had become for Maddie. He realized as their lips met that he would do anything to keep her in his life. If there were such a thing as soul mates, she was his. Everywhere he was hard, she was soft. His flaws were her strengths. She looked at him with adoration and longing, not fear or apprehension. She was beautiful, capable of being a vixen, but instead chose to be angelic in her service to her father. Maddie was the type of woman a man approached only if he had marriage in mind. He explored her mouth, silently vowing he would always make her happy.

Honk! Honk! "Chevy, come get these beasts out of the yard!" Sutton yelled from the safety of her car.

"I'll get 'em," Sierra shouted, jumping from the car amid Sutton's protests.

"Hey, Trouble," Chevy greeted Sierra in his front yard and helped her corral Placido and Porter. They took the dogs inside and locked them in Chevy's office. He left Sierra behind to play and retrieved Sutton from her car. "You need to tackle your fear of dogs."

"I'm too old to change my ways."

They went into the kitchen and he made them hot chocolate while they talked. "What brings you by?" He and Sutton were friends and he had looked at her as a little sister long before she married Greyson. They often found time to talk at his cabin about life's problems. He enjoyed his candid discussions with her, and knew he could always seek her out for advice.

She looked a little frazzled. "Greyson and I had the mother of all fights."

"Greyson loves you." His standard answer to his brother's wife.

"You always say that."

He sat with her while the milk simmered. "What's going on?"

She took her time, watching closely for his reaction. "I want Stacy Taro to find Alex's child."

He didn't like where this was going. "You don't know that Alex has another child."

"Kirkland told us Alex got another woman pregnant just before he died. Really, it was inevitable the way he messed around on me. The woman in the car with him when he died was not pregnant. I checked. This means Alex's child is still out there somewhere."

He tried to keep a neutral expression, but a million questions were pummeling him. Alex Galloway had died years ago, yet he still managed to cause havoc with the Ballantyne family.

Growing up, they'd been inseparable—the Ballantyne boys, Sutton, and Alex. Unknown to everyone but Chevy and later Sutton's father, Greyson fell in love with Sutton. At the time, she was too young to date and Mr. Hill made it plain and clear he would never allow it. Greyson tried year after year, but Sutton's father kept refusing. When she became old enough to date, Alex beat Greyson to the punch, instantly getting approval from Mr. Hill. Alex played the perfect boyfriend for Sutton, eventually marrying her—and making her life completely miserable.

Chevy harvested some guilt about Greyson's and Sutton's misery. If not for his advice, Greyson would have gone after Sutton, challenging Alex and his motives. But Chevy had held Greyson back, telling him he had no right to interfere. He hadn't done it because he favored Alex over Greyson. He'd done it because Sutton had seemed so happy. If he had known Alex would inflict years of pain on her, he would have taken a different position. As she sat at his kitchen table fighting tears, the guilt resurfaced with renewed force.

He moved to the stove to add cocoa to the milk, stirring very slowly as he tried to digest what Sutton wanted to do.

He took Sierra her hot chocolate and poured them two mugs before returning to the conversation. "Why in the world would you want to find his illegitimate child? Alex is gone. You and Greyson are happy. Why dig up all the pain?"

She scooped marshmallows into her drink. "It's been haunting me."

Alex was more of a player in all their lives since he died than he was when he was alive.

"Shouldn't Sierra know her half sister or brother?"

"You're not doing this for Sierra, Sutton. Be honest."

"I don't want them to become the best of friends, but she is related to him or her. I don't want some stranger popping up years from now causing trouble. Look at Pete Frawley and Eddie."

Two men who they'd recently discovered were the products of affairs of Mr. and Mrs. Galloway. Those situations were too complicated to intermingle with this conversation. Greyson and Kirkland had been forced to deal with those discoveries.

"I don't know." Chevy blew into his cocoa and took a long drink. "What does Greyson say?"

She ran her fingers through her hair. "Like I said, we had the mother of all fights. He's outraged. Anything to do with Alex and you know how he gets."

"He'll calm down and you can discuss it again."

She shook her head. "He won't even consider it." She sipped her drink. "He was very mad. I've never seen him so mad."

"Give it time. You should think about it some more, too. Be sure this is really what you want to do. You could be inviting a whole lot of trouble into your life. What if this woman wants something from you? If Sierra meets the kid and wants to have a relationship, how are you going to handle it? And what about you? How hurtful is it going to be to meet one of Alex's mistresses?"

"I've thought about all those things. I don't know all the answers. For a year—since Kirkland told me—I can't stop thinking—wondering." She pinned him with a pointed look. "I have to know. Even if I don't do anything with the information, I have to know."

This he could understand.

"I want you to talk to Greyson and make him understand," she blurted.

"Oh no. I'm not getting in the middle of this."

"You have to talk to him, Chevy. He was really mad…he told me he'd leave us."

Chevy couldn't hide his shocked surprise. "He didn't mean it."

Her eyes fell to her cup. She took a drink to avoid answering.

"Greyson would never, ever leave you and Sierra. Never."

"He was very angry."

She kept saying that. "And still you're willing to jeopardize your marriage to find out who this kid is?"

"Wouldn't you want to know?"

Chapter 12

With Maddie's Dad getting better, she was able to get away more often. Todd preferred to work twelve-hour shifts most days, giving her some freedom after work. Her Dad was now able to form simple phrases, and the therapists were helping him regain strength on his left side. Her conversations with him took on new meaning as he made facial expressions when she shared her day. She moved a small television next to his bed, leaving it on the news channel. Dr. Carter thought it would be a good way to orient him to what was going on in the world. Maddie agreed, knowing it had been a part of his nightly routine before he became ill. He had a long way to go, but since he was right hand dominant, his recovery seemed to be progressing at a steady rate.

Maddie used her free time doing the things she hadn't been able to do in years. She spent her mornings running with Cassidy. They were running four miles a day now, and adding every day. Chevy stopped by most days for lunch, and dinner when Todd stayed late with her father. She couldn't be happier with the way things were progressing, stealing their intimacy whenever they could.

Today, Chevy had picked her up from work and taken her back to his house for dinner. They were walking Placido and Porter through the woods backing Chevy's cabin. A fresh layer of snow had fallen during the day, painting his property as a winter wonderland.

"What are your plans for Christmas?"

Maddie shrugged. "Nothing special." She would bring the tabletop artificial Christmas tree out and spend the day watching old movies. Her father was more alert now so she might sit at his bedside and help him unwrap her gift to him. The holidays weren't as special anymore as they had been when she was a child.

"It should be special. It's Christmas. Since my parents are away on their cruise, everyone's gathering at Greyson's for dinner." *Everyone* meaning the Ballantyne family. It would be a big celebration with lots of laughs. "Can you come?"

She tensed, feeling guilty about wishing she could be with him on the holiday. "With my father…"

"I understand. Spend the morning with your father. I'll pick you up later. You'll spend the rest of the day with me."

"I can't leave my father alone so long. He's doing much better, but…" It seemed such a burden when she wanted nothing more than to be alone with Chevy. Maybe if she'd selected a more lucrative career, she'd have the money to pay for twenty-four-hour live-in help for her father. "Sometimes I feel so tired," she confessed. "I don't mean to sound like an ungrateful, spoiled child."

"You don't. I understand. I know you would be with me if you could. It has to be enough."

The snow crunched beneath Maddie's feet as Placido pulled her along by his leash. He was the gentler of the two Labs. Porter, the gatekeeper, never remembered he was 105 pounds of unrestrained energy when he bounded up to greet her.

"Come here, Placido." Chevy took his leash from her hands and joined it with Porter's, easily controlling the rollicking dogs.

She wound herself around Chevy's arm, letting him guide her on their walk through the snow-covered trees. He pointed out markings of a deer's recent visit, tracking it with the skill of a bloodhound. The deer stood in a grove, searching for food, when they came upon it. Chevy whispered the command to keep Placido and Porter quiet and still. They observed nature in its habitat, Maddie fascinated over the pleasure it brought Chevy to share this with her.

"We should get back. You're getting cold." The thunder of Chevy's voice frightened the deer and it sprinted off, which made the dogs bark wildly. Chevy regained control, turning the dogs to heel, and they made their way back to his cabin. Inside, he released the dogs from their leashes and they raced off to the kitchen for food and water.

Chevy hung his jacket and removed his Stetson. His curls wound at the nape of his neck. Stubble couldn't hide the strength of his jaw. His fingers curled around her collar and slipped her coat off her shoulders. She shivered, rubbing her hands together to warm. He wrapped his arms around her, pulling her solidly into his chest. He enveloped her in his body heat, and she warmed quickly. His palms pressed flatly against her belly. Beneath her sweater. His thumbs caressed the underside of her breasts. Underneath her clingy bra. His lips nipped at her ear. His tongue stroked the pulsating cords of her neck. She shivered again, but not from the cold. He held her hips. Pressed his hardness into her bottom. Nibbled her neck. Heated her ear with his heavy breathing.

Her knees went weak. He tightened his grip, holding her

firmly against the front of him. He moved—scandalously—scrumptiously—against her bottom. Showing her. Telling her without words he was ready.

The length. The solid ridge. The…thickness. She inhaled deeply through her mouth. If he weren't holding her up, she would've swooned. Was she allowed to swoon? She didn't want to pass out and miss one delectable minute of his skillful touch.

His hand moved downward over the button of her pants. He toyed with the zipper. He found the clasp and popped it open. She had hidden her treasure behind a fortress—button, clasp, zipper. The gate wasn't strong enough to keep him out. His fingers parted the fabric. With unhurried laziness his hand found its way to the elastic band of her frilly panties. He pushed them aside as if they were made of tissue paper…his fingers touched the soft wool between her legs…and her eyes rolled up into her head.

Placido romped into the living room with Porter close behind, nudging a ball along.

Chevy took her hand and led her into his bedroom, closing the door behind them. He positioned them at his bedside. His eyes locked onto hers with unnerving intensity as he shoved his overalls off his shoulders. She memorized every bulging muscle, her gaze meandering over the outline pressed into his underwear. She had thought he'd wear boxers. She was wrong.

Her body suffered excruciating torment as she watched him unbutton his shirt. He moved too slowly—too leisurely. As if they had done this a million times—tonight—and she could wait until he was good and ready to show her what he was made of. She couldn't. Her fingers itched to reach out and rip the cotton shirt off.

Finally the last button. He shrugged out of the shirt. She sent up a mental curse. He was wearing a white undershirt. A tank top to tantalize her further, displaying the bulk of his arm muscles. He made quick work of removing it, tossing it at his feet. His solid body was tense, fighting unspoken urges his golden eyes readily reflected. His muscles were lean and brawny, rippling and needing to be caressed—massaged. He stepped out of the overalls, grabbed the waistband of his underwear, and pulled them *slowly* down the never-ending mileage of his legs. And then he… stood…up.

His hands were fisted at his sides. His erection was straining upward, ready to explode. He wanted to let go, but restrained himself, she suspected for her benefit. His size—

She wasn't completely innocent. What she lacked in experience she made up by reading. His size was beyond the *usual*. Powerful, towering, and demanding, his erection was flanked by the weighty twin sacs cradling his seed. His skin was flawlessly brown, a chocolaty melt-in-your-mouth brown—all over. She looked up and found he was looking down at the magnificence of its upward curve.

Their eyes met.

She reached for the hem of her sweater.

Chevy pushed her hands away. He wanted to be in charge.

He watched her with hungry golden eyes, awaiting her acquiescence.

They remained this way for a long time. She thought she would scream just when he reached out and gathered the bottom of her sweater in his fists. He pulled the shirt over her head and dropped it to the floor. His eyes flared to life. He stepped forward and slipped his hands around the indentation of her waist. Upward. With one practiced move, he discarded her bra. His breathing became deep and concentrated as he slipped her pants and panties off with one tug.

She stood before him naked.

He took a step back to see all she offered. To study his playground and decide where he would start his fun. His eyes roamed her body appreciatively, and with unbridled possessiveness. She was beyond naked. He had succeeded in exposing her soul.

The masquerade was over. They were fully exposed— emotionally. There would be no hiding.

Chevy folded back the comforter, and she made herself comfortable against the pillows. He sat on the side of the bed, opened a box of condoms, and placed them on the bedside table beneath the lamp.

She thought he would cut the lights, but he didn't. He wanted to see her. She doubted she could experience him uninhibited with the lights on.

She was wrong.

He straddled her waist and she thought it would happen quickly. Their desire was at a fever pitch and they would have to quench it as fast as possible.

She was wrong.

He pressed his lips to her ear and feathered her hairline with tiny kisses. He cupped her head in his palm and fed her his tongue. He was in no hurry. She stopped trying to anticipate him. He used his tongue to taste her ears, her neck, her collarbone. He raised her hands over her head, showing her how to hold the pillow while he lavished both her underarms in kisses. She flinched with each tickling kiss. His tongue lingered in her belly button. Her stomach quivered each time his lips met her flesh. She worked her fingers into his curls, pulling him closer, conveying her need for his penetration.

Chevy helped her onto her stomach and crawled between her thighs. His fingers danced over every inch of her skin as if he were learning to speak to her in Braille. He grasped her behind as he kissed, licked, and stroked her the back of her knees. She squirmed, the frenzy too much to stand.

He covered her body with his, wrapping his hands around her chest and holding her breasts. His erection fit neatly into the groove of her behind. He tweaked her nipples while he kissed her shoulder blades. He massaged the mounds of flesh as he licked the length of her spine. She wanted him. She needed him. She squirmed beneath him, her body demanding he let her turn onto her back.

Chevy lifted his bulk enough for her to turn to face him. As she settled beneath him, he ripped open the condom. Still he was in control, disciplined, not affected by the stifling heat in the room.

He caught her wandering hands and placed them on the haunches of his behind. He kissed her thigh, opening her wide for his consumption. He balanced himself above her and flexed his hips.

She closed her eyes and concentrated on the sensation of his erection parting her moist folds. The pressure fell away and his finger replaced it, searching and measuring. The blunt tip of his penis returned, nudging into her opening. Stretching. Tugging. Pushing. Insistent. Unrelenting. Until…*ah*. She exhaled through the pain. The delicious pain of prolonged needs met.

Maddie stroked the definition of the muscles on his back as he moved carefully in and out. She placed her hands on his haunches again so she could feel the flex of muscles there as he stroked her. He kissed her, transferring his electricity. He worked her body politely, with care. In no particular hurry.

While she arched her hips, desperate to have him deeper, faster.

She felt the precise moment when she gave everything over to him. Her mind raced. Emotion mixed with lust until she didn't know fantasy from reality. Jumbled thoughts. *There.* Ecstasy. *Right...there.* Romance. *Just like that.* Security. *Again. There. That way.*

Maddie's mind wound up in a tight emotional spool. Her muscles contracted tightly. She was perspiring. Something snapped, and the dam broke. She bucked beneath Chevy, grabbing his buttocks and pulling him into her. The tingle started at her core and uncoiled suddenly, exploding and splintering her vision until she saw a million stars.

The blast sent shivers across Chevy's heated body. His rocking deepened and took on a rhythmic beat. His hips gyrated. His knees bent, bringing him deeper inside. She encouraged him with the tip of her tongue. He grasped her shoulders and lost all constraint. Now he was clutching her bottom, bringing her into his upstroke. Flex. Bend. Curve. Pushing. Deeper. His body became rigid...stressed...tight...*ahhh*...relaxed.

Chevy rolled onto his back, dragging her onto his chest so she could continue to savor the closeness of their bodies joined together. Without any words, he'd stolen her heart. He breathed rapidly, panting. She buried her face in the crook of his neck and ingested his scent until she fell asleep.

She awoke several times over the next hour, aroused to find him settled beneath her sleeping. She was sprawled shamelessly across the expanse of his chest with his arms secured tightly around her waist. She stretched with feline satisfaction and climbed down the mountain of his body. She used his private bathroom and when she returned to the bed-

room, he was gone. He was cooking. She could smell the
hearty aroma of beef.

The master bath was a showplace, decorated in contrast-
ing black and white. Black tiles alternated with white for a
startling elegant effect. Built-in shelves held plants that grew
down to the floor. The diamond pattern intersecting the walls
matched the black tiles hanging from the racks. The masculinity enfolded her. Maddie inhaled Chevy's scent from the
bottles of soap and cologne lining the sink. She stepped beneath the hot spray and showered quickly, acutely aware her
time with him was dwindling away.

She wrapped a towel around her, securing it with a knot at
her breasts. Clearing away the steam on the mirror, she saw
her disheveled, sated appearance. She smiled, searching his
cabinets for a comb and brush. Finding them, she released the
knot of hair at the nape of her neck and began her grooming
ritual.

As she brushed her hair, she ambled back toward the bedroom, distracted by a sliver of light coming from Chevy's
closet. Something pulled her to investigate, and considering
she'd seen almost every inch of the cabin except this place,
her curiosity seemed natural. She pushed open the door of the
walk-in closet and cautiously stepped inside. This "closet"
looked more like a small bedroom with a dressing area and
large freestanding mirrors. Chevy's personal things were
neatly organized on built-in shelves. Many pairs of boots and
several pairs of shoes were placed in the cubbyholes on the
wall opposite the door. The cubbyholes to the right of his
shoes held row after row of hats. His clothes were hung in or-
derly fashion: jeans, shirts, jackets all grouped together. There
were a few articles of business attire near the rear of the
closet, probably because they were used least often. She ran

her fingers over the fabric of each, imagining what process he used to select what he would wear. As she moved deeper into the "closet," she saw it.

A breathtaking vanity, recessed into the wall. The vanity mirror reached the ceiling and fluorescent lighting softly illuminated the perimeter. A Victorian influence was evident in the powerful flare of the intricately carved design. The chair was made of gold curved bars and cream-colored cushions. She sat at the vanity and stared at herself in the mirror. Chevy had built a sacred monument of what could be. Her heart raced as she considered the state of mind he had to be in to take such painstaking effort to build such a detailed display. For a woman who didn't exist. Her body shook slightly. *The rumors are true,* he had warned her.

She placed the brush atop the vanity with a trembling hand. *Don't let your imagination run away with you,* she told herself. *What did the reverend preach about just last Sunday?* "And if I go and prepare a place for you, I will come again, and receive you unto myself; that where I am, there ye may be also." The reverend had taught from John 14:3. She remembered it clearly because it would be the theme of their next breakfast.

And if I go and prepare a place for you—
I will come again—
And receive you unto myself—
That where I am—
There ye may be also.

Chevy had prepared a place—

For whom?

"What are you doing in here?" Chevy angrily growled the words.

"I-I—" No, she wouldn't defend herself. He'd allowed her

to freely tour his home. There were other, more important things to discuss. "Who—"

He stepped deeper inside the dressing area, hoarding the space and making her feel trapped. "What the hell are you doing in here?" He added as an afterthought, "Sitting *there*."

She held the towel tightly to her chest. "Why did you build this?" she asked, keenly aware she was treading on unstable ground.

"You are not allowed in here."

"Not *allowed*?" Her apprehension about his reaction to finding her at the vanity changed to fury about being barred from a part of his life. "It's a closet. Why aren't I allowed in here?"

He looked taken aback by her audacity at questioning him. He shifted his weight, and for the first time Maddie noticed his bare chest. He had pulled on his jeans, but not his shirt, and the sight of his rippled chest caused a momentary distraction.

She pressed him for answers. "Who did you build this for?" She reexamined their past conversations. "The woman you told me about—the one you were involved with—you had broken it off with her before you built this cabin."

"Maddie," he growled in warning. He thought to intimidate her into not talking?

"Maddie, and not Mandisa?"

He didn't like to be challenged. "Get dressed." He turned and began walking away. "I'm taking you home."

Outraged by his dismissal, she jumped up from the vanity. "What if I'm not ready to go home?"

He swung around, his face set with hard, unyielding lines.

"What if I want to finish this discussion? What if I need more answers?"

He stalked up to her, using his height and girth to bear down on her. "You won't get them."

Being wrapped in the towel felt too naked. She clutched the knot at her chest with both hands, refusing to be intimidated. A woman had to be firm and set limits early in a relationship with a man like Chevy. "We're not through here. You can't just take me home because you don't like the topic of conversation."

"Get dressed." He stepped backward, away from her, leaving her cold. "In the other room." He walked away. "I'm taking you home."

She ran after him, too caught up in having her way to realize the time to back off had arrived. "The rumors are true."

This stopped him cold. He kept his back to her.

"You are a—" She didn't dare use the word. He wasn't the things people whispered about him. She'd made love to him, and nothing about it had been perverse or strange. The children's rhymes were completely wrong. He wasn't an evil hermit to be feared. He was a lonely man who needed to be loved.

But she had already started the sentence—put the words out in the atmosphere so the issue had to be addressed. And he did refuse to discuss his motives for building the vanity. She wasn't *allowed* in his *closet*. His actions raised suspicion. Her mouth was dry, her tongue thick. "Chevy," barely a whisper from her lips, "should I be afraid of you?"

Without his shirt, she could see every muscle of his back stiffen. His hands were fists along the seams of his jeans. He turned in a tight circle to face her. The hurt marring his face ripped her heart apart. "I'm taking you home now, and I promise not to hurt you on the drive."

Chapter 13

After the best love he'd ever made, his first words to Maddie had been *"What are you doing in here?"* Seeing her sitting at the vanity had come as such a shock to him. He wasn't prepared for the onslaught of emotions…and she kept picking him for answers. What could he tell her? How could he tell her? And now they weren't speaking and Christmas was two days away.

"Mr. Ballantyne?" The government man swung his eyes to Greyson.

"Chevy? Are you okay?" Greyson asked, worry clearly written on his face.

What had he been saying? Chevy looked up at the slide projected on the wall to jar his memory. "Working only with partners committed to reforestation, we plant one billion seedlings in the United States each year."

Greyson had heard the presentation enough to take over. "The paper mill strives not to deplete the environment. We work to reestablish at-risk species, ensuring ecological diversity and meeting the needs of the wild."

"Wildlife," Chevy corrected, pulling himself together to close the meeting. They needed the government-sponsored grant to complete a big project at the mill. It was all but won, and his presentation outlining their reforestation efforts would make it a lock—if he could stop thinking about Maddie and complete the meeting without zoning out again. It had taken a good deal of convincing to get the man to visit Hannaford right before Christmas. "Our goals include providing a healthy economy for the citizens of Hannaford Valley, along with conservation and renewal. Being proactive means working *with* the government to do our part."

Greyson walked the government man out, using his skills as a courtroom orator to put the man in the right mind-set. He knew just what to say to persuade and convince. He could phrase a proposal in such a way that investors ended a meeting begging to finance his projects. Chevy left his big brother to what he did best, hoping to escape the office before he returned.

"You're distracted," Greyson said, entering the conference room. "You've given this presentation hundreds of times, but you couldn't remember one entire sentence." He propped his hip on the edge of the table. "What's going on?"

Knowing the amount of teasing Greyson could dole out, he thought of not telling his brother what was bothering him. He remembered the long talks they used to have, and how Greyson always stood in his corner. If Greyson could help— and Chevy needed all the advice he could get when it came to unfamiliar matters of the heart—he would help.

"Maddie and I had a fight."

"Is that all?" Greyson stood and shoved his hands in the pockets of his slacks.

"We haven't spoken since."

Greyson winced. "Well then, better get to apologizing."

"I'm not sure I was wrong."

"Who cares? Make it easy on yourself. Women hold the cards in matters like these. Apologize and get on with it."

"With what?"

"It. Your relationship. Life. Your life with Maddie."

"What kind of convoluted advice is this?" Chevy asked, truly exasperated.

"Look, when it really comes down to it, is whatever you're fighting about worth never seeing Maddie again?"

Profound words to contemplate.

"It's Christmas," Greyson added if the season explained it all. He exhaled harshly. "If you want to persist with who's right and who's wrong, take a long objective look at the situation. Talk to Maddie. Whatever you do," he added with a grin, "don't break up with her. You've been doing a good job at keeping her under control and too busy to cause havoc with my wife."

"Maddie's not the firecracker in that bunch."

"Hmm." Greyson rocked back on heels, watching Chevy with all-knowing eyes. After a moment he asked, "Okay?"

He nodded.

"See you on Christmas." The paper mill would close at the end of the day until after New Year's.

"Greyson?"

"Yeah?"

"You and Sutton doing all right?" He hadn't forgotten his promise to talk to Greyson on her behalf.

"She came to you?" He wasn't angry, only curious.

He nodded. "I think she's going to do it. Or be forever miserable because she didn't."

Greyson cursed. "You see where I'm coming from?"

"He's like poison ivy."

"Alex won't leave my family alone."

"What are you going to do?" Surely, Greyson would never leave Sutton and Sierra. He loved them too much. He'd barked and made threats, but he would support Sutton any way he could.

"Talk to Stacy."

As soon as Greyson left the room, Chevy's thoughts turned to Maddie. Greyson hadn't been diplomatic in handling his problem with Sutton, and Chevy hadn't handled the situation with Maddie any better. He'd immediately become defensive when he saw her sitting at the vanity, looking like an angel—taking her place on the throne without consulting him first. It wasn't like she hadn't tried to apologize—she'd called within an hour of him taking her home—but he hadn't been in the mood to accept it.

"I'm sorry," Maddie said. "I shouldn't have implied—I'm not afraid of you, Chevy."

"Good to know," he answered tightly. He offered nothing else. He held the phone, knowing she was searching for the right thing to say to make everything better.

"And I know…" She paused. "In my heart, the rumors about you are not true."

"But they are."

"No." There was a small hitch in her voice when she added, "They can't be true."

"You wish they weren't true, but what you know is that they are. You thought I would hurt you because of the rumors you've heard about me." He'd never been anything but gentle with her. Even when they'd made love he'd fought every animalistic urge he had to salve his hunger and throw her onto the bed, possessing her with forceful hands and rough strokes. It still hadn't been enough. In the end, the one person he felt knew him better than anyone didn't know him at all.

"*Chevy, I never really believed you would hurt me—or force me to do anything I didn't want to do. We were arguing. I got caught up in the fight and said the wrong thing. If I could take it back—*"

"*You can't take back the fear in your eyes when you looked at me.*"

Her feisty temper slipped into place, and she forgot her tone should be apologetic and remorseful. "*You* want *me to be afraid of you. You* keep bringing up the rumors. *You in-sisted on being so mysterious about the vanity. You want me to be afraid of you so I'll push you away, and you won't have to admit the way you feel about me.*"

She had hung up on him, not allowing him the chance for rebuttal. Hung up on him! Mandisa Marie Ingram needed to be put across his knee. She was exhausting with her endless questions, trying to get to know everything about him. She was stubborn, refusing to go home when he insisted it was time for her to leave. She was too independent, not needing him to do anything for her—she even refused to allow him to help with her father's medical bills. She dreamed too much, too big. The only thing she ever talked about was seeing the world, experiencing what it had to offer. Mandisa Marie In-gram was just *too much*. She was a temptation, made to keep him in a continuous, painful state of arousal—only to find the real thing was much, much better than his fantasies. And worst of all, she was absolutely right about his anger in find-ing her sitting at the vanity.

All his musing brought him back to the same spot. He had to admit Mandisa was too much woman for him to handle, and leave her alone—forever. Or, he had to admit his feelings for her were too strong to let her get away.

He couldn't reason letting her get away. He wouldn't ever

have peace. He saw her face and smelled her perfume every single minute of the day and night.

Begrudgingly, he confessed to being hopelessly under her spell.

Now he had to get her back in his arms before she strayed too far away.

Chapter 14

Maddie's father sat up in a chair while she decorated the tabletop Christmas tree. She'd presented him with his gift early that Christmas morning—a set of novels by his favorite mystery writer. Breakfast had been light, and she wasn't planning a big dinner since her father's diet was so restrictive. The activity exhausted him, and Maddie helped him back into bed afterward. She sat as his bedside, watching television with him and reviewing her notes from the reverend's sermon of John 14:3. She couldn't get it off her mind, the mystery of the vanity and how easily it could be related to the good or evil intentions of its maker.

"What…reading?" her father asked. His words were still muffled and elongated, as a deaf person might speak. Maddie was overjoyed he comprehended the world around him and was making an attempt to become part of it again.

Maddie held up her King James Version of the Bible.

Her father smiled. "Good…girl." The "g" words were easiest for him to pronounce. "What…?"

"What am I reading? The Book of John. Actually, I've

been reading and rereading the same passage for the past few days, trying to make sense of it."

He bobbed his head toward the book, signaling he wanted her to read aloud.

It was a beautiful passage and she'd come to appreciate the simplicity of the profound message. "'And if I go and prepare a place for you, I will come again, and receive you unto myself; that where I am, there ye may be also.'" She looked up at her father, hoping for a sign of his previous wisdom and insight.

"Good…girl." He turned back to the portable television next to his bed.

And if I go and prepare a place for you—

Prepare a place for you. Those were the most meaningful words of the passage. They haunted her. Chevy had worked long hours to complete the intricate carvings of the vanity. He was preparing for someone's return, and judging by the heightened anger of his discovering her there, he wasn't waiting for *her*. Her heart was so entangled in her feelings for him, the thought made her want to fold up into a ball and disappear.

I will come again. He hadn't even called. Not after her botched attempt to apologize. He was being so stubborn and unforgiving she'd hung up on him. Her upper lip stiffened. He deserved to be hung up on. The man could be completely unreasonable when he set his mind to it. She'd extended her apology. He'd rejected it. Still, she missed him.

And receive you unto myself. The imagery made her shiver. Okay, so Chevy was the man in the relationship, and she should look to him to lead her—she couldn't even feed that line to herself with any credibility. Maybe she'd been wrong to push when he told her he didn't want to discuss the hidden vanity. She'd been completely wrong in bringing up the ru-

mors and alluding to being afraid of him. She wasn't, could
never be. It wasn't possible. He treated her with care and respect, always protecting her.

That where I am— Where is he? she asked herself. How
was he spending his Christmas? He had mentioned a family
dinner at Greyson's house. She pictured him there—alone—
while his brothers had their families at their sides. *Won't he
be lonely?* She couldn't help worrying about him. She cared
for him.

—*There ye may be also.* Maddie pushed down her emotions. She wanted so badly to be with him.

So there it was. She'd read the passage again and again, and
now she knew the message had been *for* her, not *about* Chevy.

"F-f-f-fone," her father pushed out.

She hadn't heard it ringing. She raced to the den to answer.

"I'm so sorry," Todd said. "Time got away from me, but
I'm in the car. I'm only ten minutes away."

She didn't understand. "My father isn't scheduled to have
a nurse today. Besides, I thought you were off today." She took
care of her dad when she wasn't working.

"Chevy Ballantyne called the agency days ago to make the
arrangements. He requested me. I talked to him myself. He
was very specific about what your father would need."

Several days ago, and probably before their fight. She
searched for a delicate way to tell Todd his services wouldn't
be needed after all. "I think there may have been a change of
plans, and Chevy forgot to call and cancel. We don't have any
plans for today. I'm here, and able to look after my father."

"Oh, man. I hope not. He offered a nice bonus. Maybe I
can come anyway. Everything has been arranged. Isn't there
something you'd like to do for Christmas? Visit a friend or
something?"

Obviously, Todd needed the money for the visit, and her father was fond of him. She could use the company to ward off the holiday blues. "Okay, I'll see you in ten minutes."

Less than ten minutes later, the doorbell rang.

Maddie's mouth dropped in disbelief. Chevy was standing at her door, but that wasn't the shocking thing. What made her sway with jolting surprise was Chevy dressed in a black tuxedo covered by a black, wool overcoat. She openly stared, memorizing every detail of the three-button notch lapel, the way the single-breasted jacket strained to tame his muscular physique, and the razor-sharp pleat running the length of his legs. Layered beneath the jacket were a five-button vest, crisp white shirt, and traditional tie. Her fingers itched to dance across the pattern in his vest, over the terrain of rippling muscles and flat abdomen. His shoes were shiny, despite the snow-covered walk to her door.

"Merry Christmas." He removed the black hat—this hat more subtle than his everyday wear. It was made of black wool with a matching silk headband circling it. His face had been shaved clean, softening the hard lines of his chiseled chin. His hair still fell to the nape of his neck, but the thick curls weren't as unruly as usual. He was simply mouthwatering.

"Merry Christmas," she managed.

"I accept your apology, and offer mine."

She was too dazzled by his audacious handsomeness to even remember what their fight had been about. Her heart was chugging along faster than a runaway train.

"Do you have plans for the rest of the evening?"

Had she stepped into old-world London? The dream was so real she thought she heard horse-drawn carriages clopping by.

Todd's horn sounded as he pulled up into the driveway next to her house. Maddie looked around Chevy, and gasped. A shiny black limousine was parked in front of her house. She looked up at him, askance. "What are you up to?"

"How long will it take you to get dressed?"

"I don't own anything like—" Like the fabulous designer tuxedo he was wearing. Wherever they were going, she would be out of place.

"I'm wearing this for you," he said as if the matter was simply resolved. He watched her, bewildered.

She let the men in, made sure Chevy was comfortable in the den, and went to change. Completely dismayed with her wardrobe, she flopped down on the bed hoping for a miracle. She recited the only scripture she could remember: John 14:3. Before she finished the verse, the idea hit her. She rushed to the bedroom next to hers where her mother and father had slept. The room was mostly used to store her father's extra medical equipment now.

"How much longer?" Chevy called as she darted inside the room.

"Not long," she answered, focused on her mission.

She opened the closet, pulled the cord for the overhead light, and shoved aside her father's suits. In the back of the closet were her mother's old clothes. "Vintage clothing," the fashion magazines would call the wardrobe. It took only a minute to find a dress she could wear. It was her mother's favorite cocktail dress. Her grandparents had purchased it for her mother in the late 1960s for her first formal dance with her father. The velvet dress had a jet-black top and funky 1960s floral-print skirt.

The straight cut fit Maddie's frame, hugging her body snugly. Her top was a little bigger than her mother's, but the busts were darted for a tailored fit. Fully lined, with long sleeves, the dress was perfect for the cold weather. She reached behind her and pulled up the zippered back, rounding out the neckline. She discarded the belt, and found the dress to look better without it.

She weaved a tomato-red silk scarf through her hair, sweeping it upward away from her face. After dusting her cheeks and lips with color, she presented herself to her father.

His tears spoke volumes.

The interior of the black stretch limousine was as elegant as Chevy's tuxedo. He helped her inside and offered her a drink.

"Beer."

He smiled at her selection and retrieved two longneck bottles from the refrigerator.

"Where are we going?"

"Have you eaten? I thought we'd have dinner with my family."

"All of this for dinner?" She ran her hand across the seat.

"All of this for you."

She sipped from her beer. "Chevy, I'm really sorry about the other day."

He took her hand in his. "We'll talk about it later."

Greyson's eyes bugged out when he opened his front door. He examined them closer before his gaze slipped to the limousine parked in front of his house. Recovering, he took Maddie's hand and pulled her inside.

Chevy hung their coats and they followed Greyson into the formal dining room where everyone had gathered and were waiting for Chevy's arrival. Everyone was buzzing around, laughing and having a good time. The table was set with dish after dish, dessert after dessert. They stepped into the room, Greyson cleared his throat, and everyone looked up. The room fell into a stunned silence.

Kirkland looked over at Cassidy. "I didn't know we were supposed to get dressed up."

"Shh." She elbowed him.

"You're just in time," Sutton greeted them. "Greyson, get everybody seated while I set a place for Maddie."

She glanced up at Chevy, but he was busy finding her a place at the table. They weren't expecting her, but a lot of planning had gone into hiring Todd, renting a limo, and dressing like Prince Charming. She slipped into the chair between Cassidy and Chevy.

Cassidy leaned over and whispered in her ear, "What did you *do* to him? Chevy in a tux?"

Sutton arranged a place setting for Chevy and took a seat next to Greyson at the head of the table. Everyone still seemed a little disoriented by Chevy's appearance and Maddie's invitation to Christmas dinner. She knew food was a big deal to the Ballantynes. Inviting a date to a holiday family dinner must be out of the stratosphere.

"Well," Greyson started, "I guess I'll be the one to say what everyone is thinking. Maddie, how did you get my brother out of his jeans?"

The table erupted in laughter.

"Maybe not the best choice of words," Greyson added, kissing Sutton's cheek.

The warmth Maddie felt at sharing dinner with friends could never be duplicated. She mourned her mother, the person who made them hold to family traditions. She missed the vibrant, boisterous man her father used to be before the massive stroke left him fragile. Dinner with the Ballantynes would never replace having her own parents, but they filled a void she'd always thought impossible to fill.

After the meal, the men wandered off to the entertainment room to watch a football game on the big-screen TV. Maddie suspected they were grilling Chevy more than watching the game. Sierra and Courtney sat beneath a Christmas tree that touched the tall ceilings of Sutton's home and played with their new toys. Cassidy and Sutton each grabbed one of Maddie's arms and hauled her into the living room.

"What fairy-tale story did you two step out of?" The perfect hostess, Sutton offered drinks.

"Sleeping Beauty in reverse," Cassidy answered. "Maddie kissed Chevy and he awoke from his thirty-two-year nap."

She smiled with the pride of thinking she might have been partially responsible for the debonair man who had escorted her to dinner.

"Tell us everything." Sutton sat next to her on the sofa.

"And hurry up before Chevy tramps in here to see if you're all right."

"What?" Sutton grinned, anxious to hear the explanation.

Thank goodness, Chevy did come check on Maddie, because Cassidy and Sutton grilled her for as much detail as she would give about their relationship. She didn't mind sharing her happiness with her friends, but after her fight with Chevy, she knew how much he valued privacy.

Chevy whisked her off to the limo, with the entire Ballantyne family crammed in the doorway watching.

"They're really happy for you," Maddie told him.

"They're nosy." He instructed the driver to pull off.

"I can't believe you did this for me. Arranging for a nurse, the limo—it's too much."

He pulled her into his arms and she fell lazily into his embrace. She burrowed into his coat, next to his heat. She was so content, she hardly noticed when the driver missed her street.

"The night isn't over," Chevy told her. "The driver is taking us to Charleston for the Festival of Trees."

The Festival of Trees occurred in a park in the capital. Christmas light scenes were elaborately displayed, and the trees were decorated for the season. The two-mile ride through the park was a dazzling spectacle of lights. The per-car entry fee went to support the upkeep of the park. They removed their coats and settled in for the show. Maddie pressed her nose to the window, watching the scenery with the enthusiasm of a young child. Chevy's hand rested at her back, encouraging her response.

"You're the most beautiful woman I've ever seen." He made the statement as if it were the most profound finding of the century.

She returned the compliment. "You're too handsome for words."

"I got very angry with you the other day." Finally, he would discuss their fight. "I shouldn't have." He fell back against the seat. "I was surprised to find you—the vanity is very private."

"Why?" she ventured. "Did you build it for someone?"

He nodded and her heart dropped to her toes.

"What happened to her?"

His eyes narrowed with confusion.

"What happened to the woman you built the vanity for?"

"Nothing happened," he answered softly. "I built the vanity for the woman I'll spend my life with. It was meant to be unique—my gift to her. I used the tools I'm best with and poured my heart into building her a special place."

"I don't think I want to hear any more of this." She slanted her body toward the window, but Chevy placed his thumb beneath her chin and forced her to look up at him.

"You are the only woman to ever see the vanity. My brothers are the only ones who know it exists. Mandisa, you looked so perfect sitting there—natural, as if I built it for you before I knew it was even for you." His lips were a breath away from hers. "It *is* meant for you."

He kissed her and she felt it to her toes. To think a thing as beautiful as the vanity was meant for her...it sent her emotions into overdrive. She returned his kiss, telling him without words how special the gesture was to her.

He stroked her cheek. "Are we finished with this fight?"

"I didn't mean what I said to you. I'm not afraid of you—"

"Some of the rumors are true, Mandisa."

She refused to believe it, but allowed him to finish.

"I have a voracious appetite when it comes to sex. I've seen everything, and tried most. If you let me, I'll do things to your body that will shock you—things you didn't know were possible—but you'll enjoy every one. I wouldn't force you to do anything you're not comfortable with, but I *will* teach you things." His fingers traced the collar of her dress, releasing the steam rising from her neck. "How does that sound to you? Does it scare you?"

Her body tingled with the possibilities.

"Do you want to walk away from this relationship?"

"No. Never."

He trailed a finger down the front of her dress, and the velvet quivered as it parted to accommodate him. "You're not afraid of me?"

"No. Never." They were the only words she could manage with him cupping her breast.

"When would you like to start your lessons?"

Her lips parted, but there was no sound.

"I was thinking now would be a good time." He converged on her mouth, covering her body, pushing her down against the cool leather seat. He gathered the cloth of the skirt of her dress in his fist as his mouth tutored her on the nuances of his kisses. His touch became more sensual as it glided across the thin silk of her hose. He slipped within the waistband and discarded them. While she was in an erotic haze, he shoved her underwear aside and his head disappeared between her thighs.

She was too sensitive to withstand the manipulation. She jumped and jerked with every flick of his tongue.

"Calm down," he instructed as if it were easy to follow his command when her body was quaking.

"I…can't…too…too…too much." She couldn't even form intelligent sentences. Her body was completely under his control, and she had no say in it.

He returned to his work, this time slower, more thoroughly tasting her. He laved at her with long, sensuous strokes. He avoided touching the place that made her spasm, drawing a circle around the nub. He drew circles and she saw stars. Bright, brilliant, exploding stars. She was melting into a boneless heap, but he kept at her.

"Scream," he encouraged.

"No." She didn't want to scream—yet. And there was the driver on the other side of the privacy window.

He showed her the consequences of disobeying. He gripped her thighs, and attacked the tiny, swollen nub. Everything in the world shrank down to the tension gathering in the growing engorgement between her legs. She couldn't think. She couldn't speak. She couldn't move. Her body jerked with tonic-clonic movements. Her body bounced up and down on the seat. She grabbed Chevy's hair, gripping it in her fists. She pulled, but Chevy did not back off. He took both her hands in one of his, locked them against the seat, and finished his work, uninterrupted.

When she collapsed into a mindless heap, unable to catch her breath, tiny sparks tingling her skin, he grasped her behind and delved deeper.

Chapter 15

Totally sated, Chevy held Maddie as she slept. Her body was wildly sprawled over his, shamelessly claiming ownership. They didn't need a sheet or blankets to cover them. It was cold and snowy outside, but their lovemaking had heated up his bedroom with their flame. He had thoroughly worked Maddie's body, leaving her exhausted. She hadn't stirred when he left the bed to start a fire, and she never opened her eyes when he pulled her to cover his body with her nakedness.

Maddie jumped awake, her head popping up with a start. "My father. I have to get home."

He soothed her, caressing her spine. "Todd is with your father. You don't have to be home until morning."

"Todd is staying with my father all night?"

He nodded.

"You made those arrangements?"

He nodded again.

"So I can be with you?"

"So I can be with you—all night. Your father is fine. Relax."

She watched him for a long, assessing moment. Her lips

parted and he thought she might be ready to admit the depth of her feelings for him. The night had been designed to demonstrate how much he cared about her. He wanted to test the waters. He needed to know if she was falling as fast, and as hard, as he was falling for her.

"I have something for you," she said. She scooted to the edge of the bed and padded into the living room. Two dimples, positioned as watch-guards above the healthy flesh, accentuated her heart-shaped bottom. Her hair was barely secured as the scarf she had weaved through unraveled. From every angle, Maddie was a beauty. She rejoined him on the bed, sitting against the headboard as she scavenged through her purse.

"What is it?" he asked, hoisting himself up against the headboard next to her.

"Open it."

He took the tiny package wrapped in Christmas foil. "Women shouldn't buy men gifts."

"I didn't know your policy, so you'll have to accept this one."

"This one. Not again."

"Fine." She pouted, but he wasn't fooled. Defiance simmered behind her droopy lip.

"Mandisa, I'm serious about this."

"What about Christmas, and your birthday?"

He shook his head.

"All right."

"Promise."

"Promise? What is it with you? You don't want me to buy you a gift? *Never*?"

He narrowed his eyes, giving her the answer. How could he make her realize her love was the only gift he ever needed from her?

"All right. I promise. I won't buy you any more gifts. But open this one."

He carefully pulled away the ribbon and bow, and then removed the tape securing the package. He opened the lid and removed a layer of square cotton. There was a certificate inside. He glanced at Maddie's anxious face before unfolding it. "You bought me a star?"

She watched eagerly as he read the "official" document. He didn't have the heart to disappoint her. Only the International Astronomical Union had the authority to name stars, and the companies claiming they could were deceiving the public for profit.

"What? You think it's stupid? Too sappy?" she asked, forlorn.

"No." He wrapped her in his arms. "It's great."

"Something's wrong. What?"

He hesitated, but couldn't let her be fleeced by some unethical company out to make a bunch of money off naïve consumers. She had her father's medical bills to pay.

"Honey," he started softly, "I don't want you to be disappointed, but you can't *buy* a star. The International Astronomical Union has a system for naming stars. The names have been long established, waiting for the discovery of new stars. You might have been taken. How much did you spend on this?"

"You're worried I might have been taken?"

He nodded. "It's okay. How would you know?"

"Why do you worry about me so much?"

"I care about you." *And so much more.*

"It's okay. I did the research. I became suspicious when the first company I called told me the name would be registered in Switzerland. No, I didn't get taken. I had Cassidy drive me to the planetarium at the botanical gardens you took me to.

They were holding a fund-raiser to support wildlife in West Virginia. For a donation, they named a star after you. For a year, this star on their map at the planetarium will have your name on it."

"You went through all of that to do this for me?"

She smiled, hopeful, and wanting his acceptance.

"We were fighting."

"I knew the argument wouldn't last."

He read the certificate again. "You're incredible." What else could he say? He would never be able to articulate how much her thoughtfulness meant to him. She had selected a gift she knew would please him. When it didn't work the way she wanted it to, she'd done the research, bummed a ride into the capital, and made it happen anyway—the right way. She'd made a donation to support wildlife, and given him a piece of the greatest wildlife of all—outer space. "Mandisa, I—"

"Did you say you care about me?"

"What?"

"A minute ago—did you say you care about me?"

"I'm not a poet. I wish I were. For you, I wish I was a lot of things."

"Did you, Chevy? Did you say it? Or did I want you to say it so badly, I heard what I wanted to hear?"

He twisted his body around to face her, taking her face between his hands. "I care about you, Mandisa. So much." Even with her hopeful prodding, there was a part of him that still realized she was too good for him. He didn't chance her rejection of his feelings. He kissed her long and tender, lowering her to the bed.

She batted her long lashes at him, her brown eyes swimming in unshed tears. "I care about you, too. Make love to me."

"Make love to you?"

"Yes. Right now. Make love to me."

He covered her body with soft kisses in an attempt to prove how special she was to him. He touched her with feather softness, stroking her inside and out. He feasted gently on her nipples. He pushed her legs apart and found the place where he belonged. He slipped on a condom and entered her in one continuous stroke, reuniting them. He rocked her body, trying desperately to say the things a poet would have said long ago. He claimed her, released her, cherished her, and ravaged her. He restrained himself, insisting they come together to celebrate this milestone in their relationship. For once, Maddie obeyed him without questioning, erupting so explosively she caused his heart to shatter into a thousand pieces.

As he held her in the aftermath, he pondered the things a man considers when he finds the woman of his dreams: marriage, kids, stability—his future…with her. She disappeared in the bathroom and returned wearing his pajama top. She perched next to him on the bed and cleansed him while he watched, her sure stroke pumping him up to monumental size.

"If you don't stop, I'll be at you again."

She grinned, wickedly.

"Come here. I have something for you."

She scampered to the head of the bed. "Should I search your pockets for it?" She pressed her hands to her mouth in feigned Betty Boop surprise. "Oops, you don't have any pockets."

He couldn't help but laugh at her.

"You don't do that enough—laugh."

He didn't. He couldn't argue. "I have a Christmas gift for you."

"You gave me my gift—the limo, everything tonight."

"There's more." He searched his bedside drawer. "I didn't wrap it as nicely as you did."

She took the envelope from his hands and shredded it. He made a note of how much she liked receiving gifts. He couldn't write a poem, but he could shower her in gifts, putting his money to good use.

"What is this?" she asked after seeing the contents. "Is this a joke?"

"I hope you don't consider going away with me for the weekend a joke."

"But I—this is—I can't—and then there's my father to consider."

"No buts—and it is—you can—arrangements have been made for Todd to care for your father while we're gone. You and I are going to spend New Year's weekend in Virginia Beach, Virginia."

"But, Chevy—"

"'But, Chevy,' what?"

"Virginia Beach is seven hours away. This is too exorbitant. It's too much."

"Mandisa." He stopped her rambling by placing his hand on her cheek. "You're going away with me for New Year's."

She looked as if she would swoon.

"We're going."

In the morning, Chevy left Maddie sleeping while he started breakfast. Their time together would end soon and he'd have to return her to her father. He wished she never had to leave. He could see himself cooking breakfast for her every morning, driving her to work before he went to the lodge, and returning at the end of the day to bring her to their home. His parents would have the kids while they worked.

Porter nudged him, bringing him back to reality. He turned the food down to simmer and took Placido and Porter out for a quick morning walk. Maddie was standing in the kitchen waiting when he returned.

"Good morning." He approached her for a kiss.

"Telephone." She threw the cordless across the room like a missile, turning on her heel and stomping away.

Would he ever understand this woman?

"Hello."

"Hey, number two." Stacy's bubbly voice resonated across the line. "Couldn't get in touch with the mountain man, or your little brother. Who was the chick who answered the phone, and *what* is her problem?"

"What did you do?"

"*Moi*?" she asked innocently. He doubted anything about the pistol PI was innocent. "I only asked for you."

"How did you ask for me?"

"I can't remember *exactly*. I think I said I wanted to talk to the big gorgeous brother they refer to as the tree hugger."

Chevy groaned. "Why did you call?"

"I've got some info about your father. Can you meet me in my hotel lobby tomorrow? Bring your brothers. We can make it one big"—she coughed when she said—"orgy."

He had never met a woman as wild as Stacy Taro. Briefly, he wondered about Greyson's past relationship with her. There was no way he could have gotten around her bodacious flirting without dating her. The only question was how far it had gone before Greyson came to his senses.

Chevy made the arrangements and disconnected. He sought Maddie out and found her sitting on his sofa, not happy.

"Who was that crazy woman?"

"Stacy, the PI I told you Greyson hired." He had no secrets from her. She was his friend as well as his lover.

"Hmm. It didn't sound like she was calling about business. Does she always refer to you as Triple A?"

"Triple A?"

"I asked the same question. The animal advocate with the big—"

"I get it." Not what Stacy had told him when he asked. "Listen, Stacy is *different*. She flirts a lot. She knows I have a girlfriend."

She crossed her arms over her chest and threw him a skeptical glare.

"Are you jealous?"

"Jealous?" she sputtered. "Don't be ridiculous."

"Doesn't look so ridiculous from where I'm sitting." He loomed over her, waiting for a confession.

"Okay, but you would be too if Richard called me at this time of the morning calling me his Triple A."

His blood curdled at the thought. He eased next to her on the sofa. "We're not going to fight about this, because there's nothing to fight about. Stacy flirts with everyone."

"I don't like it."

"Me either. I'll talk to her about it the next time I see her."

Her bottom lip dropped. She hadn't realized he actually spent time with her.

"Mandisa, I'm all yours. I can't be any plainer than that. You have free range here. You can answer my phone, and stop by whenever you want. I'll show you where I hide the extra key." He traced the shell of her ear and her body trembled. He liked her response to his touch. "You're the only woman I want in my life."

Chapter 16

As if Christmas wasn't overwhelming enough, Chevy surprised Maddie every day with some demonstration of his deepening affection for her. She was falling shamelessly in love with him. Her life was definitely on the upswing, and she took advantage of everything she could to make it better. She never tried to suppress her joy in seeing him. She chomped up every minute of his time she could. Her friendships with Cassidy and Sutton were growing, and they felt more like sisters. With Todd's help, her father was getting a little better every day. Maddie couldn't ask for any more blessings.

"Maddie," her father called when the doorbell sounded.

"I've got it, Dad." She smiled at him as she passed his bed. "Chevy, what are you doing here?"

He held up two grocery bags. "I want to have dinner with you and your father."

"You're being a bit forward, don't you think?" she teased.

"I have to get to know your father better if I plan on getting serious about his daughter." He kissed her cheek and stepped inside.

She worried her father's restricted diet and physical weakness might make the evening awkward for Chevy. He greeted her father and barreled into the kitchen, taking over. He made do with the mishmash of pots and pans she had—nothing like the designer cookware he owned. He had the presence of mind to inquire about her father's diet and made accommodations in his menu for it—with her help.

"I'm not doing much," he said, almost apologetically.

She looked over his shoulder. He didn't consider baked chicken, green beans, corn-on-the-cob, and rolls "much"? Her mouth was watering just looking at the golden chicken.

"I never eat like this."

"Except when you're with me," he added with a satisfied grin.

"I'll have to run an extra mile in the morning."

He turned his attention on her, stepping away from the stove and pulling her into his arms. She buried her head against his chest. This was becoming a familiar, welcoming place for her.

"Do you think you could do this every day with me?"

"Have you cook for me? Yes."

"Cooking, yes, but more. Could you stand me coming home to you every day? Would you want to keep my house?"

"Yes." *Have your babies. Share your bed.* She could imagine it all.

"What about your career? I'd want you at home raising our kids."

Her stomach did a cartwheel. "You've thought about this?"

He nodded, not giving her any more information. "Have you?"

She smiled up at him. "I dream about it." Being his wife, having his babies—these were the things her fantasies were made of. She understood their relationship was still new, and she'd never pressure him into commitment, but she was glad to know he thought about their future, too.

His body relaxed around her. He liked her answer. "You're not going to give me any flack about being a housewife?"

"I like working at the library, but when I plan my perfect future, I don't see myself shelving books. I'm an old-fashioned girl. Having a family is appealing to me. Being a housewife isn't a dirty word."

"You could be happy?"

"With you, yes."

"When you're planning your perfect future, what do you see?"

"I want a home with a husband and children, but I want to travel and see the world."

"I remember."

"I know you do." He'd planned a trip to Virginia for them for New Year's.

"I should finish up."

After a heated but too short kiss, she left him in her kitchen, cooking her dinner.

From Christmas to New Year's Day, Hannaford Valley shut down. There was no school. Most of the city services were closed, including the library. Local businesses followed, giving their employees a long Christmas break. The movie theater, diner, and grocery were open, but the town seemed deserted. With Maddie's father's independence increasing, she grew bored over the break. She continued to run every morning with Cassidy, but most of her days were long if Chevy was too busy to come around.

"My legs are killing me," Cassidy said, slowing down. "Whose idea was it to do a long hill run?"

"Yours," Maddie reminded her, "and it feels great!"

"This is the last hill, and I need a break at the top."

"Okay."

"We'll walk back," Cassidy panted.

"That's no fun."

Cassidy rolled her eyes, but pushed on. She lagged behind, but they both reached the top of the snow-dusted hill. At the top, they stretched, catching their breath.

"Chevy's taking you to Virginia Beach next week?" Cassidy asked as they started walking the five miles back to the high school.

"I can't wait."

"Isn't it closed for the season?"

"I don't think it'll matter."

"Shame on you." Cassidy swatted at her. "Chevy spoils you."

"He does." She smiled, recalling the ways.

"He's in love with you."

"Is not!"

"And you're in love with him. Deny it."

She didn't bother. After a moment she said, "I don't think I've ever felt this way about a man. We're taking it slow though, so I'm keeping a tight rein on my feelings."

"You can't do that. The heart wants what the heart wants. Don't fight it. Let it happen."

They walked quite a distance with her contemplating her relationship with Chevy. Cassidy chattered on about Courtney and Kirkland, and her work.

"I want to show you something." Maddie reached inside her jacket and pulled out a colorful postcard. "I got it in the mail a few days ago."

Cassidy examined it.

"I'm thinking we should do it."

"We? I can't run a marathon."

She moved closer as they walked, pointing out the important information on the card. "They'll train you to run the marathon. We'll be getting in shape while raising money for a worthy cause."

"The American Stroke Association is a great cause." Cassidy scanned the postcard. "We can run in support of your father."

Her enthusiasm increased. "We can see California in the bargain."

Cassidy threw a suspicious glance her way. "San Diego to be exact. Isn't that where Richard lives?"

"This has nothing to do with Richard. It's an excellent opportunity for me to travel while raising money for the organization that helped my father get better."

"We'd be gone for four days. What about your dad?"

"I talked to Todd. He's willing to stay with him. I'd have to raise the money to pay his salary for the extra hours, but he's willing to work with me to make it happen."

"Do you really think we can do this?"

"I really want to. There's an informational meeting in two days. We could go, and then decide."

"Count me in." Cassidy handed her the postcard, and Maddie gave her a big hug.

"This could be fun."

They made it back to the high school in good time. Walking with a partner made the time and miles fly. They were completing their stretch routine when Cassidy inquired about Maddie's plans for the day. She shared her new onset of boredom. "I'm glad my father is getting better. I just didn't realize how much of my time was spent caring for him. Now I have all this free time and nothing to do with it."

"Chevy would be happy to occupy your time."

"He's busy with the lodge. I miss him when he's tied up at work." The best idea came to her. "Can you give me a ride to his cabin?"

"Sure, but I thought he was at the lodge."

"He told me how to get in."

"Well, well, well."

Cassidy drove her home to change before dropping her at Chevy's cabin. She found the spare key and let herself inside by way of the kitchen. Porter came to investigate, and once he gave his approval, Placido greeted her. She took the dogs out one at a time—they were too much to handle together. Afterward, she put them in the dog walk. She knew their routine, and how long Chevy kept them outside on cold days. They came inside and collapsed in a heap in the kitchen for a nap. Having settled the dogs, she ventured into the living room to get comfortable with being in Chevy's cabin alone.

"Oh my—" She clamped her hands to her mouth. "He didn't."

Chevy had rearranged the living room to accommodate a brand-new flat-screen television. The boxes for the new satellite dish and television were scattered as if he left before he was able to discard them. She searched the room for the remotes, turning on the system. Chevy didn't watch television. *She* was the TV junky. He had done this for her. He never stopped surprising her.

Maddie dialed up Sutton. "Do you know how to reach Chevy at the lodge?"

"Is something wrong?"

"No. I just need to talk to him."

"I'm not sure if the phones have been installed. Hold on. I'll ask Greyson." She put the phone down, but returned shortly. "Greyson has a number, but he's not certain the phones are on. I've told Chevy a hundred times to get a cell."

"I tried to make him carry one at the paper mill. He leaves it in his desk most days," Greyson added in the background.

"Thanks," Maddie said. "I'll try this number. If you speak to him, tell him to call home."

"Call home?" She didn't miss the mischievousness in Sutton's voice. Sutton wouldn't let her get off the phone until she answered key questions about how serious they were becoming. Sutton squealed with delight, prematurely congratulating her for becoming part of the family. She disconnected and dialed the lodge, crossing her fingers that Chevy would answer.

"Ballantyne Wilderness Lodge." His deep bass vibrated to her toes.

"Chevy, it's Maddie."

"What's wrong?" He was clearly alarmed.

"One question. Why did you buy a TV?"

He scoffed about her scaring him half to death since she'd never called him at work before.

"The TV?" She pushed him back to the subject at hand.

"You told me you're a cable junky. I can't get cable that far out, but the satellite works."

She sank into the sofa with the remote in one hand and the phone pressed to her ear. "Do you know how special that is?"

"The TV?" He sounded bewildered.

"You don't even watch television but you went out and bought one for me to watch when I'm at your place. Anyone can buy flowers and candy. Not many men work so hard to keep their girlfriends happy." There was a hitch in her voice she hoped he didn't hear.

"Mandisa," he said softly, "don't you know I'd do anything for you by now?"

"Why?" she managed.

"Because I could never repay you for the way you've changed my life." He paused. "Everything is so much better since you came along."

She battled shedding tears and carrying on a coherent conversation.

"You're at my place?"

"Yes," she squeaked.

"Why?"

"I missed you."

He held the phone too long. He always said the right thing—the most romantic things—but he still struggled with the raw emotions of expressing his feelings.

She let him off the hook. "Go back to work."

"Will you be there when I come home?"

"I'll stay as long as I can. The nurse leaves at six."

Chevy came home for lunch, and didn't return to work that day.

Maddie held her breath when he surprised her, sitting at the vanity, brushing her hair. "It's so beautiful," she said in explanation.

He did not greet her with explosive anger. He eased up to her and kissed her forehead, then took the brush from her hand and brushed her hair in long, even strokes.

Maddie enjoyed every minute of their New Year's celebration. Having made arrangements with Todd to care for her father, and giving him all the information to contact her in the case of an emergency, she was determined to have a good time without worrying. It didn't take much to clear her mind of any troubles.

Chevy arrived in his truck and they drove to the Charleston Airport. Greyson did legal consulting work for a client who owned a private plane, and Chevy had somehow finagled an invitation to have it at his disposal for the weekend. The weekend couldn't have started off any better. The seven-hour drive was cut dramatically short by flying.

Still buzzing from the luxury of flying in a private plane, Maddie was giddy when she stepped into the fancy hotel suite. She was so sexually charged by his lavish treatment, she couldn't wait for the bellman to leave them alone. As the man showed them the features of the rooms, she stayed behind in the bedroom and started stripping off her clothes. When Chevy glanced back to see why she wasn't at his side, his eyes almost fell out of this head. He hastily ushered the man out of the room and joined her.

Chevy liked her spontaneous admiration, but he insisted on being in charge of their lovemaking. He obtained his pleasure in tutoring her. His mission was always to make her body rock in new and different ways. Sometimes he slowed things down and made love, but he preferred to walk on the wild side. After a few of his tutoring sessions, Maddie did too.

"What are we doing?" she asked with a giggle. She was completely nude—Chevy too—draped across the humongous bed.

He kneeled next to the bedside. "Scoot to the edge." His voice held laughter and mischief, but his arousal was solidly wedged against the hairs trailing from his navel to the root of his erection.

She did as he instructed.

"Lie on your belly."

She did, looking over her shoulder to see what he was up to.

"Wrap you legs around my neck."

"What?" What he was proposing was impossible.

"You'll like this."

"What are you going to do?"

"I'll call this move 'the tastefest'—so you can ask for it by name."

With some measure of acrobatics, Maddie wrapped her calves around Chevy's shoulders. He stood, dragging her across the bed. He wrapped his arms around her waist. He stood to his full height, causing Maddie to yelp and wrap her arms around his thighs. Dangling upside down, her parts lined up perfectly for his *tastefest*. As he lapped mercilessly, the blood rushed to her head, heightening the experience. Too quickly, her body was rippling with pleasure.

Chevy laid her across the bed, too satisfied with her response. He teased her about her brazen reaction to his moves as he discarded the condom wrapper. She challenged him to use his willpower, but his lips were already sucking her breast into his mouth.

"You can't wait, either," he chastised.

"Can—too—"

He inserted a finger into her nest of curls. She yelped at the wonderful sensation.

"Liar." He showed her evidence of her fib on the tip of his finger.

She tossed her head back and laughed, enjoying the way he played with her.

"Be a good girl," he told her, fitting himself between her legs and sheathing himself in a condom. He grinned down at her, the rumble of laughter escaping his sensual mouth. "You might need to bite down on a pillow," he said as he pushed inside her.

After they both climaxed, they showered and ordered dinner by room service. It wasn't until late the next afternoon before they stopped playing their games, experimenting with foods, locations, and other things that made Maddie blush to recall. She'd always known good sex was part of a long-lasting relationship, but their sexual compatibility was beyond anything she could expect to have experienced. The gossips in town spreading rumors about Chevy and his bizarre and dangerous sexual appetites had been wrongly informed. She was glad the secret was all hers.

When midnight came, Maddie was sitting between Chevy's thighs in a bathtub filled with hot water and bubbles, drinking champagne. They toasted the longevity of their relationship and clinked glasses. She leaned against him, feeling small but cherished as she rested back on his broad chest.

"Do you want to go out on the balcony and watch the fireworks?"

"I could stay here forever," she told him.

He removed the pins holding her hair in its tight bun. Placing the pins on the edge of the tub, he dragged his fingers through her hair, using the tendrils to frame her face. He massaged her scalp, arousing her in a way she hadn't believed possible.

"Chevy, I want to talk to you about something."

"What is it?" His voice was soft and forgiving without his knowing what the matter could be.

"I want to run in a marathon to support the American Stroke Foundation." She gave him the details, including the information she'd gotten when she and Cassidy attended the runners' meeting. "It's going to be in San Diego."

"San Diego is so far away." He lifted her hair and kissed her shoulder. "How long will you be gone?"

"Four days. I really want to do this. Cassidy and I have been running every morning and we know we can do it."

"Then you should do it. What do you need me to do?"

"I want your moral support."

"Always."

She leaned her head back for his kiss. He obliged, wrapping his arms around her waist and pulling her back tightly against his chest.

"I think I'm falling in love with you," he whispered in her ear.

"I *am* in love with you." She didn't hesitate, or play the he-has-to-say-it-first game. The moment was special. It felt right. She wanted to say it, and he needed to hear it.

"I don't believe it." The solemn look on his face said he believed the rhetoric he'd been told about his lack of character.

"You're my knight in shining armor."

"My armor is cracked, and the queen is *on* crack if she thinks I'll ever be good enough for her."

She twisted and swatted at his chest.

He caught her hands in his fist. He was smiling, and it was the most perfect smile she'd ever seen.

"I love you, Mandisa."

She didn't have to ask if he really meant it, or if he was just reciprocating. His smile, and the sparkle in his eyes, told the truth.

"Mandisa," he said matter-of-factly, "I'm going to marry you one day."

Chapter 17

"You told Maddie she could go to San Diego and now I have to let Cassidy go." Kirkland was sitting in the front seat of Chevy's truck, pouting as they inspected the cabins of Ballantyne Wilderness Lodge.

"I don't give Maddie permission to do anything. She's her own woman."

"Yeah, well."

"And I'm sure Cassidy didn't ask you permission to go either."

Kirkland didn't reply.

"What's wrong with them running in a marathon? It's for a good cause." A cause dear to Maddie's heart since her father had suffered a massive stroke.

"I don't care about them running. The problem is with them going to San Diego. I don't know if I can take off—we're too busy with the paper mill and the lodge. Besides, someone has to watch Courtney."

"They're grown women. They'll be fine together."

Kirkland scratched his sandy brown curls. "You don't know, do you?"

"Know what?"

He grinned like a wise old cat. "Richard lives in San Diego."

Chevy chewed on this bit of information the entire day. His focus was shattered by images of Richard making a play for Maddie. He wasn't sure his encounter with Richard at the library had been enough to deter him from hitting on her. Warning her about Richard wouldn't do any good. Either she'd discount the seriousness of it or she'd feel she was tough enough to handle it herself. Neither option was satisfactory.

After they finished their work at the lodge, they picked Greyson up from home. He climbed into Chevy's pickup, sandwiching Kirkland in the middle.

"Any idea why Pop wants to see us?" Kirkland twisted to face Greyson with his question.

"None. He might want to thank us for the cruise. Mama's probably cooking a big dinner."

"He didn't sound too happy when he called last night," Kirkland said, his voice wary.

Chevy joined the conversation. "I'm just happy Stacy didn't turn up anything."

Greyson thumped Kirkland in the head. "I should have known better than to listen to you. I don't know what Alex meant by telling you he took care of Eileen Putnam, but there was never anything going on between her and Pop."

"Just like I tried to tell you," Chevy gloated.

"I should have listened to you, because it cost me a bundle of money to have Stacy look into it only to find there was nothing to look into." Greyson dropped his voice reflectively. "Pop would never cheat on Mama."

"Never," Chevy confirmed.

Kirkland shook his head. "I want to believe what Stacy found, but it doesn't make sense. Mama was so distraught during that time. Alex did go see Eileen, and she did move away. That has to mean something, right?"

"I don't know what it means," Chevy said, "but it doesn't have to mean Pop had an affair."

They lapsed into silence during the drive, each dealing with his suspicions and regrets.

"Sutton still looking for Alex's baby?" Kirkland's question shattered the silence.

"Yes," Greyson answered tightly. He offered no more conversation on the subject, and his brothers didn't question it further.

Chevy pulled into their parents' driveway and they filed into the house. After greeting Mama, they joined Pop in the den. They tossed each other inquisitive glances when Pop welcomed them with angry stares. He crossed the room and closed the door, returning to his seat without a word. Chevy sat on the sofa across from Pop, wedged in the middle between his brothers.

"How was the cruise, Pop?" Greyson asked.

"Good," Pop answered, barely parting his lips. He studied them individually, scrutinizing them without saying a word. His feet propelled the leather rocker-recliner back and forward.

Chevy was about to ask what was going on when his father spoke.

"I have never been so ashamed of you in all my life."

Chevy's palms began to sweat, and suddenly he was twelve years old, in trouble for doing something he shouldn't have. He had the tough, unyielding pride of a man, but Pop still had the power to bring him down to size.

"Pop?" Greyson was the oldest and should be the one to clear up the mystery.

"You hired a private d'tective to dig up my past."

They didn't bother denying the truth.

"Did y'all think I wouldn't find out? First thing I get home, I got Eileen callin' me about some Asian woman snooping around asking questions about my relationship with her. Is that why you sent me and your mother on the cruise? To get me out of the way so you could get in my business?"

"Pop, it wasn't—" Greyson started.

"I know what the hell it was!" Pop raised his voice, but quickly recovered. Mama hadn't been invited to sit in on their meeting, so he didn't want her to know what was going on. "How'd you find out about Eileen and me?"

Kirkland spoke up. "I told Greyson." He was still protecting their mother. She didn't want her husband to know she knew about the time he was spending with another woman.

Greyson grew bolder. "What do you mean by 'Eileen and me,' Pop?"

"None of your business! None of this is your business. *I'm* the parent. You don't have the right to stick your nose in what I do."

"If what you do hurts my mother—"

Chevy cut him off, speaking in a hushed tone meant to calm the situation. "We were worried about Mama. We didn't want her to be hurt."

Pop's eyes squinted down to red-hot slits. "If you cared about your mother you wouldn't be digging this up."

"Digging what up?" Greyson challenged, his search for answers renewed.

"Let it go," Kirkland urged.

"I won't let it go." Greyson's voice was rising. "What did you do, Pop? All the lectures—all the self-righteous lectures you've given us about how to treat women with respect and you go and hurt my mother? I want an explanation."

Pop moved to the edge of his seat. "You don't demand anything from me."

Greyson looked to Kirkland, and then Chevy, before forging on. "We deserve to know what you've done."

"Kirkland," Pop said, "you feel that way?"

He hesitated, but answered firmly, "It's my mother."

"What about you, Chevy?"

He hadn't wanted any part of investigating his father's past. When it came to Alex being involved, he'd known it was bogus. Stacy's findings supported his father's innocence. It hadn't been until his father lost his temper, defending his right to have a secret life, that Chevy had truly become suspicious. This made Greyson right—he wouldn't let anyone hurt his mother. He wouldn't listen to Pop lecture them about the nuances of a relationship when he was destroying his own. He wanted answers, too.

"I want to know what went on with you and Eileen. If you hurt my mother, you'll answer to me."

Everyone stared at him in utter shock. He was quiet-spoken, and a lover of nature and people. He would be the last to threaten their father.

Kirkland tried to calm the situation with an explanation. "Mama knows something was going on. I spent the days when you were with Eileen holding her while she cried. Alex was the one who ran Eileen out of town."

"Your mother knows—how did she find out?" His eyes dropped to the floor while he contemplated it all. "Alex was the one who ran Eileen off?"

"Tell us what happened, Pop," Greyson demanded.

"You three have done it now," Pop spat. "I'm not the one who hurt your mother. Y'all hurt your mother by stickin' your fingers in the wrong pie. If you had questions, you should've come to me in the first place. I wouldn't have answered them—just like I'm not going to answer them now—but at least I would have respected y'all trying to protect your mother."

"What happened?" Greyson wouldn't let it go, and Chevy was growing antsy to uncover all the mystery.

"I don't answer to you!" Pop was out of his chair, spittle flying from his mouth as he shouted. "You had no business doin' what you did. I have no respect for any of you!"

Greyson kept pushing, and Kirkland kept trying to smooth everything over. Chevy joined in the shouting, siding with Greyson, but trying to give his father the benefit of the doubt until he explained.

All four men stood nose-to-nose asserting their will until Pop yelled the words that quieted the room. "*You are not my sons!*" The only sound in the room was Pop's heavy breathing. "Not anymore." His chest heaved with anger. "I want you to leave."

Knowing the argument had gone too far—no one had ever challenged their father—they moved as a unit to the door.

Mama tentatively stepped into the den. "Jack? What's going on?"

"Get out of my house!" Pop was so mad, even Mama couldn't squelch his anger.

"Jack!" Mama was shocked. "Our sons are always welcome in our home. What are you doing? What is this about?"

"These are not your sons anymore," he answered with a sweeping wave that grouped all three of them into the same traitorous group.

Mama's mouth fell open.

"They're not your sons. They're not my sons. Get out of my house, and don't ever come back. I don't want to speak to any of you again. I don't want to see any of you again."

"Pop, you don't mean—"

"Kirkland, stop. Don't say anything else. Let your shoes do the talking."

The notion of Pop disowning them was so foreign, Chevy couldn't process the words. He had witnessed his father's anger before, but never on this scale.

To end any doubt about his seriousness, Pop added, "If y'all ain't out of here in two minutes, I'm calling the sheriff."

They drove home in silence. Chevy stopped at Greyson's first. When he climbed out of the truck, he turned back and said, "Pop didn't mean what he said. I'll call him in the morning and apologize. It was my idea to hire Stacy. I'll make it right."

When Chevy pulled up to Kirkland's place—the refurbished home they'd grown up in—Kirkland was reluctant to get out of the truck. "We really messed up," he said before closing the passenger's door.

Chevy felt strangely isolated as he drove back to his cabin. How strange the way his life could be going so good, only to be turned upside down. Placido and Porter greeted him when he arrived home, but their companionship wasn't enough. He felt a growing void, as if he had lost his entire heritage tonight. His family was splintered, and he was in disfavor with his father. He loved Pop, and the thought of never seeing him again was too much to digest.

He called Greyson and Kirkland called him. They rehashed the scene, making sure it wasn't a nightmare or some sort of evil group hypnosis. This was so far beyond comprehension, no one knew how to handle it. The entire extended Ballantyne family seemed in jeopardy without the patriarch standing watch. They ended their conversations with regretful sadness. They had no idea how they would live with what they had done. Suddenly, whether Pop had an affair with Eileen Putnam didn't feel important.

"Mandisa?" He called the only one who could help ease the pain.

"Chevy, what's wrong?"

"I had a terrible day."

"Come over."

She didn't hesitate to offer him solace.

"It's late."

"Come now."

Twenty minutes later, Chevy was sitting in the den sharing his night with Maddie. They spoke quietly, careful not to disturb her father. She listened intently, expressing her shared hurt over the situation. He let her hold him. She kissed him and stroked him. She didn't offer pat answers or reprimand him for his foolishness. She just gave him a soft place to lay his head. He fell asleep on her sofa. When he woke in the morning, he was underneath a blanket, and Maddie was asleep in a chair she'd pulled up to the sofa.

A week later, Pop hadn't changed his mind, although he'd stopped taking any phone calls from his sons immediately. He stopped taking his sons' phone calls, then forbade their mother to speak to them either. Kirkland's persistence resulted in Pop changing the phone number.

"Chevy," Maddie started. They were sitting at his kitchen table eating an early dinner.

He looked up at her, encouraging her to go on. He could tell by her hesitation the topic wasn't one he'd want to discuss.

"How long are you going to let this go on?"

"What?"

"This thing with your father. You were so happy... The hermit who barricaded himself in the cabin had all but disappeared. You were becoming a part of Hannaford. You were even laughing. It was a miraculous transformation, really."

"Thanks," he said sarcastically. He couldn't argue. He'd noticed the change in himself too. Since dating Maddie, he'd become a different person.

"I'm just being honest. You don't want anything less from me. Since the fight with your father, you've been so unhappy."

"I love my parents," he said. His reason for his changed behavior was clear.

"So are you going to let him just kick you out of his life?"

"It's his decision. Pop is very stubborn. Once he makes up his mind—"

"Hmm. Who does that remind me of?"

"I'm not stubborn."

She wisely didn't pursue that argument. "All I'm saying is that what your father has done can't be a solo decision. What you guys did was wrong. You should've confronted your father with the information and given him a chance to straighten it out. It was wrong, but he can't disown you because of it. He has an obligation to his children. You have an obligation to your parents. And it'll take all of you to keep your family as strong as it is."

"What are we going to do? What am *I* supposed to do?"

"I don't know," Maddie said softly. "All I know is that I lost my father after his stroke, but I refused to let him go. Now I have him back. I've been without my mother so long—but it still hurts. Cassidy has been battling to fix her relationship with her folks. I can't excuse anyone who would voluntarily let their parents go when they live only minutes away."

Chevy loved his parents, but more than anything right now he needed Maddie's respect.

"You and your brothers have huddled together and are trying to establish a new family—your bothers with their wives and the kids, and you with me. It's a way of coping, but in the end, you'll all need your parents."

Greyson had stepped up and was trying to fill the shoes of their father. He kept close tabs on his brothers, and encouraged Sutton, Cassidy, and Maddie to spend more time together. They were all having dinner at his house next weekend.

"You're right," he admitted.

"At dinner this weekend, take your brothers aside and find a way to make it right with your father."

"The worst part about all of this is we did it for nothing. We still don't know what truly happened between my father and Eileen. One part of me wishes we could take it all back." He shook his head reflectively. "Another part is more curious than ever to get to the bottom of the mystery. If you could have seen how upset Pop got when he found out the details of what we'd done... If he's hurt my mother in any way, I'd be the first to turn my back on him."

"How are you going to resolve this when you feel this way?"

"I don't know. Maybe it can't be resolved until we find out the truth."

"I don't like this."

"Me either, but I think it's something we're going to have to do. If we want to save the Ballantyne family, all the secrets have to be revealed—Pop and Eileen, Alex's child. There are too many unanswered questions, which keep popping up to cause problems. Once and for all, everything has to be accounted for."

She covered his hand with hers. "I want you to be careful here. I love you, and I see what this is doing to you. I don't want you to lose your parents forever."

Chapter 18

Maddie's life was so entangled with the Ballantyne family that she felt Chevy's loss as if it were her own. His mood was always so solemn and reflective, although he tried to keep his spirits high when he was with her. Greyson and Kirkland were hurting. Cassidy and Sutton were also feeling the sting of the stubbornness of the Ballantyne men. Greyson was trying too hard to hold everyone in a close net of togetherness. He started putting the pressure back on Sutton to have a baby. Kirkland adored his mother, and his bad mood reflected the depth of his loss.

The entire valley seemed to take sides. No one outside the family knew the reason for the rift, but this didn't stop them from entering an opinion on the subject. In the middle of the winter when the town was closed down more than it was open, people needed something to do and talk about. People first noticed Marybeth Ballantyne's sudden absence from church. Mr. Ballantyne knew his sons would try to contact her there—especially since Chevy accompanied Maddie every time she went—so he barred his wife from attending services and doing her volunteer work.

Maddie heard the whispers every time she went into town.

"Those boys always have been a handful."

"I don't know what they did to fall out of favor with their parents, but children have to know their place. Even adult children."

And then there was the other side of the coin.

"Some people are so ungrateful. After the house those boys bought…not to mention the big cruise they just took. They probably wanted a mansion and a small island instead."

"Parents acting more foolish than their children—it don't make no sense."

The entire saga was being played out with the Hannaford gossips, all itching to get the inside story. Each time Maddie heard bits and pieces about what was going on within the family, the story grew to epic proportions. Speculation would do in the absence of truth.

"We have to do something," Cassidy said. She'd dropped by the library to discuss the situation with Maddie and Sutton.

"I tried to talk to Pop," Sutton said. "He refused. He kindly informed me he had to stop communicating with me as long as I was married to Greyson. I tried to remind him about his granddaughter, but he cut me off before I could lay my guilt trip on him."

"I got the same reaction," Cassidy said. "These Ballantyne men can be difficult when they want to."

"I'm not a part of the family," Maddie reminded them. "It might be best for me to stay out of it."

Sutton jumped in. "You're as much of this family as Cassidy and me. Don't try to back out now that the going is getting rough. We need to put our heads together and find a way to save this family."

Maddie's heart warmed at being considered a part of the

Ballantyne family—no matter that it was fractured right now. They loved each other completely and always supported each other. With her mother gone, she needed Mrs. Ballantyne's gentle companionship.

Sutton continued. "The hardest part of all of this is watching how much this is hurting Greyson. He's trying to pretend he's dealing with it, but it's tearing him up inside. He and Pop were really close. They could talk about anything and everything. Now he can't just pick up the phone and call. He wishes he never started this whole thing."

"It was a hard decision to make," Cassidy added. "Kirkland didn't want to do it either, but they were trying to protect their *mother*. In any other circumstance, Pop would have insisted they come to her defense."

"It looks so suspicious—Pop getting so angry about what they did. I mean, I can understand why he'd get upset, but to kick his sons out of his life? Out of Mama's life? What he did affects all of us, including his grandchildren."

Cassidy nodded her agreement. "Whereas they were ready to let it drop, his reaction stirred the whole thing up again."

"Well, we're the wives, and we're going to have to step in and end this. We need Mama to join in with us, and then we need to make the four of them sit down and work it out."

"But Mama didn't want Pop to know she knows about Eileen," Cassidy reminded her.

"It's too late for that," Sutton rebutted. "When Pop kicked the boys out, I'm sure they talked about it. He has to know now."

"I could talk to Mrs. Ballantyne" Maddie offered.

Sutton and Cassidy stopped chattering and turned to her.

"She and I get along well. Mr. Ballantyne doesn't know how close Chevy and I are. Mrs. Ballantyne isn't sitting with my father anymore since she hasn't been attending church, but it would make sense for me to drop in on her. It's a way inside."

"It could work," Cassidy said. "Pop will think you're coming on behalf of the church."

"I'd want to discuss it with Chevy first. If he's against it, I can't interfere."

Sutton looked hopeful. "We understand."

"The sooner we stop this madness, the better," Cassidy agreed.

Sutton embraced Maddie. "Welcome to the family."

Maddie stood in the middle of her parents' old bedroom surrounded by mementos and vintage clothing. She had sorted the goods, organizing them according to what she would donate to charity, store as antiques, and the things she'd have appraised. Her father sat in his transfer chair in the doorway, watching with tears in his eyes.

"We don't have to give anything away, Dad. I can just rearrange it and keep it all."

He shook his head. "It's time…to say…good-bye."

It was a time for new beginnings. He was able to assist the nurse when transferring from the bed to his wheelchair. His speech, while still slurred, was getting easier to understand and he was putting together complete sentences. He still had many deficits, but he was determined to work hard to overcome them.

"I want—I want—I want," he stuttered.

"Take your time, Dad."

"Want to move…back—" He nodded, indicating the room.

"You want to move back into your bedroom?"

"Yes."

"I guess it would be all right."

He nodded his head once, firmly.

"I'll make it happen."

Her father tried to maneuver his facial droop into a smile. She kept tons of framed photos of her family around the house, and in each one her father was a strikingly handsome man. Her mother was equally attractive, but it hurt a little more to see the lingering effects of the facial paralysis mar his good looks.

"I'm tired," he told her.

"I'll help you back to bed."

After Maddie got her father settled, she returned to the bedroom to finish her work. After everything was properly boxed and labeled, she changed the drapes and rugs, giving the room a simple makeover. Helping her father start another phase of his life made her eager to do the same for herself. Without any rational reason, she went into the garage and tried to start her father's old car. It had been sitting since his accident, and didn't surprise her when it refused to turn over. She wasn't even sure she remembered how to drive—her license had expired long ago—but suddenly she needed the freedom of being able to go where she wanted to go without depending on others.

"Hi, Mandisa," Chevy said when he answered his phone. "I was just thinking about you."

"You say that every time I call." And she enjoyed hearing it.

"It's true. You're always on my mind."

"You're a charmer now?"

He laughed.

"I need to ask you a favor."

"Anything. What is it?"

She told him about wanting to drive again and how uncooperative her father's old car was being. "Do you think you can take a look at it for me?" Her funds were budgeted tightly. She couldn't afford the cost of putting the car in the shop.

"No problem." Chevy didn't hesitate to help her. "I'll stop by after work tomorrow."

True to his word, he came by the next day to take a look at the stubborn car. After tinkering under the hood for a few hours, he came inside to announce he'd pinpointed the problem. "It's a big job. I'll have to get Grey and Kirk to help me. We could start this weekend."

"That would be great." She was in the kitchen finishing dinner. "Can you stay and eat with me?"

Chevy got cleaned up and talked with her father while she set the table for them. One of the things she admired most about him was his willingness to forge a relationship with her dad. Most people avoided her father because of their fear. They didn't know what to expect, seeing his physical condition was so bad after the stroke. Chevy treated her father like a regular person. Trying to convey his thoughts with jumbled words and slurred speech could frustrate her dad and he sometimes shut down with the therapists and nurses. Chevy easily interpreted what her father said, making conversation more welcome with him.

"How's the training for the marathon going?" Chevy asked over dinner in her small kitchen.

"We ran for two and a half hours this morning. Our trainer says we're right on schedule."

"Congratulations."

She needed to ask his opinion about her speaking with his mother, and eased into the conversation. "I was cleaning out my parents' bedroom today, and my father told me he wants to move back into his room."

"This is good news?"

"I know he's coming to terms with my mother being gone. The doctor said his stroke was brought on by his grief. He had other risk factors, but my mother's death pushed him over the edge. He was so stressed his blood pressure went through the roof and couldn't be controlled." She had already told Chevy how close her parents were in their relationship.

"I'm glad he's doing better. When we come to work on the car this weekend, we can rearrange the furniture too. If you want."

She smiled, her heart spreading warmth throughout her body. "I love you."

He looked up, locking his eyes with hers. "I love you, too."

She stared at him for a long time. How could one man be so perfect? He was handsome and protective; supportive and intelligent; ambitious and sensitive. He deserved to live his life without strife or controversy. And she wanted to help him in any way she could.

"What?" he asked, tilting his head in question.

"I'd like to talk to your mother about everything that's going on, but I don't want to do it if you're uncomfortable with it." She went on to give him a sketch of her conversation with Sutton and Cassidy. "I see how upset you are about it. Greyson and Kirkland are too. I'm in a position to at least *talk* to your mother. Don't you want to know if she's okay? If there's a way to resolve this, wouldn't you want to know what it is? I might be able to help. You know how fond I am of your mother. Especially since my mom isn't around anymore—"

"Mandisa." He stopped her rambling. "I don't have any problem with you going to see Mama."

She sighed her relief. "I didn't want you to think I was interfering."

"Never, but don't push too hard. If Pop gets upset, back off. This thing with Pop—we'll work it out. I don't want you jeopardizing your relationship with my mother."

Mrs. Ballantyne was a plump woman with a big heart. She wasn't flashy with her dress, hair, or makeup, but she was very pretty with eyes that lit up when she spoke about "her boys." She embodied everything Maddie believed a mother should be. She loved her husband and cherished her sons. She strived to set an example for her family by volunteering in the community. She spoiled her grandchildren, and although they were her step-grandchildren, no one would ever know they weren't hers by blood. Her mission was to make sure her family was cared for. She looked for any occasion to cook a huge meal, bringing them all together over food.

She had bonded with each of her children differently, but significantly. Greyson was smart, very cerebral. She nurtured his desire to learn as a child by supporting and encouraging him entering every science fair, spelling bee, or any other display of intelligence he could become a part of. It had paid off when Greyson became the first black partner at the upscale Chicago law firm. Kirkland was her self-determined protector. She encouraged his love for working with his hands, resulting in his successful construction career.

"But Chevy was special," Mrs. Ballantyne told Maddie over tea in her kitchen. "Growing up, he was very quiet while the oldest and the baby hogged all the attention. I wanted him to know I loved him just the same, so we spent a lot of time together doing mother-son stuff. He gets his love for nature and animals from me."

"You're responsible for him loving to cook, too."

Mrs. Ballantyne smiled. "I guess I am. You'll have to come

over when my roses bloom." Everyone in the county knew about her sensational rosebushes. They colored the front of Greyson's home. She'd even crossbred several specimens and invented her own rose.

"I'll take you up on that."

The oven timer sounded and Mrs. Ballantyne removed huge chocolate chip cookies. The smell made Maddie's mouth water. Chevy had definitely gotten his cooking abilities from his mother. She placed them on a rack to cool and returned to the table. "I'm really glad Chevy found you."

She freshened Mrs. Ballantyne's tea. "Believe me, I'm the lucky one. Not many men would put up with a woman who's tied so closely to home because she's taking care of her sick father. He's so understanding, and patient." She caught Mrs. Ballantyne's gaze. "I really love him."

"This is good news. All my sons with women who truly love them. They're good boys. This is the least they deserve."

"Mrs. Ballantyne—"

"Call me Mama. All the girls do."

Maddie assumed she meant Sutton and Cassidy. "Mama, I didn't come just for a visit."

"I know. You're wondering when I'll be able to sit with your father again." She sipped her tea. "It's hard right now."

"I understand. My father is doing much better. He doesn't require as much care as he used to, so it frees up more of my time. I appreciate all you did do. Without you and the other volunteers from the church stepping up, I wouldn't have been able to spend any time with Chevy.... It's not the reason I came."

"What is it?" Even as she asked, Maddie could tell Mama Ballantyne knew exactly why she'd come.

"Your sons are miserable."

She clutched her chest, and with an audible intake of

breath, the tears formed in her eyes. "I miss them so much. This is such a mess. Jack—he won't listen to common sense."

Maddie held her hand across the table, fighting her own tears. "Tell me if I'm interfering, and I'll back off right now."

"No. No. You're Chevy's girlfriend, and you care that he's miserable."

"What can we do about this? Sutton and Cassidy sent me"—she tried to smile and lighten the mood—"as a delegate to try and negotiate a peaceful resolution."

"I wish I knew the answer. I've never seen Jack so mad! He's angry, but he's sad, too. He's set on never speaking to them again. He refuses to back down."

"What if we get them together—"

"Not now. Jack isn't ready yet. It could make it all worse. I think we're going to have to give it more time."

"I should tell them to lie low?"

"Yes. Yes, tell them to 'lie low' for now. I'll get a message to them through you when I think the time is right. In the meantime, I'll keep working on Jack."

"It's not an instant fix, but at least we have a plan now."

Mama went to the stove and started placing the cookies in a basket. "We women have to put up with so much when we agree to love these Ballantyne men."

Maddie treaded lightly. "Mama, how are you holding up? Are things okay between you and Mr. Ballantyne? The guys are really worried you might be hurting…."

She turned to Maddie, spatula in hand. "Tell my boys I'm fine, I miss them, and I love them. When this is over, we're going to have the biggest celebration ever."

Chapter 19

Stacy crossed her short legs, studying each of them in turn. Her flirtatious stares made Chevy uneasy, but Greyson and Kirkland seemed to have gotten used to it. While "investigating" Pop's involvement with Eileen Putnam, Stacy found her way to the town's barbershop. The men were more than receptive to her aggressive flirting. Punchy abandoned his daily checker game with Rabbit, and he and Stacy had been seen together almost every day since.

"Mountain man, you still want to go through with this? It doesn't matter that someone tipped your father off to my investigation?"

Greyson looked torn, but stuck with their agreement. "We'd like you to be more discreet, but yes, we want you to continue investigating."

"You got my bill last week, right?"

"If you decide to continue, you'll have an advance by the end of the day."

The ever-present flirtatious smile slipped from Stacy's face as she studied them cautiously. "You're sure you want to do this?"

Stressed over his decision to pursue the investigation, Chevy had enough of the procrastination. "We've gone too far to turn back," he said firmly. "We've made up our minds. Do you want the job?"

"All right, you've got me."

Greyson, knowing her best, asked, "Why the hesitation?"

"Mountain man, I'm good, and I'm not bragging on myself. I'm the best in the business. I dug deep and came up with nothing. Somebody has gone to a lot of trouble to hide the truth. Now I'll do whatever it takes to get to the bottom of it." She paused briefly. "You guys are more than just clients to me. I'm worried I might find out something you *really* don't want to know—or weren't expecting. Can you handle that?"

Chevy spoke up. "We'll handle it because we have to. Dig deep. Find the truth, and tell us everything."

Stacy glanced over his shoulder. "I'll report back as soon as I know something. Call me if you need me." She stood up. "I have a dinner date."

They collectively turned to see Punchy waiting sheepishly near the entrance of the hotel.

"Gotta go." Stacy bounced off.

"She'll eat him alive," Chevy said.

"What could she see in Punchy?" Kirkland asked. "She's *so*…and he's *so*… The world has gone crazy."

They watched Stacy and Punchy leave the hotel together.

"I have to get going." Kirkland stood and dug his car keys from his jacket pocket. They exchanged good-byes and he left, leaving Chevy and Greyson together in the lobby of the hotel.

"How's Mama?" Greyson asked, knowing Maddie kept in regular contact with her.

"Maddie says she's doing okay. She didn't see any signs

of problems between Mama and Pop when she stopped by the other day."

"Good." The sadness in Greyson's voice reflected how much he missed the closeness they all had with their parents.

"Kirkland was right. The world has gone crazy. Who would have ever thought there would be a time when the only way we could communicate with our parents was through my girlfriend?"

"Who would've ever thought you'd have a girlfriend?" Greyson laughed, and Chevy joined him.

"Mandisa's great." He braced himself for Greyson's reaction. "I'm in love with her."

"Does she know?"

"I told her."

"What did she say?"

"She's in love with me, too."

After a congratulatory brotherly hug, Greyson asked, "What's next?"

"With everything that's going on, we're taking it slowly."

"What's going on?"

He relaxed back in the chair, crossing his legs at the ankles. "The thing with Pop. Maddie's father being sick. Finishing up the lodge. We both have a lot going on."

"It's called life, and there will always be another obstacle to face. Don't let Maddie get away while you're waiting for things to be perfect between you—it'll never be perfect."

"It's pretty perfect right now."

"There you go. What more could you want?"

Chevy wanted a lot more. He wanted Maddie to love him as much as he loved her. He wanted to start a family with her. He wanted her in his life forever. He couldn't measure how she'd changed him. He couldn't name all the new emotions she'd introduced him to just by being herself. No woman had ever made him feel so special. When she looked at him as if he were a living miracle, his knees buckled. The things he did for her he considered not enough to prove his love—to Maddie, they meant the world. She demanded everything, but never asked for more than he could give. She made him want to be *better*—a better man, a better businessman, a better provider.

If not for Maddie's support, he wouldn't have handled the situation with Pop very well. Emotionally, she offered him unconditional support. Physically, she soothed his weary body. She never told him what he wanted to hear to appease him, but she remained nonjudgmental.

As he drove home alone in his truck, he replayed a familiar scenario—Maddie at his cabin waiting for him to come home. When he opened his front door, Placido and Porter were there. The dogs had been a great comfort, but since Maddie claimed her place in his heart, they weren't enough. He turned on the television before leashing the dogs for their walk. He wasn't interested in watching it—not without Maddie. Having the television on awoke the warm feeling he got when he was puttering around the cabin while Maddie stretched out on the sofa watching the "junk food" shows.

Two beers, and several hours later, Chevy lay in his bed, staring up at the ceiling, still thinking about Maddie. He could hear the faint chattering of voices coming from the television in the living room. One of the dogs was moving around in the kitchen. Porter soon pranced into his bedroom, jumped up on the bed, and flopped down next to him.

"You miss Mandisa, too," Chevy said, stroking the dog's shiny coat. Both of the dogs loved her, but Porter never left her side.

Without warning, a sudden panic—he couldn't think of another way to describe the urgent feeling—washed over him. He needed Maddie beside him—now. Greyson had given him good advice. There was no sane reason for not making his intentions crystal clear to her. If he had learned anything from the mess with Pop, he'd learned time was short and those you took for granted could disappear from your life without warning. He had to take every precaution against losing Maddie. He had to show her how much he loved her, and needed her. He had to drop his guarded exterior and open himself up for possible rejection, giving Maddie a chance to accept him.

Impulsively, he jumped up from the bed. When had he become impulsive? He had no time to ponder the question. He dressed quickly, hopping around the living room as he pulled on his boots. This was on his heart to do—he had to seize the sudden influx of courage. He packed an overnight bag, jamming clothes into it. By the time he shoved his arms into his jacket, Placido and Porter were barking wildly with excitement—as if they knew what he was about to do and offered their approval. After securing the dogs, he jumped into his truck, and at three o'clock in the morning he drove to the capital.

He checked into a hotel and set the alarm clock to wake him at dawn. Being in Charleston, close to achieving his goal, decreased his anxiety. Knowing the huge step he was about to take made his nerves a wreck. He wished he could talk to Mama, and get approval from Pop, but those options weren't available. He was long on independence, and realized he loved Maddie so much their opinions couldn't really sway him.

He tossed for a while before falling asleep, fighting the jittery feeling in his chest. He imagined how his life would change after today, and serenity lulled him to sleep. He understood he had other things to do to make himself worthy of Mandisa, but he was ready for the challenge.

* * *

"Good morning, sir. Welcome to my store." The shop-keeper swung open the door and flipped the sign to OPEN. The middle-aged man had a pudgy middle he tried to hide beneath an expensive suit. He was bald on top, and the hair surrounding the perimeter was closely and neatly shaved. He was doused in cologne and his shoes looked as expensive as the suit he wore. "What can I do for you this morning?"

"I want to purchase an engagement ring." Chevy stepped inside and the door automatically locked behind him. The safety feature disclosed the unlimited value of the shopkeeper's goods. Glass cases framed the small specialty shop. The early morning sunlight streamed through the windows, causing the gold, silver, and diamonds to sparkle. There were two women working in the back of the shop—one around the same age of the man, the other much younger.

The man took his place behind the counter. "Do you have any idea what you want?"

Glancing at the large variety of jewelry made Chevy's task daunting. "She's a very special lady, and I want something to show her how much I love her."

"Beyond that, you have no clue." The man chuckled. "What price range?"

This was a test. Anyone entering into the exclusive jewelry shop and haggling over price was either clueless or more interested in casing the store. Hamric Jewelry was well known for its high-end diamonds and unique settings. The shop catered to wealthy individuals who needed armed guards to escort them home after a day's shopping spree. Hamric had loaned jewelry to three presidents' wives for their husbands' inauguration. This was a store people chartered private jets to visit. This was not a place where you looked at the price tag before you selected your purchase.

"Price is no object." Chevy had heard the line used before, but never thought he'd be in a place in his life where it would have any meaning to him.

A pleasant smile spread across the man's face. "Let me show you some rings. Once we narrow down what you like, I can focus in on helping you select the perfect ring for the perfect woman."

The man patiently explained the importance of clarity and cut as he showed Chevy ring after ring. Once he had a better idea of what Chevy was looking for, he called his wife from the back to assist.

"You'll know the right ring when we find it," she told Chevy.

"That one." He pointed to a ring with a round diamond in a tulip setting with a platinum band. The ring was simple, but elegant—quietly stunning—just like Maddie.

The shopkeeper's wife removed the ring from the display case and placed it atop a black cloth on the counter. "It's one of our best pieces. It's beautiful," she added in a hushed tone as if it were a sacred artifact.

Chevy only needed to slip it on his pinky to know the ring would be perfect for Maddie. "I'll take it."

"Wonderful," the shopkeeper said. "Do you know your young lady's ring size? If not, don't worry. You can obtain the information and give me a call later. It'll be two weeks before the designer completes the ring."

"Two weeks? I need the ring today."

"I'm afraid that's not possible. This ring was designed for display at our store. It's an exclusive—you couldn't find it at any jewelry store for ready purchase. I have to take a deposit and place the order. We need the correct size—"

"This is the correct size." He'd held Maddie's small hand in his enough to know what size ring she wore. "I want to take it with me." He hadn't yet planned how he would ask Maddie to marry him, but he knew he had to have the ring and he had to have it today. He needed it with him when he returned to Hannaford, because whenever he asked Maddie to be his wife, he wanted it ready for presentation.

The shopkeeper shook his head. "To replace it in the display case would entail commissioning the designer to make another. I'd lose the opportunity of any other possible clients wishing to purchase it, because they wouldn't see it proudly displayed at Hamric…" His rambling died as he looked over at his wife. He took in Chevy's determination and conceded. "I would have to charge you extra, and I'd need full payment immediately."

"I'll take it."

"Sir, this ring is quite expensive."

The five-figure price didn't cause Chevy to hesitate. He removed his credit card and handed it over to the man. The shopkeeper took the card and left to verify its limits.

"Would you like to see the matching wedding set?" the owner's wife asked.

"I would."

By the time the shopkeeper returned—all smiles—Chevy had placed an order for the matching wedding band for Maddie, and a band for himself.

"She must be an amazing woman," the shopkeeper said, handing Chevy the engagement ring. "We look forward to meeting her when you come for your sizing."

"She is amazing, and I appreciate her coming into my life more every day."

Chapter 20

Chevy arrived at Maddie's house Saturday morning dressed in tan Dickies hauling his toolbox. After talking with her father, he went to work on the car. Maddie joined him until he chased her away, telling her she was too distracting. He was in an exceptionally good mood, and full of special smiles just for her. It was nice to see him this way since he'd been so troubled by the situation with Pop.

"Still think you can fix it?" Maddie asked when he walked into the den.

"It's going to take more work than I thought, but we can fix it. I need to go get some parts, and I'll have to wait for Greyson and Kirkland to get here. I can build a house with my bare hands, but when it comes to repairing cars I need a little help."

"I didn't know it would be such a big job. I should have it repaired later—at a shop."

He wound his fingers in the fabric of her sweater and hauled her to her feet. He pressed his forehead to hers. "You don't want me to help you?"

"I do, but—"

"You don't think I can do it?"

"I know you can do whatever you put your mind to, but—"

"Are you trying to get rid of me? Do you have a hot date planned?" The growl in his voice had nothing to do with anger.

"You know better."

"Then let me keep doing what I'm doing." He sealed the deal by pressing his lips to hers and demanding she accept the caress of his tongue. His knuckles pressed into her chest as he pulled her closer, exploring her mouth deeply. He claimed her, adding another tattoo to her body and soul. When he released her, he looked down at her with a thoroughly satisfied, devilish grin. "Be back shortly."

Maddie swayed on her feet, unable to speak. When she heard the front door close, she snapped out of her trance. She didn't know what had gotten into Chevy, but she couldn't wait until they were alone so she could investigate further.

Chevy returned shortly after lunch with his brothers. They briefly greeted her and then went to work on the car.

"That man…crazy…for you," Maddie's father said.

"I hope you're right, Dad, because I'm in love with him."

He watched her for a long moment. He didn't say anything—she'd expected a father's warning to guard her heart carefully. Instead, he shocked her beyond imagination. "If you have to make a choice, choose Chevy."

Maddie would have thought she'd misinterpreted her father's words, but for the first time in a long time, his speech was clear. "Chevy wouldn't ask me to make a choice, and if he did, I wouldn't."

"He won't ask."

"I know. Chevy isn't selfish."

"But there might come a time…when what he wants…

from you—" He struggled with the words and they came out garbled, but Maddie understood. "You won't have the life he offers if you have to take care of me."

"Dad, you're tired."

"Not tired!" He raised his voice. "I see how much he cares…for you. If you have to choose, choose Chevy."

"No. I'd never, ever leave you."

"Done enough. Sacrificed enough. No more. I won't… have it. Time…for you to…live."

"Dad—"

He stopped her by sandwiching her hand between his. "Time…for you to…live…your own…life." He tried to end the conversation by turning toward the television at his bedside.

Maddie couldn't let him believe he'd ruined her life. "Dad, I'll admit I haven't done all the things I've wanted to do, but I don't have any regrets. There'll be time for me to do other things. Right now, you need me."

"When time?" he snapped. "When I'm dead?"

"Don't talk like this."

"I'm dead…then you start…living. No. Not good."

"I *will not* leave you. It's not an option. I'd never place myself in a situation where I had to choose between you and—"

"And I'd never ask you to."

Maddie whirled around to find Chevy standing in the doorway, anger clearly etched on his face. He approached her father's bed, situating himself firmly between them. "Mr. Ingram, family is very important to me. I would never try to come between you and your daughter. Frankly, if Maddie would allow me to pull her away from you she wouldn't be the person I think she is." He glanced at her and his features softened. "I love Maddie. Part of loving someone and building a relationship with them is learning how to relate to their family. Any plans I make for Maddie and me will include our families."

Her father was speechless. She swallowed the lump in her throat and kissed his forehead. She approached Chevy and signaled for him to bend for her kiss. His eyes flashed over her head to her father, but he wanted her kiss badly enough to fight the embarrassment of her public display of affection.

"Did you need something?" she asked him.

"Sutton and Cassidy just pulled up with the kids. They're carrying shopping bags."

She looked between Chevy and her father and hurried out on the front porch, leaving them to end the conversation.

"What's going on?" Maddie asked, grabbing a shopping bag from Cassidy so she could take Courtney out of her car seat.

"Our husbands have been here all day working on your car. We knew they'd be hungry and it wasn't fair to ask you to feed them."

"We know their appetites," Sutton added.

"Can I go with Daddy?" Sierra asked.

Sutton pointed her in the right direction and she ran off to join the guys in the driveway.

"You didn't have to do this," Maddie said as they went inside.

"We wanted to. Sutton and I thought it'd be a good excuse to hang out together. The guys have been so down about Pop, maybe this will cheer them up."

Sutton agreed. "We're going to have to come to the realization that Pop may never get over his anger. We have to start rebuilding the family and, ladies, the new Ballantyne family starts with us."

They went inside and began cooking dinner amongst laughs and plenty of good conversation. Maddie's house hadn't bustled with activity since her mother passed. Her father enjoyed every minute of the attention the "pretty girls" gave him. He got to his wheelchair and actually had the guys take him outside. Maddie was worried—it was still winter and cold—but he insisted with Chevy's support and promise to keep a close eye on him.

"I don't know how we're all going to fit in this kitchen," Maddie worried aloud. She was aware Cassidy and Sutton were blessed with big homes. Maddie's house was very small, even compared with the others in the neighborhood. She felt a little ashamed she couldn't provide elaborate table settings at a table to seat ten.

"We'll rearrange," Sutton said.

"I just wish I had more room and more furniture."

"Don't sweat it," Cassidy told her. "We'll make do, just like we've all had to."

"This will be nice and cozy," Sutton told her, going off to start moving things around.

Maddie became overwhelmed by the raw intensity of the day's emotions. These people really cared for her. Chevy had come to spend the day working on her car without asking for repayment in any form. He'd purchased the needed parts and called on his brothers to help. Kirkland and Greyson had come without question. Sutton and Cassidy spontaneously showed up on her doorstep with dinner. These things might seem small someone else, but to Maddie, who had been left isolated for so many years to care for her parents, they meant the world.

Her father hadn't looked so content in a long time. He was enjoying having leisure time with men who treated him as "one of the boys." She recalled his sacrifice earlier, and tears came to her eyes.

"What is it?" Cassidy was there in an instant, hugging her.

Maddie tried to put it into words, but failed miserably. "I'm blubbering."

"It's okay." Sutton joined them in a group hug. "I felt the same way when I realized how much I loved Greyson."

And it was all about her love for Chevy. Without her relationship with him, she wouldn't have become a part of such a great family.

"Mandisa?" Sutton and Cassidy broke away so Chevy could take her in his arms. "What did you do to her?"

"We didn't do anything to your girlfriend," Sutton scolded. "She's just happy."

"She's crying because she's happy?" Chevy sounded totally baffled. "Give us a minute." Sutton and Cassidy left to begin rearranging furniture.

"This has been a big day for you," Chevy said. "I can take my family and leave so you can get some rest."

"Don't do that. I got a little overwhelmed. It's nice to have a big family—it's been just me and my father for so long."

"Are you sure?" He swiped a tear from her cheek with his thumb. "My family can be a little overpowering."

"I'm sure. I'm having a good time, really." She quickly changed the subject. "Why'd you come inside?"

"Your father was ready to come in. Sierra's keeping him company." He laughed. "She's chattering away, and he seems to enjoy it." He kissed her cheek. "We're done with your car. It's running like a charm. Tonight, you'll take me for a ride."

"I'm too anxious to wait until tonight."

"You have to. I'm not letting you drive without me when you haven't done it in so long, and right now we're going to move your father's bedroom."

"Chevy—"

He pressed his finger to her lips. "Call us when dinner is ready."

Dinner held more lively discussion, and plenty of laughs. Everyone found a place to lounge, and no one seemed put off by the limited space. After dinner, everyone migrated into the den. Chevy sat on the floor, his back against the wall. He pulled Maddie down with him, situating her between his outstretched thighs and wrapping his arms around her middle. Every time he planted a kiss on the back of her neck she shivered.

"It's getting late," Chevy announced. "Let's finish up the bedroom." He herded Greyson and Kirkland away to move the last of the furniture and medical supplies into the bedroom.

The women moved to the kitchen while Sutton was placed in charge of picking up in the den. Maddie couldn't have enjoyed Cassidy's and Sutton's company more. They were the sisters she never had growing up. Cassidy had a twin brother, but Sutton was also an only child, which probably accounted for how quickly she bonded with Maddie when she started working at the library.

"Mommy," Sierra said, "Daddy said to come get you and Aunt Cassidy and Aunt Maddie."

Sutton knelt and grabbed a napkin to clean Sierra's face. Maddie watched them interact and couldn't help entertaining the idea of having her own daughter. Sierra and Courtney were sweet kids, full of life and very curious. Maddie wanted a family, but always considered it a distant reality. Before Chevy came along, she'd only had one boyfriend and that circumstance didn't increase her likelihood to become a parent.

"We'd better go see what Greyson wants," Cassidy said, drying her hand on a towel. She placed Courtney on her hip and they trouped into the den.

The stage had been set. Chevy, Kirkland, and Greyson were

still dressed in matching overalls, but their suits were meant to be stage costumes. Maddie leaned against the arm of her father's chair, settling in for the show. Sierra dropped Sutton's hand and took center stage. The men lined up behind her.

Chevy hit the button on the stereo, and a familiar tune started to play. The breakout song from the movie *The Five Heartbeats*, "A Heart Is a House for Love," began to unfold. The men did a fancy version of the two-step. They weren't Vanity 6, but they were pretty spectacular. Sierra used the television remote for her microphone as she started to croon the words to the record. Maddie had no idea she could sing so well. She was a vision of Countace Vaughn. Sutton and Greyson beamed with pride. The chorus rose up and the men changed their dance step, reminiscent of the group from the movie.

As the record went on, the men took their turn singing the lead. Chevy became Leon, oozing the same sex appeal as he took Maddie's hand and brought her up onstage. His heated version of the chorus left her mouth dry, and her heart thumping. As the song came to an end, she moved to Chevy, collapsing on the floor in a heap as she clung to the leg of his tan Dickies. Everyone howled with laughter. Chevy—very gently—helped her up, pretending to revive her from the vapors. When the music stopped, she was draped around his neck. They seemed to be in their own world as he leaned down and kissed her.

"I love you," Maddie told him, hardly able to stop laughing.

"I love you, too."

"It's been too long since I've been here." Maddie snuggled deeper into the crook of Chevy's shoulder, relishing the feel of skin-to-skin contact. It had been two weeks since she'd been able to sneak away and spend time at his cabin, and she missed him terribly.

"We have to make a point to never let it happen again."

"Sounds like you missed me."

He kissed the top of her head. "Was there any doubt?"

Porter padded into the room and flopped down on the floor next to the bed.

"I thought I shut the door," Chevy mumbled. "I don't want to share Mandisa with anybody right now, and that includes you, Porter." He commanded the dog to return to the kitchen, and Porter begrudgingly sauntered out of the bedroom. "Don't forget who rescued you, dog."

"Stop being mean."

"I have to be when it comes to protecting you from the predators." He slid up in bed, sitting against the headboard. He maneuvered her body with a firm touch until she was sitting between his muscular thighs.

"What predators? Porter is the gentlest of any creature I've ever met—including you."

"Funny. What about Richard?"

"What about him? If I remember correctly, you attacked him. For no reason, I should add."

"Oh, there was a reason. And what is this I hear about him living in San Diego? Does him living there have anything to do with why you're running in the marathon there?"

"Of course not. It's a coincidence."

He made a sound of skepticism.

"Although exciting things happen when you're jealous."

"You're enjoying this too much."

"Guilty," she shamelessly admitted.

"Then I hope you'll enjoy it when I tag along to California with you."

She whipped around to see his face clearly. "You're kidding."

"Kirkland's going, and I want to be there too. Not just to protect you from the predator, but because I want to support you. You and Cassidy are doing a good thing. I want to be there with you."

She lay back against him, a huge smile spreading across her face. "You coming along means a lot to me."

His hands cascaded around her waist, down her thighs to her calves, and back up. "Running has done great things to your body." He repeated the gesture, his fingers awakening each of her nerve endings. "Your legs are so muscular and strong. I'd like to have them wrapped around my waist, but there'll be plenty of time for that tonight." He lifted one leg and then the other, draping them over his and leaving her fully exposed. His hands moved over her belly. "Your belly is so tight." His fingers danced across her breasts. "Your breasts," he growled next to her ear, "are perfect." He kneaded her breasts until her nipples responded, becoming hard and alert.

Maddie had noticed the improvement in her figure, but Chevy's touch brought a whole new appreciation. His hand dipped between her thighs while she was still writhing from his fondling. He moved his legs apart, dragging hers along, opening her wider. Brazenly, he stroked the soft curls between her thighs, taking his fingers on a deeper journey with each touch. As her mind vacillated between the pleasurable sensations on her breasts and between her legs, he started to kiss her neck. He nipped her ear, momentarily distracting her from the penetration of his fingers. Her head fell back and he captured her moans with his mouth.

She felt him growing, elongating into a tower of strength against her back. She fought to flip around and straddle him, taking him deep inside, but he steadied her by plunging his finger deep and adding another. He widened his stance, locking her in the best position for his explicit exploration. His thumb burrowed into her nest of curls, finding her core throbbing and wet. He stroked lightly with unhurried ambition until she was begging him to end the torture.

"Chevy," she whimpered when he removed his hands and set her away from him.

"You really have to work on your patience," he teased.

"Don't torture me if you don't want me to respond." She watched with overly eager eyes as he safeguarded their future. "You're doing that on purpose," she scolded as he moved at a pace too leisurely for her liking.

He glanced up at her with a devilish grin. "Of course I am."

"Oh, you want to play games." Maddie had become pretty good at growling herself since spending time with him. "You shouldn't provoke me." She gave him a brief warning before taking the skin of his thigh between her lips. She fed from the sensitive area until his hands fell away from her desired target. She spent a very long time kissing and caressing his thighs—coming close, but not quite *there*—until his willpower melted. He had never let her taste him before, always redirecting her efforts and later explaining how he wouldn't allow it until they were married. He had provoked her this evening, and as she pressed her fingers to the area behind his scrotum that made him wiggle and groan, she declared her revenge.

She used her other hand to unroll the condom, but he had the presence of mind to forbid it. She'd thought him thoroughly sedated by her seduction, but he still wasn't the mass of putty she wanted to control. She came to her knees between his legs. Momentarily, she forgot her wicked game when she looked at him. He was so handsome it was striking. With the added glow of sexual desire, he was stunning. She continued to fondle him as she pressed her mouth to his. The gesture was so tender compared to what she was doing to his towering erection, it surprised him and his eyes flew open.

She pulled away and smiled. He grinned—pure happiness without words.

Maddie bent low, sliding him slow and steady into her mouth. She quickly realized she'd never be able to consume every inch and added the up-and-down movement of her hands.

His hands grasped her head. He released her hair from the knot at the nape of her neck and tangled his hands in her locks. Him forbidding her the right to give him this pleasure seemed far away, and long gone. His entire body tightened. He bent his legs up, giving her unrestricted access. His loss of control caused her to place her hands on his thighs, bracing against his upstroke.

He gripped her shoulders and tossed her to the bed, covering her quickly. He quickly slipped on a condom. She lifted her hips to meet his, wanting to savor the delight. She had unleashed a barbarian-like wildness in him.

"Come quick," he demanded between clenched teeth as he entered her in one unending stroke. He plunged into her with scandalous drama that held no remorse. She cried out as he filled her to capacity, touching places she'd never been touched before. As he pounded into her, taking her on a rough ride, her nails bit into his back. He placed his finger under her chin and turned her head to meet his kiss. As savage as his stroke was, his kiss was more gentle.

Her muscles coiled. Her heartbeat scampered. Her back bowed as every nerve producing pleasure sent a message to the core of her body. She exploded, falling onto the bed in a quivering mass. She jerked uncontrollably, the climax refusing to end.

Chevy continued to rock his hips, but slowed his stroke as his hands petted her body, bringing her down from her high. Once he quieted her, his hips shimmied. He seemed to grow longer and penetrate her more deeply. She wrapped her legs around his waist and he grabbed her bottom, pulling her up into his stroke. She felt the muscles in his back bunch. His haunches contracted as he pushed, digging his feet into the mattress. He froze—one second, two—and then his body shook. He let out a long groan that set the dogs barking.

He remained inside her as he gathered her in his arms. "This is too excellent."

She was thinking the same thing herself.

Chapter 21

Chevy was sitting in Greyson's den when Kirkland arrived. He had called his brothers together to discuss the future of their family. He and Kirkland sat on opposite ends of the sofa, and Greyson was perched behind his desk playing the new role of family patriarch. They made small talk about the businesses, and Kirkland brought up the marathon. "Cassidy is going to leave Courtney with her brother over the weekend. Her parents will keep her Friday and Monday."

"No kidding?" Greyson asked. "Her parents are going to keep the baby?"

Kirkland nodded. "Being around Maddie and her father, and watching the trouble we're having with Pop, has made Cassidy put more effort in her relationship with her parents. It seems to be working out."

"How's Maddie going to swing going to San Diego with her father?" Greyson wanted to know.

"Now that he's getting better," Chevy said, "he's able to stay with his sister for a couple of days. The nurse will still come, but he doesn't need much medical care anymore."

"Nothing from Pop?" Kirkland asked him.

Chevy shook his head. Maddie was in constant contact with their mother, who promised Pop was softening because he missed them as much as they missed him. "What I want to talk to you about—I would've gone to Pop, but since he isn't speaking to us…"

"What's up?" Kirkland asked. He shared a curious look with Greyson.

Knowing he could show them better than tell them, Chevy fished the box holding Maddie's engagement ring out of his pocket. He handed it over to Kirkland.

"Is it an engagement ring?" Greyson came from behind his desk and pried the box from Kirkland's hand. He whistled. "Wow."

"How much did this set you back?"

When Chevy answered Greyson, his eyebrows shot up. He told them the story of how he'd gotten up in the middle of the night and driven to Charleston and bought the ring.

"I didn't know you could get a limit that high on a credit card," Kirkland said. "Exactly how much money do you have stashed at the cabin?"

Chevy ignored his bratty little brother. "How do you feel about me asking Maddie to marry me?"

"It's great," Greyson said. He sat between Chevy and Kirkland, wrapping Chevy in a bear hug.

"It's about time." Kirkland came around to grab him from the other side. Before long they were wrestling around on the floor of the den like kids. Exhausted, they remained on the floor talking.

Kirkland ran his fingers through his curls, ruffling them back to life. "When are you going to ask her?"

"In San Diego after she finishes the marathon. I want it to be special. Don't tell Cassidy. I want it to be a surprise."

Kirkland assured Chevy he could keep the secret.

"I have some good news, too." Greyson was beaming, so it wasn't hard to guess what it could be.

"Sutton and I are trying to get pregnant."

The announcement set off another wrestling match.

"You know," Chevy said after they calmed down, "our problem with Pop has made us make major changes in our lives."

"Our parents should be here," Kirkland said.

"They should, but they aren't and we've managed to keep living. You and Cassidy are doing well. Sutton has agreed to have the baby Greyson's been wanting. I'm going to ask Maddie to marry me. Maybe we needed to break away from Pop in order to be our own men."

They were quiet a moment, contemplating the sheer genius of it.

"Do you think Pop knew this when he disowned us?" Greyson asked.

Chevy shrugged. "Could be. All I know is that when this is all over, he'll be proud of what we've accomplished."

Kirkland was skeptical. "Let's just see what he does when he finds out Stacy is still investigating him before we get all philosophical."

Chevy didn't want to get down about Pop when he had just announced his plans to marry Maddie. "I need your help." He looked at each of his brothers in turn. "I'm thinking of making an offer on the nursing home. I have to go look at it this week. Greyson, I want you to negotiate the sell. I want you to come along, Kirkland, to help me figure out what needs to be done to renovate it."

"You're going to buy the nursing home? What about the lodge?"

"Construction on the lodge is done. We'll be ready to open by next summer. That reminds me, bring the pictures Cassidy painted so the interior decorator can get to work. You put together the Ballantyne Wilderness Lodge. It was Greyson's idea to reopen the paper mill. I need to invest my money and my energy into something."

"Yeah," Greyson said, "I just thought it'd be something associated with animals, or forestry."

"Spending time with Maddie's father showed me how hard a major illness can be on a family with limited resources. The elderly here in Hannaford don't have adequate housing, or a senior center. I've been fighting so hard for animal rights, I forgot how important *people* are."

Sutton knocked on the door before entering the den. "What are you guys doing on the floor?"

Greyson went to her. "Brother stuff. What's up?"

She placed her hand on her hip. "Chevy, where's your cell phone?"

He felt the heat rising, traveling up his neck. "I left it at work."

"Uh-huh. Maddie's on the phone."

"She has a habit of tracking you down, doesn't she?" Kirkland goaded.

He ignored Kirkland and grabbed the phone off Greyson's desk. "Is something wrong?"

"Is that how you answer the phone?"

He turned his back to the room and mumbled, "Sorry. Hello, Mandisa."

"I miss you. I haven't seen you in three days. I called your cabin and you weren't around."

"Come see me."

The smile in her voice transcended the phone line. "When?"

"Now. I'll meet you at my place. I'll cook dinner. We'll go to a movie."

She hesitated. "Todd's leaving soon."

"Ask him to stay. Tell him same deal as usual."

She put him on hold, but quickly returned.

"You coming to see me?" Chevy asked.

"I'm on the way."

They arrived at his cabin at the same time. He stood in the yard and watched her navigate the big car beside his. The first thing he would do once they were married would be to buy her a more manageable car. She shut off the engine and skipped across the yard, jumping into his arms. She threw her arms around his neck.

"I like this greeting," he told her. He wrapped his arm around her waist and carried her inside. Placido and Porter rushed up to them. "Back, dogs."

"Leave my dogs alone."

He set her on the floor and she gathered the dogs in her arms.

"They mind you better than me. You've spoiled them. I'll start dinner after I take them for a walk."

"Grab my bag." She smiled up at him, a mixture of soft feminism and devilment.

He leashed the dogs, stopping at the door to look back at her.

"You have a strange look on your face."

"This is nice, isn't it?"

"This." She pointed between them. "You and me?"

"Yeah."

"It's great. Hurry back."

When he returned, Maddie was at the kitchen sink shredding lettuce. Since training for the marathon she ate a lot of salads and pastas. Chevy wasn't complaining because he benefited from the shapeliness of her body just as much as she did.

"What are you cooking?"

"Chicken and rice primavera. Grab the broccoli and carrots—and an onion."

She did as he asked, leaning against the counter watching him work. "I can make the rice."

"Then get to it." He swatted her behind, liking the way she jumped up on tiptoe, causing her thigh muscles to flex. "We won't have any pie."

She lowered her voice. "Your mother's doing fine."

It didn't stop him from missing his parents. Pop had been suspicious at first about Maddie's regular visits, knowing she had dated Chevy, but she never discussed their relationship and over time Pop thought they were no longer seeing each other. It was good to have Maddie on the inside, keeping an eye on his parents, but the closeness his family had would never be the same without his parents' support.

"You're thinking about your father," Maddie said. She set the rice on the counter and came up to him. "Look at me."

He turned to face her. Half his size, Maddie never had a problem keeping him in line. She was a spitfire, but she was also kind and soft and loving.

"Stop worrying about your father. You've done all you can do. You've apologized, and asked for his forgiveness. You've pleaded with him to explain his relationship with Eileen Putnam." She pressed her hand to his jaw, and he felt the tension melt away. "There comes a time, Chevy, when you have to say enough is enough. How long can you keep trying when your father isn't willing to even talk to you?"

"He's stubborn."

"And so are you, but you made the first move." She pulled

her hand away. "I'm concerned about you—Greyson and Kirkland have Sutton and Cassidy to worry about them."

He understood. They had all agreed to do the wrong thing, but doing the right thing would have to be an individual decision.

Undaunted by his silence, Maddie went on. "You're his *son*. You made a mistake. He has to forgive you—it's what parents are required to do. If he's not willing to meet his responsibilities, you can't make him."

"You're telling me to walk away?" He couldn't believe a woman who valued family and cherished her father would give him such advice.

"Yes," she answered without hesitation. "You know how important family ties are to me, and I'm telling you to let it go. You've done all you can do to change your father's mind. For whatever reason, he's not ready to let you back into his life." Seeing his reaction, she took his hand between hers. "You're not turning your back on your family. If Pop asks to see you, go. But in the meantime, fix this within yourself."

Hadn't this whole thing been about his selfishness to know the details of his parents' marriage? What business of his was it what went on in their relationship? If Pop had pried into his relationship with Maddie, he would've been just as angry. Maybe he should do a little introspection to find what had been missing in his life that prompted him to try to live someone else's.

"You might be right," he admitted.

"Did you ever consider Pop might be waiting to see how you handle this? Maybe he had to step out of your life so you could become your own man."

She placed her hands on his shoulders and pulled herself up to kiss his cheek. She walked away, leaving him in a cloud of contemplation while she cooked the rice.

Her words offered a new insight on his family dynamics. Pop was the patriarch of the Ballantyne family. A strong disciplinarian, he kept a tight rein on his sons. As kids, they had needed the threat of a father figure's scorn, but as adults they needed to live by their own rules. Pop had done a good job instilling values in his boys. Mama had been there to nurture and support them through the hard times. But now they were men, and it was time to let go of the past. Problems from their childhood followed them into adult life, and often had the power to direct their future. Maddie was right. It was time for him to break away from his father's hold, and his brothers' choices, and become his own legacy.

Renovating the nursing home was a project he could embrace. Watching Maddie with her father had been the catalyst, but he lived to defend those not able to stand up for themselves. He'd watched the land destroyed, and went to college to major in forestry. Animals were being displaced, and he'd become a spokesperson for animal rights. As he watched the future of Social Security crumble and elder abuse rise, he felt compelled to take up their cause.

He wouldn't tell Maddie about the project until he knew how feasible it would be to complete. As he cooked dinner, he imagined how much he could do with the dilapidated buildings near the old nursing home. One semester of anatomy and physiology summed up his medical knowledge, so he'd need help from someone he trusted. Todd might be up to the challenge. If not, he could provide a referral.

After Maddie finished the rice, she started setting the table. "Are you mad at me?"

"What? No."

"You haven't said a word."

"I'm thinking about what you said. I can't put my life

on hold until Pop comes around. I've missed out on enough."

Maddie found the candles and linen napkins Mama had left behind from the last family dinner at his cabin, and set a romantic table. They dimmed the lights and had a quiet dinner together. Just what he needed to wind down after a busy week at the lodge.

"Would you be mad if we didn't go to the movies tonight?" Maddie asked, tracing a small circle on the back of his hand.

"We can do whatever you want to do."

"I'd like to sit in front of the fire and watch TV. Let's just cuddle."

"Cuddle only?"

"We'll see." She lifted a longneck beer to her mouth and his body took immediate notice, stretching and elongating and wishing it were the bottle.

After eating, they watched a little television, but after an intense kissing session, they abandoned it and took a long, hot shower together.

"You're in a romantic mood tonight." Chevy rubbed lotion into her back as she sat at the vanity.

"I know." Her voice was low and sultry.

"Why?"

"I love you."

They climbed into bed together, shutting off the lights and watching the moon streak across the bricks of the fireplace. The glow warmed the room, adding to the romantic atmosphere Maddie needed. She lay in his arms, her head against his chest. He held her for a long time, enjoying being with her.

"You and Cassidy together are three thousand dollars short of your donation to the American Stroke Foundation for the marathon."

"We haven't been working as hard as we should be to reach our goal. We plan to step it up."

"I have something for you."

"What? Where could you be hiding it?" She ran her hands across his abdomen, lower, and exciting things began to happen.

"Look under your pillow."

She rolled away long enough to dig beneath the pillow and pull out a tan envelope. She opened it, glancing up at him. "Are we going to Virginia Beach again?"

"They don't want us back. We burned up the sheets."

She laughed, but gasped when she found the check. "You *cannot* give me three thousand dollars, Chevy. I won't accept this."

"My brothers and I each gave a thousand."

"So that makes it better?" She shoved the check back in the envelope and pressed it to his chest. "This is too much money."

"We give to charities every year. You and Cassidy are doing a good thing. We want to do our part."

"You and Kirkland are traveling with us."

"Mandisa." He pulled her into his arms. "Listen to me. We want to do this. We've done it. Just say 'thank you.'"

She watched him behind hooded eyes. "Thank you."

"I'm investing in you. Make love to me, and we'll call it even."

She lifted an eyebrow. "I'm worth three thousand dollars?"

"Your love is worth a million."

Chapter 22

Late Spring

Maddie couldn't believe she was in California. She looked out the window of her hotel room down onto the pool. Families were romping in the water. People were tanning in lounge chairs. Others strolled by enjoying the scenery. The trip had gone smoothly. On the plane, Kirkland and Cassidy sat across the aisle from Maddie and Chevy. She and Cassidy chattered the entire flight, nervously excited about running in their first marathon. Chevy stayed at her side, quiet and unassuming as he carried their bags up to the hotel room. She could see how proud he was of her at the marathon registration desk. He stood with the other family supporters, telling them how she'd come to run in the race.

Chevy entered the room through the door adjoining their room to Cassidy and Kirkland's. "They want to know if we're going to dinner with them. I told them you might be tired after the trip."

"No! I want to do it all! I don't know if I'll have the opportunity to visit California again."

He laughed at her enthusiasm. "You don't have to do it all in the first day."

She was well aware she was behaving like an excited child at Disney World. "Cassidy and I are going to be tied up with the marathon."

"We're staying an extra day after the race." He'd surprised her with this announcement on the plane.

"It's just not long enough. Let me check on my dad, and then I'll get ready for dinner."

He shook his head as he went to take a shower, but she could see he was enjoying her excitability.

She spoke to her dad and her aunt. Everything was going fine. Her aunt was enjoying her chance to visit. After plenty of discussion, and much planning, Maddie's aunt came to stay with her dad until her return from San Diego. Her father was getting around much better with the help of a four-wheel walker. His speech was still slurred, but not as garbled as before speech therapy. He tired quickly, so Maddie was careful not to let him overdo, even though he felt he could do anything and everything. Todd was scheduled to work during the days Maddie would be away. He'd taken over the primary care of her father with good results, and was showing the other nurses his tricks of the trade. For the first time since her father's stroke, she didn't feel guilty about leaving him.

They had dinner in the Gaslamp Quarter in typical tourist fashion. They requested a city map from the hotel front desk, and grabbed a cab to what the brochures called "San Diego's liveliest neighborhood." The Gaslamp Quarter was located in a historic area of San Diego. The mixture of eateries, shopping, and entertainment drew many people to the area. They ended up at Dakota Grill and Spirits. The restaurant served

American with southwestern flavor. After steaks, seafood, and beer they returned to the hotel for the official welcome party.

Chevy shed his jeans and dressed in a tan linen suit. He even let Maddie talk him into leaving his Stetson behind. There were hundreds at the welcome ceremony, and for the first time, she felt overwhelmed.

"You didn't expect this many people?" Chevy held her hand tightly as they moved through the crowd.

"Our trainer told us there were over a thousand registered, but I didn't realize how *big* that number is until now." She'd never been this far from home. Even her college was small and private, in the suburbs of a tiny town. The throngs of people, coupled with the media and publicity cameras, made her nervous. "I might have taken on too much."

Chevy found a corner not packed with people, and made her sit down to catch her breath. "You have the night-before jitters. Once you start running, this will seem very *small*."

"I hope you're right. I don't want to let everybody down." She was running in the name of her father. The Ballantynes had contributed three thousand dollars to make this happen. The American Stroke Foundation was counting on her to live up to her commitment.

"You look a little green. Let's go back to the room."

"We can't leave yet. I'm rooming with Cassidy tonight, remember?"

"I remember you and Cassidy made that decision." He stroked her hairline until his finger disappeared behind her ear. "I want to sleep with you."

"I have to get some rest tonight. If I'm in the room with you, I doubt that'll happen."

He stroked her hair, pressing his fingers into the back of

her neck. "Stay here. I'm going to find Cassidy and get her room key. I'll bring you some water on the way back." He backed away. "Don't move. I won't be able to find you in this crowd."

Maddie watched him go, his muscles flexing and contracting beneath the soft linen. Women watched him over the rims of their glasses. Some smiled, boldly trying to get his attention. Chevy's eyes were only for her. When he came around, her insides shimmied like Jell-O. Their relationship had evolved nicely, becoming a solid friendship surrounded by the commitment of mutual love.

"Maddie." Richard's laughter gave away his identity before she looked up at him.

"What are you doing here?"

He swooped into the chair next to her. "I live here."

"I know, but what are you doing at the welcoming ceremony?" The invitation-only event was for the runners and their families.

"You inspired me. I started training to run as soon as I got home."

"You're running tomorrow?"

He nodded. "You look a little flushed. Are you okay?"

"It's been a long day. And my stomach is rocking." She pressed her palm into her belly to slow the movement. "I'm nervous about the run."

"It happens. You'll be fine once we start running. Have you had a chance to see San Diego?"

She told him about their brief trip to the Gaslamp Quarter.

"We'll take care of that after the race. You have to see the beaches. The San Diego Zoo is one of the best in the country. I'll show you around. Where's Cassidy?" He craned his neck, searching the crowd for her.

"Chevy's looking for her."

Richard's happy demeanor faltered. "Chevy's here with you?"

"He's supporting me."

He scrubbed his chin. "I guess I won't be able to show you San Diego after all. I had hoped I could show you all the things we talked about."

"Maybe I'll be able to find the time." Maddie didn't want to miss out on the opportunity of her lifetime, but the chances of Chevy letting her go off on a private sightseeing tour with Richard were zero.

"Yeah, maybe. After what happened at the library the last time we tried to get together…"

The crowd parted, and Chevy appeared. Concern turned to rage in an instant. He marched up to them, ready for trouble.

"Richard's running in the marathon," Maddie said before he could say anything.

He cut his eyes at Richard.

"Chevy." Richard stood, extending his hand.

Maddie prodded Chevy with the toe of her shoe.

He shook Richard's hand. "We have to be going. Mandisa has a big day tomorrow."

"We both do." Richard turned to her. "See you at the starting line." He sauntered off, purposefully adding too much strut to his step.

"He's in the race? Since when did he become such a good Samaritan?"

"No, I did not know he was running," Maddie said, shutting down Chevy's anger.

He pulled his eyes away from Richard. "I don't like him. He doesn't respect what we have."

"Are you going to fight him again? Normally, I would

enjoy the show of powerful masculinity, but I really am a little clammy right now."

"Sorry." He took Richard's seat, handing her the glass of water. "Let's get you up to the room."

Once they left the crowded party, Maddie felt much better. She was a little tired, but it had been a long day. Chevy sat on the side of the bed while they watched the television coverage of the marathon. He kissed her temple. "You're going to do fine tomorrow. I'll be on the sidelines the entire time."

"Meet me at the finish line?"

"I'll be right there. Waiting."

She closed her eyes, sleep coming easy now that she was safely under Chevy's watch.

"Good night, Mandisa," he said as she drifted off. He kissed her temple again. "I love you."

In the morning, Chevy was gone—and so were the nervous stomach and sweaty palms. Maddie awoke invigorated and ready to run. She and Cassidy completed their morning rituals and made their way to the marathon.

"Do you see them?" Maddie scanned the crowd of thousands, searching for Chevy. She knew he was there. She could feel him reaching out to her, wishing her luck with her first marathon, but she needed to see him before the starting pistol was fired.

"Mandisa!"

She jogged in a circle, searching all directions for Chevy.

"Mandisa, over here!"

To her right, Chevy was there, jumping up and down, waving his arms above his head.

"Chevy!"

He weaved through the crowd, trying to reach the front. "Good luck. I love you."

She blew him a kiss.

"I'll be waiting at the finish line," he said just as the pistol exploded.

Maddie took off at a good clip with Cassidy at her side. A troublesome feeling washed over her. The sound of the pistol was so final—instead of signaling the beginning of the race, it seemed to mean the ending of an important chapter in her life. She couldn't make sense of it, and didn't want to lend credence to what she feared it might mean. She and Chevy were doing well. Every day she fell more in love with him. The marathon was an event that would bring them closer, not tear them apart. She admonished the negative feelings and turned her focus internally, concentrating on her stride.

"Ladies," Richard huffed, falling into line between them. "Mind if I run with you?"

Instinctively, Maddie glanced at the sideline. She couldn't see Chevy. She liked Richard, and he had never really been inappropriate with her, so she didn't object when Cassidy gave him the thumps-up sign.

The first ten miles went by without notice. Maddie and Cassidy had been running fifteen miles every day, no matter the weather. Richard was well trained too. He didn't even start perspiring until they were twelve miles into the race.

Cassidy jogged around, placing Maddie in the middle. "Remind me whose idea it was to ever start running?"

"Don't make me laugh. I can hardly breathe."

At the twenty-mile mark, Maddie began to doubt her sanity. "I'm starting to feel it now. My legs are burning."

"Let's slow down," Richard said. "The important thing is to finish. We don't have to finish first."

They slowed their stride.

"My breasts are hurting, Richard," Cassidy said. "What kind of cure do you have for that?"

Despite the need to conserve oxygen, Maddie and Richard answered with short bursts of laughter.

Cassidy jogged closer, lowering her voice so only Maddie could hear. "I bet if your boobs were hurting, he'd have an answer."

Maddie was drenched in perspiration by the time they reached the twenty-five-mile marker. Exhaustion triggered her mind to play dirty tricks on her. Her legs were aching and her arms were tired. She had to concentrate to breathe, and the only words she could pronounce were "shower" and "bed."

"Are you hanging in there?" Richard asked them.

Cassidy grunted, but nodded. "I'm never doing this again."

"Maddie?"

She felt her focus shrinking to myopic size. The runners in front of her looked like wavy cartoon characters. Her arms and legs were moving because they had been programmed to. Not because she had any control over them.

"Maddie?" Cassidy's voice sounded miles away. "Maddie, are you okay?"

She tried to answer, but obviously she was unsuccessful because Cassidy grabbed her shoulder and kept calling her name.

"Go ahead," Richard told Cassidy. "I'll stay with Maddie. We'll catch up."

"No, we promised to stay together."

"If she can't finish—"

"She'll finish. She made me promise not to let her quit."

Maddie heard the conversation taking place around her, but her mind was focused on following the preset program—lift your feet, move your legs, pump your arms, breathe.

Richard jogged close, using his shoulder to guide her to the sideline. He grabbed a cup of Gatorade from a volunteer. "Slow down."

Sandwiched between Richard and Cassidy, she slowed to a leisurely jog, but kept moving. Richard placed the cup to her lips. "Drink—slowly." He patiently fed her the cup of juice, replenishing her electrolytes. After she finished, he asked, "Can you talk?"

"Yes," she sputtered.

"How many fingers?" Richard held his hand in front of her face.

"Three."

"Can you go on?" Cassidy asked.

She nodded.

"We could walk the rest of the way."

Maddie shook her head. "I'm fine. I want to run."

Richard snagged another Gatorade and passed it to Cassidy before taking one for himself. "Okay, ladies, let's do this."

Richard became their cheerleader and trainer, pushing them to finish the race. He was in amazing shape. When he announced they were hitting the thirty-mile mark, he hardly looked tired.

"We should have been training with you," Cassidy managed.

"Next time," he told them, hardly short of breath.

"Eight more miles," Maddie announced.

When she approached the end of the marathon she became reenergized. Her legs weren't heavy logs anymore. Her stride was light and graceful. She wiped the perspiration and had Richard dump a cup of water over her head. She joined hands with Cassidy for the last mile. They were determined, but astonished they were finishing their first thirty-eight-mile marathon. Maddie thought of how her efforts would help other people with her father's illness and tears welled up in her eyes.

She saw Chevy standing at the finish line, waving her in, and took off at a clip to meet him. She crossed the line amid the cheers of onlookers, receiving their congratulations as she jumped into his arms.

"You did it, Mandisa." He held her tight, swinging her in a wide circle. "I'm so proud of you."

"I did it."

When he set her down, Kirkland was kissing Cassidy. Richard was standing nearby, his hands on his knees, trying to catch his breath. Maddie went over to him and offered a hug. "Thank you for helping me through it."

"Any time."

Chevy slipped his arm around her waist. "Let's get you back to the hotel."

She nodded, still struggling to catch her breath. Chevy ushered her out of the crowd. She stopped and turned to Richard. "We'll see you later at the celebration party?"

"Definitely."

Chapter 23

Taking care of Maddie had become one of Chevy's favorite things to do. He shared in her joy when she called her father to tell him about the race. While she gave him all the details, and their schedule for the evening, Chevy ran her a hot bath. When she finished her call, he untied her shoes and pulled them from her feet. He peeled the Lycra tank top and shorts from her body, being careful to save her assigned number as a memento. He lifted her weary body into his arms and placed her in the tub. He sat next to her on the floor while she soaked her aching muscles. He washed her back, quieting the excitement from her busy day. He helped her from the tub, dried her, and massaged lotion into every muscle of her body. When he was done, she was tired, so he helped her into bed and let her sleep.

The next morning, Chevy awoke early, but did not disturb Maddie. He watched her from a nearby chair. Tonight he would ask her to marry him. He wanted the occasion to be special, and what could be more special than this? He had never seen her so happy, so proud of herself for helping others. As she crossed the finish line and ran into his arms—ignoring the well-wishers to receive his congratulations—his heart was full. Beaten and tired, she never looked more beautiful. This was the woman he wanted to have his kids. This was the woman he would sacrifice everything for. This was the woman he wanted in his life forever.

He planned the perfect time to propose—at dinner, on the plane, back home—he couldn't decide. Should he ask the MC to make a special announcement when she received her marathon completion medal? No, he didn't want to over-shadow her moment. Later, in private. When they returned to their room and she thought she was as high and as happy as she could ever be, he would ask her to marry him.

He made the arrangements while she slept: a bottle of champagne and plenty of roses. Afterward, they would make love until they had to leave for the plane—if her body could tolerate his vigorous expression of thanks. They'd celebrate their announcement over dinner with Kirkland and Cassidy after touring San Diego. And then they'd return home to begin planning their life together.

Chevy dressed in a lightweight summer suit for the medal presentation party. He'd been making additions to his ward-robe as Greyson had advised. Being with a woman like Mad-die meant representing her properly. They'd spent the day seeing as much of San Diego as was possible to cram into one day—the zoo, Balboa Park, and the finest shops. They rode the trolley, had lunch at a sports bar, and walked through the historic district. They returned to the hotel with just enough time to dress for the medal ceremony.

Maddie emerged from the bathroom wearing a slinky dress the color of the blush that dusted her cheeks after making love. The thin fabric stopped above her knees, mercilessly hugging the curve of her hips. Her runner's-tanned skin glowed into the deep cleavage of her breasts. This was the type of dress he wanted to take off her in the privacy of his bedroom—not the kind he wanted her to parade around in a room full of salivating men. Especially since Richard would be in attendance.

"How do I look?" She twirled in a circle, displaying too much of the skin only he should see.

"Take it off."

"What?" She laughed.

He unclenched his teeth so she could clearly understand. "Take it off."

"Why?" She glided over to the mirror, examining her body from every angle. "Do I look too hippy?"

Hippy? Was there such a word? "I don't want you to wear that dress. If you don't have anything else with you, I'm sure Cassidy has something. Or we can stop by the mall."

"The mall?" She parked her hands on her hips, staring him down. "What exactly is wrong with my dress?"

"It's too revealing." And Richard would be at the party, taking in every inch of his private playground.

"Chevy, everything is covered, and I have a jacket. This dress belonged to my mother. It can't be too revealing."

Strong arguments. "I don't like it."

She folded her arms over her chest and her breasts rose up, threatening to seep over the neckline. "What's going on? The truth."

"I don't want you to wear *that* dress to the party. You're with me. No one else should be staring at everything you have to offer. All your—your—your curves are showing."

She exhaled, completely ignoring him and grabbing her jacket. "Are you ready?"

"Oh, I don't have any say-so in this?"

"No, you don't. Since when did I give you permission to veto my clothing? Are you ready?"

"Stop asking me if I'm ready. I won't be ready until you change."

"You're being totally unreasonable. You've never objected to what I wear."

"You've never worn anything like this out in public."

"This is getting silly. I'm going to the celebration. Are you taking me?" When he didn't answer she moved to the door.

"Wait."

She turned to face him. "What do you think is going to happen, Chevy?"

Only that the bronzed California men will flock to you and you'll realize there's better out there.

"I trust you. Trust me."

It was clear he would not win this fight. With a curse, he gave in, putting his heart in her tiny hands again.

Downstairs, the reaction was what he anticipated. Every man in the room focused his attention on Maddie. Some were brave enough to approach, despite Chevy's constant grip on her hip. He didn't let her out of his sight. Richard crossed the room as if she held a giant magnet. He was all grins and laughs as he reminisced with Maddie about the race. Chevy's blood came to a slow boil as he learned the details of how Richard had coached her through finishing the marathon. Before he could stop it, her gratefulness led her to invite Richard to dinner with them. Not wanting to be in the same cab with Richard, Chevy hastily changed their plans and they had dinner in the hotel restaurant.

Chevy felt as if he could chew glass as he watched the dynamics at the dinner table. Kirkland and Cassidy were so wrapped up into each other the fifth wheel directed most of his conversation to Maddie. Chevy draped a possessive arm around her shoulder, fingering the medal lying against her cleavage.

Richard was courteous, occasionally asking Chevy's opinion of something. Rather than make polite conversation, he'd like to take Richard outside and remind him of their confrontation at the library. He hated pretending to be civil when everyone at the table knew it wasn't real. He faded out of the conversation, hoping Richard would exhaust himself and leave. The conversation moved from reliving the race to the culture of San Diego. The next thing Chevy knew, Maddie was inviting him along on their extra day in San Diego. They would have a long talk once they returned to the hotel room.

"We're going to bed," Kirkland announced.

"I'll get it," Chevy said when he signaled for the check.

"It's been a long day," Cassidy said. "See you in the morning."

Kirkland and Cassidy left hand in hand.

"We should go up, too." Chevy pushed his chair away from the table.

"Already?" Maddie looked up at him with the disappointed eyes of a child who didn't get the present she wanted for Christmas.

"It's getting late, and we have to be at the airport early."

"Too bad," Richard said. "We have so much to catch up on, and I'm still stoked from the medal celebration."

"Me too." Maddie stood and placed her hands against Chevy's chest. "You go on up. I'll be right behind you."

He glanced over at Richard. "I'm not leaving you here alone."

"She won't be alone," Richard piped in, clearly not caring that he was eavesdropping. "I'll look after her. Matter of fact, let me pay for dinner, too. You're guests in my town."

"This might be my only chance to visit California. I want it to last as long as possible."

When she looked at him in a certain way, he couldn't deny her anything. As awestruck as she was by traveling, he doubted he could pry her away without making a huge scene. He kissed her lips, trying to sound more trusting than he felt. "Don't stay too long. I want to spend some time alone with you before we go back."

"I won't." She sat down, destroying his planned proposal.

As he rode the elevator up to his room, he tried to be mature about the situation. Maddie was filled with untapped adventure. Now that her father was getting better and she had fewer responsibilities at home, she was able to do things she'd never done before. Of course she'd want to spend as much time as possible in San Diego. He wouldn't be jealous of Richard. Maddie was in love with him. So they were talking, when Chevy proposed he'd have her for the rest of his life.

In the early morning, when purple slices of sunlight cut through the window, Chevy didn't feel so charitable, or understanding.

"Where have you been?" There was no putting a cap on his rage.

She dropped her shoes on the floor. "Richard took me sightseeing."

Chevy bolted out of bed. "You've been out with Richard all night?"

"Don't make it sound dirty. We were talking, and he told me about this place—" Her excitement was squashed by the baring of his teeth. "I wanted to see it."

"So you went running around in a strange city with another man?"

"This is San Diego, not the Amazon. Why are you being so controlling?"

Her accusation opened his eyes. Maddie had been changing over the last month. As her burdens were removed, she blossomed into a woman who busied herself with running, hiking, and ladies' days. She wore makeup and let her hair hang freely, shedding the tight bun at the nape of her neck. Her independence grew by leaps and bounds. Often, she'd take her father's car and drive into the capital on solo excursions. Completing the marathon had reassured her that she could do anything.

"I'm not changing, Mandisa, you are."

"Maybe I am changing. Maybe I've found a way to do the living I've never been able to do."

"Have I been holding you back?" It would hurt him to know she thought so.

"No, but you've been strange since we got here—my dress, hovering over me at dinner."

"You used to like having me around."

She didn't answer. Her silence annoyed him because he was angry and he needed a fight. He needed her to fight as passionately as possible, to show him some emotion. "Now you like having Richard around."

"This isn't about Richard." Her passion flared, and he didn't like it. "Richard is a friend. Even after you attacked him at the library, he's tried to be a friend to you."

"Not to me, Mandisa. And not to you. He wants to be something to you, but it isn't a friend."

"You're wrong. We were together all night. If he wanted to make a move, he could have. He didn't. Richard understands me in a way most people don't."

His insides twisted. He wanted to find Richard and do ter-

rible things to him, but it wouldn't end with Richard's destruc-
tion. Maddie had tasted freedom, and like any freed captive,
she didn't want to be imprisoned again. Chevy felt it coming—knew the train was getting ready to run off the track—
but he was powerless. Armed with his anger and his
disproportionate love for Maddie, he was helpless to stop the
massacre ahead.

"Richard listens to me, and when I talk about seeing the
world, he helps me plan a way to do it."

"I haven't been there for you? I haven't supported you in
everything you've ever wanted to do?"

"You have. I know you have." She exhaled loudly, as if she
were tiring of him. "It's just that…I need to be who I want to
be without worrying about upsetting you. For once, I have to
think of myself first."

"People in a relationship don't have that luxury."

She glanced up at him before her eyes dropped to the floor.

"What are you saying, Mandisa? You don't want a relationship with me anymore? What the hell happened here?"

"I love you." She moved deeper into the room, noticing the
flowers and the champagne. "But how can I appreciate you
if I don't know myself?"

He ran his hand over his face. "I don't understand what's
going on."

"I have to take the same advice I gave you. I have to become
my own woman. There are things I'm not willing to give up."
Her eyes fell on the ring box next to the vase of white roses.

"Damn, Maddie. I'll take you on a trip around the world
if that's what you want."

She stepped over to the table and stared at the ring box for
a long moment.

He felt it all slipping away. He didn't know what had been

the thing to make Maddie realize she was bigger than Hannaford Valley could ever be, but she'd finally learned the secret he'd been keeping for months. She was too special to be locked up in a town that was stuck in the nineteenth century. The old-fashioned values he cherished were a noose around her neck. She'd been denied the opportunity to fly, and now she wanted to soar.

He snatched up the ring box, and prepared to drop to his knees and beg her to marry him if he had to.

"I'm staying in San Diego for a while."

His heart hit the floor faster than he could bend his knee. "What do you mean?"

"I'm not ready to go back to Hannaford."

"I'll tell Kirkland and Cassidy to leave without us."

She watched him.

He dropped to his knees.

"Don't do it," she whispered.

"Mandisa, will you—"

"Don't do it!" she shouted. "I told you not to…" She backed away. She was crying.

"Mandisa, will you—"

"I'm trying not to hurt you any more than I have to, Chevy." She crossed the room, moving too far away.

Chevy rose from the floor and stalked over to her. "I love you. I want to spend the rest of my life with you."

"I love you, too." The silence punctuated what she did not say.

He thrust the ring box at her and she shrank back, as if it were a snake, aiming to strike. He threw it across the room onto the bed. "I've been up front with you. I told you where I wanted this to go. I thought we were in the same place. What are you telling me? I was wrong? All these months, you didn't want the same things I wanted?"

"I didn't plan this."

"I'm not enough for you anymore."

"You're too much for me to handle right now."

"What does that mean?"

"You overshadow me."

The room was so quiet he could hear his heart pounding in his ears. He had to find a way to make her see things clearly. "How are you going to stay in San Diego?" he asked, knowing the answer. "Your funds are limited. You didn't bring enough clothes to stay. What about your father?"

"My father is with my aunt, and don't you use him to make me feel guilty. I've sacrificed everything to care for my father. Now it's time for me to live!" she shouted.

"How are you going to stay here, Mandisa?"

She swallowed hard, her throat bobbing up and down. "Richard has a house and he's offered to let me stay with him for a while."

Chevy shot across the room, leaving a string of curses in his wake. He had to move away from her. The hurt she was hurling around was pummeling him from every direction. "You're not staying!" he shouted. "You think I'm going to leave you here with Richard? You're so wrong. Pack your clothes."

"You can't force me to leave," she shouted back.

"If I have to drag you to the airport and put you on the plane, I will."

"I'll fight you all the way."

Another string of curses aimed in her direction.

Kirkland tentatively opened the door adjoining their rooms. "What's happening?"

"I'm not going home," Maddie announced.

Cassidy was at Kirkland's back. "What do you mean?"

"Don't listen to her. She's going back if I have to drag her back." Chevy meant every word. "It's not an empty threat, Maddie. Start packing."

"Hold on." Kirkland stepped between them.

Cassidy ushered Maddie into their room.

"What's going on?" Kirkland asked. "Did you get into a fight?"

Chevy filled him in on what had happened. "She stayed out all night with Richard, and then she shows up talking about how she's staying here with him."

"She's what?" Kirkland's indignation matched his.

"I'm not letting her stay behind." He gave his little brother a pointed look, which meant they'd do whatever they had to do to get her on the plane.

"I'm not going to jail for dragging a woman through the airport. I have a wife and little girl. Cassidy will talk some sense into her."

When Cassidy rejoined them, Maddie moved past her and started packing her things. "Maddie's got her mind made up. She wants to stay in San Diego."

"Talk to her some more," Kirkland said.

"I tried."

"You didn't try hard enough. I'm tired of talking." Chevy advanced toward Maddie, but Cassidy jumped in front of him.

"You can't make her go, Chevy."

"The hell I can't."

Kirkland grabbed him from behind, restraining him. "You have to let her go."

"Chevy, stop! Please." Maddie locked her suitcase. "You're making this a lot worse than it has to be. I'm not a teenager running away from home."

"You're acting like one," he shouted.

"You're angry. This is about *me*, not you. I don't want to hurt you. I just want to live my life."

"Mandisa…" The words died on his tongue.

"I'm going to go before this gets any harder."

"Mandisa, I love you." He stopped struggling against Kirkland's hold and Cassidy moved out of his path. "Don't go."

She stepped up to him, pulling her suitcase behind her. "I have to." She kissed his cheek and was gone.

Chapter 24

San Diego

Richard lived in a quiet neighborhood lined with trees whose leaves were thick and green. The grass was lush and full and blanketed the front yard with manicured precision. There were two bedrooms upstairs with a bathroom. The first level comprised a small living room, dining room, kitchen, and half bath. The trolley was within walking distance, so even when Richard was at work, Maddie could go exploring.

It didn't take long for her to learn the way of Californians. She shed her prim clothing for shorts and sunglasses. No more tight buns fastened to the back of her neck. The sun made her hair glisten as it fell across her shoulders. She ran on the beach in the morning, and drank cool drinks made from guavas in the evening.

Maddie called her father weekly, but stopped calling Chevy when the conversations became too anguishing to continue. Cassidy's phone calls were much lighter. Cassidy kept her informed about what was going on in Hannaford, and hardly ever asked when Maddie was coming home.

The truth was, Maddie didn't know when she would go back to Hannaford Valley. The more she explored San Diego, the more she realized how much of her life had passed her by, fueling her desire to stay in California. When she accepted a librarian position at the Catholic high school nearby, Richard helped her find an affordable studio apartment and she began to ask *if* she would ever go home.

"Hi, Dad. How are you?"

"I feel good."

"Dad, guess what? I got a librarian job nearby. Richard had some connections and pulled me an interview."

"You're working? I thought you were coming home."

"I am." Her heart ached. She missed seeing him every day. "I just don't know when, and I didn't want Richard to keep paying my way."

"You're living with him?" Her father didn't approve of couples living together before they were married.

"He and I are only friends."

"What about Chevy?"

The question took her aback. "Chevy?"

"He stopped by."

"He shouldn't put you in the middle of our relationship."

"He didn't say a word, but he's unhappy."

She hadn't planned on telling her father about her place— it made everything seem too permanent when she hadn't really decided what the future held for her. But she couldn't talk about her feelings for Chevy without turning into an emotional mess. "Richard helped me find a place," she announced.

"You're not coming home."

"I wanted to be on my own. This doesn't mean I'm staying in San Diego forever, but I couldn't keep taking advantage of Richard."

He didn't sound like he believed her. "When will you decide?"

"Soon." She couldn't take hearing the sadness in his voice. "Dad, I have to go. I'll call you next week. Call me if you need anything." She hung up before he could keep her on the line with more hard questions.

Her relationship with Chevy was complicated. She loved him, and didn't want to lose him, but realized she had no right to ask him to wait for her. How could she make him understand how badly she needed a chance to be on her own? When he dropped to his knees with a ring box in hand, she almost changed her mind. But she'd made the right decision, because if she had accepted his proposal, she would've resented him when she was caring for a family and unable to see the world.

"Hey, you're here." Richard wasn't surprised to see her at his place. She often stopped on her days off.

"How was work?"

"Same old, same old. What about you?"

"The same. I enjoy the kids, but it's much busier than the library at home."

"You'll get the hang of it. Hey, you want to go running?"

He drove her home to change before they headed to the nearest beach. They jogged along the water, and when the sun began to set they sat on the sand and watched.

"Can't watch a sunset like this in Hannaford," Richard said.

"Do you ever miss the mountains?"

"And the snow and ice and cold weather? Never. I do miss my family, and the small-town atmosphere." He nudged her with his shoulder. "Are you getting homesick?"

"I miss my father."

After a long moment, he asked, "And Chevy Ballantyne?"

She smiled, always remaining vague about the details of her relationship with him.

"He makes you sad when he calls."

She didn't deny the truth. Her heart broke each time she spoke to him.

"When are you going back?"

She brought her knees up to her chest and wrapped her arms around them. "I've been thinking about staying."

His head snapped around in her direction. "What about your father?"

"He can't live with my aunt permanently. She'll start getting restless with having to take care of him soon. A month is too long already. If I decide to stay, I'll have to make arrangements to bring him out."

"I can help."

"You've done enough already." The dusk rushed up, and the sky dimmed. "Why have you been so helpful?"

"You're a hometown girl. I didn't want you getting into trouble out here."

"I thought you might want more than friendship."

"Are you offering?"

She'd braced herself for his advance the first night, but it didn't happen. When things got rough with Chevy she wondered what it would be like to know another man. On the nights when she was lonely and doubting her decision to stay in San Diego, she considered seeking comfort with Richard. But it never seemed right. Her heart still belonged to Chevy. She didn't know how long it would take to get over him—or if she ever would.

"I like the way things are between us," she told him.

"Maddie, I'm attracted to you, but I wouldn't approach you in that way unless you gave me a signal it would be all right."

She rested her chin on her knees. "Everything is so confusing right now."

"So we'll be friends, but I haven't been out on a date since you came."

"I understand."

"I can't wait for something that might never happen."

She stood up and pulled her foot up behind her, stretching. "Race you back."

Chapter 25

Chevy went on. Men went on. They didn't waste away because their heart had been broken. The Ballantyne Wilderness Lodge was completed and the grand opening was being planned. He'd acquired the nursing home and surrounding property. Today, he was meeting with his brothers in Greyson's home office to go over construction plans for a retirement community.

"What do you think, Kirkland?" Chevy asked as they pored over the drawings.

"My guy came through. I'd go with it."

Greyson slipped into attorney mode. "I'll give him a call in the morning and have him draw up the contracts."

Sutton breezed into the room, not looking her usual chipper self. Instinctively, Greyson went to her.

"Stacy Taro just called. She has news about Alex's baby."

Kirkland started rolling up the drawings. "I'd better get going." He and Sutton had been getting along better, learning to put their differences over Alex aside, but he knew better than to add kerosene to a smoldering flame.

Sutton walked up to Kirkland. "I'm not going to hold this against you. Whatever Stacy found, I'm not going to blame you anymore for what Alex did. We have to concentrate on keeping this family together."

Chevy watched in shocked surprise as Sutton and Kirkland embraced. He had hoped, but never thought he'd see the day those two buried their differences and learned to trust each other again.

Kirkland peered at her with raw sincerity. "I'm going home to my wife and daughter. They need me more than Alex's memory." He kissed Sutton's cheek and left the den. He had entered into therapy to help deal with the loss of his best friend. His silent suffering had almost cost him his life. If Cassidy hadn't stepped in and provided him with unconditional love, he might not have been strong enough to correct his past mistakes and rebuild his life.

"I'd better get going, too." Chevy fit his hat on his head.

"No, don't leave yet." Sutton looked between Chevy's and Greyson's bewildered faces. "Greyson, I don't want you with me when I meet with Stacy, but I don't want to go alone."

The implications of what she was asking would have long-term consequences.

"You don't want me to go with you. You want Chevy to go?" Greyson clarified.

"Yes."

"Absolutely out of the question." Greyson didn't take a hard stance with Sutton often, but when he did it usually had something to do with her ex-husband. "I only let you go through with this because you were so insistent. You agreed to let me deal with Stacy directly."

"And I have, but this I need to do without you."

"Why?"

"Look at how angry you are already. You always get this way when it comes to my marriage to Alex. This is going to be hard enough to hear as it is. I can't have you there being angry."

Chevy cleared his throat. "Sutton, I should stay out of it."

"You'd let me go alone? Although I'm asking you as a friend to come with me?"

He knew whatever she found out would be hard. He didn't want her to go through it alone. He also didn't want to be placed in the middle of Greyson and his wife.

"You don't want me there?" Greyson asked again, his anger visibly growing by degrees. "Are you going to tell me what Stacy found out? Or is it going to be a secret between us?"

"Of course I'm going to tell you. But I want you to hear it from me. Not the PI."

"What am I supposed to do in the meantime? What exactly do you want me to do?"

Sutton sauntered up to him and wrapped her arms around his waist, dropping her voice low enough to soothe a wild tiger. "I want you here waiting for me when I get back. You shouldn't be associated with this in any way. When I come home, just hold me. Be there for me. Can you give me this?"

Chevy knew ultimately, Greyson would give in to Sutton. He always did.

Greyson pressed his finger into Chevy's chest. "Take care of my wife."

Before he could emotionally ready himself, he and Sutton were in his truck on the way to Stacy's hotel. Greyson was sure to pull Chevy aside and warn him not to let Stacy drudge up the friendship he had with her in Chicago. Again, Chevy wondered if Greyson and Stacy had ever been anything more than just friends, but Greyson assured him they hadn't. Chevy knew enough about Stacy to understand that fact wouldn't stop her from insinuating they had been.

They met Stacy in the bar of her hotel. Chevy escorted the women to a table some distance from the few patrons sitting at the bar and ordered a round of beers. To his surprise, Stacy remained professional, never hitting on him or giving Sutton a reason to question her relationship with Greyson.

"How much do you already know?" Stacy asked, coming right to the point of their meeting.

Sutton fidgeted, twisting the strap of her purse. "Alex Galloway had several affairs while we were married. Other than a few who were bold enough to track me down, I don't know any of their names. He gave away everything we owned to various mistresses, but I don't know what kinds of relationships he had with them." She glanced at Chevy, seeking moral support. He touched her shoulder, encouraging her to continue. "The latest rumor is he has a child from one of his affairs."

"Do you need to know the gritty details of those affairs?" Stacy fingered a green folder.

"No. I just want to know about the baby."

With Sutton's answer, Stacy removed the green folder from the top of the stack and placed it on the seat next to her in the booth. "I'll destroy this immediately."

Curiosity distracted Chevy from the conversation. All the evidence of Alex's affairs was probably contained in the folder. He remembered his violent reaction to Richard's overt flirting with Maddie. How could Sutton have been strong enough to put Alex's indiscretions behind her and find love with Greyson? Chevy imagined the pain of betrayal had to cut deep. He'd always admired Sutton for persevering through her troubles, but he now had a new respect for her.

"Alex had an affair with a woman in Chicago," Stacy was

saying when Chevy rejoined the conversation. She slid a photo of a brunette beauty across the table.

With no more than a glance, Sutton spat, "Belinda."

Chevy looked askance. He vaguely remembered seeing the woman in Hannaford. She'd caused a stir outside the barbershop, which left Sutton sobbing in his arms, and Greyson knocking on his cabin door.

"Alex went to Chicago to visit Belinda, but they fought so much he ended up checking into a hotel."

"Is their fight connected to Alex's baby in some way?" Chevy asked, wanting to hurry Stacy along. She had the habit of doing a grand summation. He wanted to end the pain and embarrassment for Sutton as quickly as possible.

Sutton answered, "They were fighting because I made Alex send her away." She looked over at Chevy with sad eyes. "She was the one mistress who never understood her place. We all played a part in Alex's life. It was his show and we were only as important as our performance in the next act."

Stacy looked to Chevy for permission to continue. He nodded, and she went on. "Alex met a woman in the hotel bar. They spent the night together. He never contacted this woman again. She found him." She handed Sutton another photo, and continued. "Carla Winslow. Single, never married. A little younger than Alex. Twenty-two at the time she met him."

Chevy took the photo from Sutton. The woman was pretty, but flawed. Her charcoal skin had a raised scar above her right eye. Her body was perfection, and Chevy felt the pull of her sensuality from the photo.

"Carla wasn't the most stable person. She turned a one-night stand into more than Alex intended. She told anyone who would listen about her 'relationship' with him. When he never called again, she got his contact information from one of the hotel clerks—he was later fired—and took off to Ohio. The only thing she brought from her apartment was the clothes in her closet."

"She found Alex?" Sutton asked.

Stacy nodded. "She showed up at his office, demanding to see him. From what I've heard, Alex protected his reputation at all costs. He couldn't have a strange woman showing up, making a scene, when he was a happily married man."

Sutton made a noise, but Stacy continued.

"It didn't take long for Crazy Carla to catch on. She used his fear of being found out against him. She twisted Alex's arm until he put her up in an apartment. After a while, it seems, Alex became amenable to the idea, and he started spending more time with her."

"Did Kirkland know about this?" Sutton asked.

"Sutton," Chevy started, but the hurt in her eyes hushed him.

"I can't be sure," Stacy answered, "but it didn't seem like Alex told anyone. Carla couldn't keep her mouth shut, but Alex was trying to repair his marriage. He confided in his supervisor about having trouble at home. He wanted to make it work with you."

Sutton glanced at Chevy, then back to Stacy. "Go on."

"In the meantime, Alex got caught up with several other women. And Belinda refused to lose him to another woman. Carla was becoming more possessive, finding the other women and threatening them. Belinda was getting restless. Alex was juggling too many women. There was a new baby at home. It all came to a head and Alex decided he had to break it off with Carla."

Sutton snatched Carla's photo up from the table. "She looks familiar." She peered at the picture for a long time. "Did she know about me?"

"She thought Alex was married to Belinda."

Chevy hadn't realized how much of a liar Alex had been. He had discouraged Greyson from breaking up Sutton's relationship with Alex. If he had known—

"Carla had been telling people she and Alex were trying to have a baby. He ends it with her, and the next thing you know she's pregnant with his child."

"Do we believe anything this woman says?" Chevy asked, his anger rising up.

"I learned a long time in this business, you don't take anyone's word as gospel. Every fact must be checked and verified."

"How did you find all this information?" Chevy couldn't believe it. Who would hurt so many innocent people for no reason?

"A person like Carla doesn't like to be hidden. She craves the spotlight—especially when she's afraid there are other women in the picture. I started by digging up rumors about Alex from the secretarial pool at his office. There was a buzz about a woman who called regularly, but wasn't his wife. This started a few weeks after the Chicago trip to see Belinda. Like I said, Carla left a trail of stories everywhere she went. She was known for causing scenes, so people remember her."

"So Carla had my husband's baby?" Sutton asked. "We're certain it's his?"

"Alex believed it. He stayed with her during the pregnancy. She started telling people in her apartment building they were engaged, and soon after she disappeared."

"Disappeared?" Chevy asked, his stomach tightening. He didn't like where this was going.

"She had her mail forwarded." Stacy studied them before retrieving an envelope from a manila folder. She hesitated before handing it to Sutton.

"Whose address is this?" Sutton's voice sounded strained. "I know it."

Chevy swallowed the lump in his throat. "The Galloway place."

"Where Mr. Galloway was tucked away," Stacy added. "Alex took Carla there until she had her baby."

Sutton jumped up from the booth. "Excuse me." Before Chevy could stop her, she ran across the bar to the ladies' room.

"Can this get any worse?" Chevy asked as he started after Sutton.

"There's more," Stacy said.

Chevy spent the next ten minutes knocking on the bathroom door, but Sutton refused to come out. Remembering his promise to Greyson, and understanding how much she must be hurting, he barged in. The women scurried out, some offering him assessing looks before going. He found Sutton huddled on a tiny green leather love seat, crying.

"Sutton?" He squeezed in next to her.

"It's true. Alex had a baby with another woman while we were married."

"You suspected it." He placed his arm around her shoulder, comforting her.

"Knowing it's true makes it more real." She laughed, humorlessly. "So much of my life was based on lies. I feel so stupid."

"You're hurt."

"Alex is dead. I shouldn't be hurting anymore. I feel so sick to my stomach. I actually puked with the thought of Alex having another baby."

"We've always been honest with each other, right?"

"You're one of the few I could always count on to be in my corner," she agreed.

"Can I give you my advice?"

She nodded, dabbing at her tears. With his relationship with Maddie in shambles, he might not be the best person to offer advice, but he couldn't stand to see Sutton hurting. He knew the feeling too well.

"Alex was a dog, and he didn't deserve you. Greyson, Kirkland, me—we all failed you. We were friends, all five of us. We were supposed to look out for each other—you especially because you were the only girl. Instead of looking out for you, we fought over you."

Her eyebrows shot up in surprise.

"We all had a crush on you at some time or another while we were growing up. It's what kids do. But Greyson is the only one who truly loved you. He always loved you. Even when he moved away, he still loved you."

Her tears started to subside.

"Greyson gave up everything to come back for you. He didn't know about Alex's accident, and when I told him about Sierra, he didn't bat an eye. Greyson's world revolves around you." He hugged her tight. He felt emotions welling up, touching him in a way that made him want to cry for Sutton—for what he'd lost in Maddie. "If it took going through what Alex did to you to find a love as strong as that, was it worth it?"

"Greyson and Sierra are the best things that ever happened to me. I would go through anything, do anything to keep them in my life."

"All right. Hold your head up. You have never done anything wrong. Don't feel stupid because Alex was such an ass. Get the information you need from Stacy, and then let this go—once and for all. Go home and be with your family."

She straightened her back and wiped her face clean. She took his hand. "Give me a minute, and then I'll hear Stacy out."

He rose, kissing her forehead before leaving. Sutton's deep emotions triggered Chevy to think of Maddie. He missed her terribly, but he found a way to go on with his life. He told himself if he loved her, he had to let her experience the life she never had. She would come back to him when she was ready. As the days rolled by, doubt crept in, but he refused to give up hope.

Sutton rejoined them at the table, and after ordering another round of beers, Chevy told Stacy to continue.

"Alex took Carla back to Hannaford to deliver the baby. Afterward, he shipped her off on the first thing smoking. Back to her hometown in Tennessee to live with her family. There were threats back and forth, but Alex had the money to get his way."

"What about the baby?"

Stacy revisited the manila folder, pulling out documents. "Alex hired a midwife, so there are no hospital records. The birth certificate was inconclusive—only the baby's sex was listed." She passed the documents to Sutton. "It's a girl. She'd be six now."

"No pictures?" Chevy wanted to know.

"Nothing. It's like the baby never existed."

"What do you mean?" he asked before Sutton could.

"Well, we know Carla had a baby, which was delivered by a midwife, and it was a girl." She opened the folder on top of the table and fanned out the papers. "There is no record of the birth at Hannaford's City Hall. There's no photos. The trail ran cold, so I had to make a trip to Tennessee. Relatives confirm Carla came there with a baby she claimed was hers, but they disappeared four months later. No one has seen or heard from them since."

Sutton read Stacy's expression and pressed on. "What did you find?"

"Alex went to Tennessee searching for Carla and the baby. It seems that when he forced Carla to go to Tennessee, she wasn't ready to end the relationship and she took a little insurance with her—the DNA test results about the baby's paternity. He couldn't find her, so he returned home and hired one of my more sleazy colleagues to track her down."

"This is unbelievable," Sutton muttered. "How could all of this have been going on and I didn't know it?"

"Alex was never home," Chevy answered. "He traveled all around the country. How would you know when it was business, and when it was personal?"

Sutton nodded, but didn't look convinced. "Go on, Stacy."

"There was a woman in the car with your husband when he died."

"I know."

"Ava."

Sutton looked at Chevy and she appeared as confused as he was. He asked, "How does she fit into it?"

"Ava is the daughter of the midwife...."

Chevy could never have prepared himself for what Stacy told them next. A strong feeling of doom pressed into his back, but he managed to ask, "Who was the midwife?"

"Eileen Putnam."

Chapter 26

"Maddie!" Richard burst through the door, shouting her name as he searched the house for her. Her found her in his kitchen cooking dinner.

"What's going on? Why'd you ask me to meet you here?"

"Guess what this is?" He pulled a large envelope out of his briefcase and waved it in the air.

"I have no idea." She took the sealed envelope from him as he explained.

"Finally, the opportunity I've been waiting for. My company is putting in a bid for a project in L.A. All the project engineers submitted a proposal, but mine has been selected. They've asked me to go to L.A. and meet with the company. If it goes well, I know I'll be named senior project manager."

"You've been working so hard to get that promotion."

With his job as a project engineer, Richard's responsibilities included the development of construction proposals. He negotiated vendors, suppliers, and subcontractor purchases. He was minimally involved in subcontract administration and project scheduling. He'd met Kirkland while working on a project in Charleston, and they became distant friends.

"More money. More travel. More prestige. Who could ask for more?"

How about a husband and kids? Maddie asked herself. Although she was enjoying her time in San Diego, she often thought about how different her life would be if she'd allowed Chevy to propose to her.

"And you're going with me. They always let you take your spouse, and since I don't have one, you're elected. They've given me passes to a Lakers game—anything you can think of to wow the client. Don't say no. It's another opportunity for you to travel, and it'll help me to project the right image."

"You want me to pretend to be your wife?"

"No, but these people are married and their wives will be along. I don't want to go alone. Besides, I need your moral support. This is my big chance. If I screw it up, I might not get another."

"I'm in." It didn't take much to convince Maddie to take an all-expense-paid trip to L.A.

"Thank you." He hugged her close. "If I win this promotion, I'll become the first African-American senior project manager for this company."

Not wanting to ever give Richard the wrong idea about their friendship, she gave him a brief hug and stepped back to the stove. "Are we flying?"

"It's a two-hour drive up the coast. I thought we'd rent a convertible."

She whipped around. "A convertible up the coast? Sounds like something a movie star would do."

Richard sat at the table, already planning the trip. "We leave next week. We can take I-5 straight up the coast. We should spend a night in Long Beach. We'll go running. You'll love it."

"I'm loving it already. I have to get the time off from the library."

"Shouldn't be a problem." His connections at the library would come through for her again. "If I give you a list, could you pick up a couple of things for me for the trip? I'm going to be busy planning my presentations."

"Of course."

During dinner they planned their trip up the coast to Long Beach and L.A. Last weekend, they had driven down to Tijuana and spent the day eating Mexican food. At night, they danced until Maddie's feet ached too much to run the next morning. She even picked up a few Spanish phrases.

Her heart tugged her in the direction of home, but she'd never experienced such freedom to do whatever she wanted, whenever she wanted. Leaving Chevy had been a hard decision to make, but it had been the right one. She had to sample what life offered. Richard had been a good host and friend, helping her learn the ins and outs of life in San Diego, and was always ready to undertake a new adventure.

Chevy promised adventures too, but Maddie knew he loved Hannaford Valley too much and had too many commitments to leave. After a few weeks he would have been obligated to return to work and family, and she would have been forced to go with him.

Driving up the coastline with the wind whipping her hair and the sun kissing her skin caused Maddie to reflect. She was living in her own version of *Thelma and Louise*, and if she weren't careful she'd have her Brad Pitt moment with Richard. It wasn't emotionally healthy for either of them to be spending so much time alone together. Loneliness and physical attraction could be strong motivators for temptation. Even though they were miles apart, her heart still belonged to Chevy.

There were times when they were laughing or sitting on the beach together that Maddie felt it would be so easy to be with Richard. She glanced over at him sleeping in the passenger's seat. She only needed to lean in and kiss him and the dynamics of their relationship would change. With Richard, she could have adventure and blue California skies. He was destined to achieve big things on his job, and luxuries would follow. They had several common interests—running, spontaneous travel, and watching tons of junk TV. In Long Beach he taught her how to rollerskate. Were those things enough to build a lasting relationship on?

Chevy was a man of substance—mentally and physically. Some of his relationship ideas were old-fashioned, but that was part of his allure. He was quiet and dependable, romantic and bold. He was a big man, always comfortable with his size even if others were intimidated. He was a walking contradiction. Before her getting to know him, he seemed withdrawn and angry. After penetrating his protective layers, she'd discovered he was tender and gentle. He loved animals and nature not because he preferred isolation, but because they were defenseless and he wanted to be their champion. He promised a future, family, and complete devotion. Life with Chevy wouldn't be filled with wild adventures—they'd never jump out of a plane together—but he'd always love and cherish her.

Chevy was so heavy on her mind, she called him from the pay phone at the next gas stop. He wasn't at the lodge or the paper mill. She called his cabin and received the answering machine. "Chevy, it's Maddie. I'm going to L.A. for a week. I'll call you when I get back to San Diego." She held the phone close, hoping he would hear her talking and pick up. "Thank you for checking on Dad." She missed home. She missed her father. "I miss you." She disconnected before the tears started to flow.

In L.A. Maddie learned to play golf while stargazing. She had lunch with Richard and his clients. When Richard wasn't busy working, they visited all the tourist traps. If he did have to work, she sat by the pool and continued her stargazing. After the clients were wowed and went back to the office to make their final decision, Richard arranged a special dinner for Maddie and him with Magic Johnson. As envious onlookers watched them consume their meal like old friends, Maddie dreamed about living this way forever.

But she was a librarian, and librarians didn't eat dinner at restaurants where the cost of one meal equaled two months' mortgage. In the real world, women from Hannaford Valley didn't get stopped on the streets of L.A. and made into instant stars. Women like her searched most of their lives for a good man to marry and have a family with. They met their obligations, and didn't run off to live enchanted fairy-tale lives. They were content with the small things in life, which actually meant more than the big ones. And that was what California was to Maddie—too big.

Returning home to San Diego was a relief. Everything had been too glitzy and too perfect in L.A. It wasn't real. It wasn't what real life was about.

Richard carried her suitcases inside her apartment and sat at the tiny kitchen table. After reliving the highlights of the trip, Richard checked his messages from his cell. His boss was happy with the preliminary reports, and Richard should come in first thing Monday morning for a "serious discussion" about his future.

Maddie had only one message on her machine, and it brought her to tears.

Chevy's voice was earnest, sincere, and packed with pain. "Mandisa. I love you. Come home." Simple and to the point— just like Chevy—straightforward without games.

Richard brought her a tissue from the bathroom. "He has to stop calling."

"It's not his fault," she sniffled.

"It doesn't change the fact that when he calls, you get upset. He has a way of 'guilting' you into regretting your decision. I hate seeing you cry."

"I cry because I'm so torn about being here and going home. When he calls it reminds me how much I miss him. Chevy hasn't done anything wrong. I'm lucky he still calls at all."

Richard sat beside her. "I think Chevy is the lucky one. He knows it. Everyone knows it. Except you. The whole world is open to you. Very few people in Hannaford Valley realize that. They're born in Hannaford, go to school in Hannaford, marry and die in Hannaford. Watching the lives of fictitious people unfold on television is sad. They have no idea what they're missing."

"If you don't know what you're missing, how can it harm you?"

"It's self-limiting. Others who are educated—not just in books, but by life experiences—can see how ignorant you are of the world. They see it, and in some cases use it against you. What reaction do you get when you tell people in San Diego you're from Hannaford Valley, West Virginia?"

"They start talking down to me."

"Exactly. But when they have a conversation with you and

find you're intelligent they give you the respect you deserve. It's absolutely wrong to prejudge based on the superficial, but once you go out in the world and live the knowledge, you find how much you don't know. People out there living the experience have already realized how limited you are."

Maddie knew from her own experiences that Richard was right. She knew people who passed up experiences to go and do in order to stay home and watch television. Others let work define them. She loved junk food television and working at the library, but she'd never let either dictate her life. Richard was right. Better to go out and make your own life experiences instead of watching made-up characters on television live the life you wished you had.

"I've lived more this past year than in my entire life," Maddie reflected. "Meeting Chevy opened a lot of doors for me. He's taught me so much about forestry and animals and the environment. I've visited Virginia Beach, Tijuana, San Diego, L.A., and Long Beach, but I think I'm one of the people who can find everything I need in a small town like Hannaford Valley."

Richard didn't like what he was hearing.

"I definitely want to travel, but I want to do it with my family. I want to share these experiences with my children."

"You don't have a family right now, so this is the perfect time to see the world. You should think about going overseas."

"I don't think I'm ready to travel to other continents. This experience has been enough to last me for a while. There's a marathon in November in Florida. Maybe I'll train for it. It's for a good cause, and it allows me to go to places I've never been."

"And in the meantime?"

"What do you mean?"

Richard rested his hands on his knees. "You said you were torn."

"I'm going to think about it some more. I want to be sure about my decision so I won't regret it later. Either way, you've been a great friend. You gave me a safe place to stay and looked after me while I had my mental meltdown. Thank you. I don't know what I can do to repay you."

His voice was low and husky when he said, "I can think of a couple of things."

Chapter 27

Chevy stared so hard at Stacy he thought her face would incinerate. Somehow, his father had gotten himself tangled up in the Galloway web of deception and lies. It all came full circle. As Stacy explained how her investigation had led her to this point, he searched his childhood memories for anything out of the ordinary. He was looking for the connection between the Galloways and his parents. At this point, he had to include Sutton's parents, the Hills, in his scrutiny. He had always believed their parents were connected because their children played together. Now he wasn't so sure.

His head spun. Could Greyson have been right to question Pop's character? What was the real reason Mama didn't confront Pop about his "affair" with Eileen Putnam? She was a strong woman. She would never have allowed Pop to carry on. She would have put him out and raised her three boys alone if she had to if he ever dared cheat on her. And now that it was out, what was going on in their marriage? Could it be a coincidence that Pop was having an affair with the woman who played midwife to Alex's illegitimate child? Why was

Mr. Galloway tucked away in the Galloway place while Mother Galloway lived in Ohio? There were too many questions to list them all. The one thing Chevy knew for sure was that they were all pawns in an elaborate chess game. This couldn't be allowed to continue. All of Hannaford Valley's dirty secrets were about to be exposed. He refused to live his life in the dark afraid he'd trip over something that would threaten his family. Chevy did what he had to do.

"Enough," he said, cutting into Stacy's monologue. He stood and tossed some bills on the table. "Sutton, do you have your cell phone?"

"Yes. Why?"

"Call Greyson and Kirkland and tell them to meet us at my cabin."

"But what about—"

"Stacy, we'll no longer need your services."

"What!" Sutton practically shouted. She jumped out of her seat but didn't come close to matching his height. "We're just scratching the surface. There's so much to find out. I still don't know everything I need to know about Alex's baby."

"We are finished here." He turned to Stacy. "Send your final bill directly to me."

"What about my files?"

"Destroy them."

"Hold on," Sutton interjected. "I want what she has on Alex."

"Destroy everything," he told Stacy. He gave her a look that warned her against defying his orders.

Stacy gave one curt nod. "It's been nice working for you." She gathered her things and left the table.

Sutton tried to stop her, but Stacy knew who was paying her bill. Greyson threw a lot of business her way—enough to make her ignore Sutton's frantic pleas and return to her hotel room.

"I can't believe what you did." Sutton pulled out her cell and hit the speed-dial button. Chevy ushered her out of the bar with a firm grasp on her arm as she spoke. "Greyson!"

"Don't be so dramatic. He'll think I'm killing you."

She jerked her arm away from him, but kept moving. "Chevy fired Stacy before she could tell me everything."

These tantrums were reminiscent of their time growing up. Greyson would pacify her—he always did. In his eyes, Sutton could do no wrong.

"What!" she shrieked. She listened, her mouth hanging open incredulously. They were at his truck when she spoke to Greyson again. "He says to meet him at the cabin in thirty minutes."

The drive to his cabin was a quiet one. Sutton was as angry as he'd ever seen her, but they had the kind of relationship where she wouldn't challenge his judgment. She'd be mad, and she'd be upset, but she wouldn't verbally spar with him. He was the irritating big brother figure who made her do what was right even when no parents were around. He'd protect her with as much fervor as he would one of his brothers, but he'd never give in if it weren't the right thing to do.

While they waited for Greyson and Kirkland to arrive, Chevy made them sandwiches. While Sutton used the bathroom, he checked his messages. All his tension dissipated when Maddie's voice floated from his answering machine.

"Chevy, it's Maddie. I'm going to L.A. for a week. I'll call you when I get back to San Diego." She held the phone in silence for a long moment. "Thank you for checking on Dad." There was a hitch in her voice like she was about to cry. "I miss you."

He didn't hesitate to dial her back. "Maddie. I love you. Come home." He held the phone to his ear until the tape rewound, hoping she might be running for the phone. Why was she going to L.A. for a week? He didn't understand any of the women in his life.

"Was that Maddie?" Sutton asked, sitting down at the kitchen table to eat her sandwich.

"She wasn't there. She's going to L.A." He couldn't help but worry about her, but she wanted this experience alone—without his protection. He had to honor her wishes—since Kirkland thought dragging her through the airport might land them in jail.

"Why is she going to L.A.?"

He sat across from her. "The whole world is going crazy."

He drank half his beer before Sutton approached the matter at hand. "Do you want to tell me why you fired Stacy before she finished her work?"

"Greyson made me promise to protect you."

"I wasn't in danger."

"If we keep this up, we're all in danger."

"What do you mean?"

"I'll explain when my brothers get here."

From their dog walk in the backyard, Placido and Porter began barking to alert Chevy someone was in the driveway.

Greyson rushed inside with Kirkland close behind. "What happened?" Sutton had succeeded in alarming him.

"We need to talk," he answered, signaling for them to follow him.

They all gathered in the kitchen. After Greyson was satisfied Sutton wasn't the victim of bodily harm, and his marriage wasn't about to dissolve because Stacy had found some creative way to imply they were having an affair, everyone settled down.

"I fired Stacy."

"We heard," Kirkland said. "Why?"

"You want to catch them up?" he asked Sutton.

She hesitated before answering, clearly trying to decide if she was ready to have this conversation with her husband, but she gave Greyson and Kirkland all the information Stacy had relayed.

"Why'd you fire her?" Kirkland asked.

"It's enough," Chevy answered. "It's all enough. We have a stranger digging into our family's past. I understand why Pop is so mad. This is something we have to handle within the family."

"We went to Pop," Greyson pointed out, "and he refused to tell us anything. Stacy is the only avenue we have available to us."

"No, she's not. Obviously there are things going on within this family that affect us all. We have the right to have answers to our questions, and we're going to get them—directly from the source."

Greyson and Kirkland exchanged glances.

"I'm going to Pop, and he's going to tell me what I want to know."

"And you think he'll just tell you when all this time he's been refusing?" Kirkland asked.

Greyson answered, "Oh, he'll tell Chevy everything."

Sutton turned to him. "Why?"

"Because I'm demanding it," Chevy answered without delay. "I'm going to stand up to Pop, and he's going to give me all the answers I need."

"I still need answers about Alex," Sutton reminded them.

"Do you?" Chevy said. "Really?"

Sutton turned to Greyson, his face frozen with hope. After all this time, could she finally let Alex and his transgressions go?

"I love you," Greyson said. "It's the past."

"What about Sierra? What if she has a sister or brother out there?"

Greyson watched her for a long moment, all his thoughts on the matter clearly displayed by the fine wrinkles near his mouth. "We're going to give Sierra the brother or sister she wants."

Sutton glanced at Chevy and Kirkland before stepping into Greyson's arms. "Let's go home."

"I knew it would only be a matter of time before a Ballantyne showed up on my doorstep." Dressed impeccably as always, Mother Galloway opened the door for Chevy, cordially inviting him inside the Galloway home. Her makeup was flawless, but a bit too heavy around the eyes. She wore a red pantsuit with pearl earrings. Mother Galloway reminded Chevy of his elementary school teacher. Mrs. Hayes always looked like she stepped out of a fashion magazine. She was so mean dirt refused to cling to her white suits even in the winter. Mother Galloway had the same scary quality. Even now that he was a grown man she made him uneasy.

She showed him into the first room off the foyer decorated with antique furniture and dark, heavy curtains. "The last time I saw you we were in Ohio, and you were breaking into my home."

He squirmed into a high-back chair made of the rich red velvet any vampire would love.

"Tea?" she asked politely, reaching for the decanter and pouring herself a cup.

"No, thank you." He remembered his manners and tore off his Stetson, placing it in his lap. "I thought you were still living in Ohio."

"I am." She sipped her tea, assessing him over the rim of

her cup. "The detective you hired isn't as crafty as mine. When I heard someone was asking questions about Alex, I put him on her tail." She balanced the teacup on the saucer on her knee. "I thought I should be here when your investigation led you back to the Galloways."

"I'd like to speak to Mr. Galloway."

She smiled, a slow spreading of lips without the flash of teeth one expected. "You know my husband is incapacitated." She placed her teacup and saucer on the table next to the decanter. "Follow me." She stood abruptly, leaving the room without waiting to see if he was behind her.

They climbed a staircase to the second level. The Galloway home gave Chevy the creeps. He kept expecting some ghastly entity to jump from behind a closed door and take him hostage. The big furniture, heavy curtains, and thick carpeting cushioned any sound their footsteps might make. At the top of the stairs, Mother Galloway passed three closed doors before she stopped. She placed her hand on the knob and swung the door open wide, nodding for him to precede her into the room.

Chevy stepped inside. This bedroom fit the scheme of the other rooms in the house: antique furniture, and heavy drapes keeping the sun out. Drowning in the center of the huge bed was Mr. Galloway. He was much older than Chevy remembered. His hair was sparse and gray. He was thin and frail. He turned his head in Chevy's direction, but did not register anyone being in the room. Mr. Galloway's breathing was loud and somewhat labored. The stranger staring at him didn't hold his attention, and Mr. Galloway turned away without attempting to speak.

Mother Galloway showed Chevy back to the living room and continued drinking her tea as if she had not just visited her withering husband on his deathbed. "As you can see, my husband isn't able to answer your questions."

"But you can."

She nodded. "I can."

Chevy filled her in with what they had already learned. "Does Alex have another child?" he asked bluntly. The time for cordial formalities had long passed.

"That Carla creature was a real piece of work. After everything Alex did to make sure she had everything she needed to have a healthy baby."

Chevy wanted to remind her Alex had tucked his mistress away in Hannaford Valley to deliver what could have been his illegitimate child, but he let her finish uninterrupted.

"Once the baby was born Carla demanded Alex leave his wife and marry her. He couldn't, and wouldn't leave Sutton, of course. The wretched girl became more and more demanding. My husband couldn't handle her, so Alex was forced to come here and take care of business. Carla knew what she was in for, so she took the baby and ran."

"Do you know where she is?"

Mother Galloway took another sip of tea before answering, "I do."

"Where is she?"

She waved away the question. "It isn't important."

"What about the baby? Is it Alex's?"

"When my son died, she resurfaced demanding her portion of his estate—for the sake of her baby, she claimed. I knew better. I also know how women like her work. I've encountered my share of husband-stealers." She rolled her eyes in the direction of the ceiling, referring to her husband's indiscretions.

"The baby?" he asked again.

"I told Carla the only way she would see a dime of Alex's

money was to prove paternity to my satisfaction. She was on the first bus to Ohio, baby in tow. I told her there were ways to test paternity—even when the suspected father was deceased. She's a tough one, that Carla. She waited until the absolute last moment to confess the truth—the baby was not Alex's child."

"She could have been scared, and lying."

Mother Galloway shook her head no. "She identified the true father, and I had his paternity confirmed."

Chevy considered what this information would mean to Sutton and Greyson. "Where are Carla and the baby? Are they a threat to Sutton and Sierra?"

"No."

"How can you be so sure?"

"They are living in Ohio with me." After dropping the bombshell, she calmly sipped her tea. "Eddie seems to be quite fond of her and the baby." Eddie was her son by an affair.

"They're living with you? Why?"

"Alex is gone. Sierra is here in Hannaford Valley." She fingered the handle of her teacup, lost in thought. "Eddie and Carla are getting along well. It's my chance to right some wrongs with him."

Chevy didn't delve any further into her explanation. He had come to learn about his father. "What do you know about my father and Eileen Putnam?"

Mother Galloway snapped out of her deep reflection. "Your father had quite the reputation as a ladies' man when he moved to Hannaford. In those days there were only four black families in the valley, so we stuck together. Mr. Galloway became fast friends with your father—looking for a partner in crime, I suppose—but your father was devoted to your mother. When the first baby came along—Greyson—he worked hard to become a good husband and father." She shook her head, remembering. "We were all struggling, but your parents were worse off than most."

Chevy steered her back on track. "Eileen?"

"Jack still feels some loyalty to his friendship with my husband. Even after all these years. After everything that has happened…" Her eyes darted up and away from him. "I wasn't very kind to your mother then."

Chevy knew the town had shunned his poor parents, which had been exceptionally hard on his mother, who struggled to be accepted by the small town. Chevy had chosen to withdraw when he was labeled an outcast, but his mother fought for years until she became a welcomed member of the community.

"Jack found out about the pregnant girl and assumed the worst. Like I said, my husband couldn't control Carla. Alex was busy dividing his time between work, his family in Ohio, and Carla here. Jack became liaison between Carla and Eileen Putnam until she had the baby."

"Did my father have an affair with Eileen Putnam?"

Mother Galloway barked with laughter. "Jack?"

He pinned her with his eyes, conveying the seriousness of the question.

"Not that I'm aware of." She shook her head, recalling events of the past. "I can't imagine your father ever having an affair." She looked simultaneously sad and envious.

Chevy brazenly asked the obvious. "You and my father?"

She looked uneasy, but answered, "There was a time when I was very miserable in my marriage. Jack was the only one who would listen… Your father and I never had an affair. I won't deny it would have been welcome, but Jack loves

Marybeth." Her hard demeanor returned. "I learned to cope with my marital problems in my own way."

Chevy took a moment to digest what Mother Galloway had told him. "Are you telling me Pop didn't have an affair with Eileen Putnam? He was spending so much time with her because he was trying to protect Sutton from finding out about Carla's baby?"

"Noble, isn't he?" she mumbled over the rim of her teacup.

When no one else was protecting Sutton and Sierra, Pop had stepped up to the plate. "He risked his reputation and his marriage to help Sutton even before she became his daughter-in-law."

"Yes." Envy clearly tainted the word.

"This is why Alex so readily stepped in to *take care of* Eileen Putnam when Kirkland told him about Pop having an affair with her."

Immediately ready to defend her son, Mother Galloway's mouth tightened. "My son did what he had to do to control a silly waif who fell in love with him."

Chevy didn't want to dig up past problems. Sutton and Mother Galloway had made their peace. It wasn't his place to disrupt it. "You're sure about all of this?" he asked.

"I lived it. It was my life."

Chevy nodded. Her involvement had to be more than periphery. Mr. Galloway wasn't able to articulate a scheme from his bed. Someone had to keep all the wheels turning without everyone finding out what was going on. Mother Galloway was the only one crafty enough to pull it off. The fact that she had Carla and the baby living with her in Ohio was further evidence of the depth of her involvement.

"You're not covering for Pop?"

"Why would I do that?" She wasn't as noble as his father.

Chevy had heard enough. He stood and tugged on his hat. "Thank you for talking to me, Mother Galloway. No need to see me out."

Inside his truck, Chevy pulled out the cell phone he'd started carrying after Maddie's last phone message.

She'd sounded desolate. She had gone out in the world to understand her place in it, but she sounded lost and confused. He had held his desires at bay, allowing her to have the freedom to live her life the way she needed to live it. As the weeks rolled by, he wasn't feeling as generous with his understanding. Sooner or later, they'd have to make a final decision about the direction of their relationship. For Chevy, having a long-distance relationship with Maddie in California was like having no relationship at all. The problem being too big to tackle over a cell phone, Chevy turned his concentration on his family.

He made two phone calls, the first to Sutton. "The baby is not Alex's," he said when she answered.

She audibly exhaled.

"I need you to get everyone over to my parents' house."

"When?"

"Now."

The second phone call was to his parents. Mama answered. "Your sons are on the way over. Tell Pop."

"All right," she whimpered.

Chevy half expected the sheriff to be waiting when he arrived at his parents' home, but everything on the outside was quiet. He didn't wait for his brothers to arrive. He marched up to the door and used his spare key to enter. Pop had changed the phone number, but not the locks, which meant he had never intended on keeping them out of his life forever.

"Pop?" he called upon entering. Not receiving an answer,

he searched for his mother. "Mama?" He found her where he'd knew she'd be—the kitchen. Pots and pans were bubbling. Something was baking in the oven, filling the house with the smell of chocolate.

She rushed to him, pulling her into the soft warmth of a mother's hug. "We're going to have a big celebration when your brothers get here." Chevy wasn't so sure Pop would want to have a party after he was forced to have his life placed under a microscope. Mama examined him as if he were returning from war, asking a million questions about what had been happening in his life over the past six months.

"Mama, where's Pop?"

"He's in the den waiting. You can wait ten more minutes to talk to him. Sit with me. Tell me what's been going on in your life before your brothers get here."

Trying not to be distracted by the confrontation ahead, Chevy told his mother about the completion of the Ballantyne Wilderness Lodge and his plans for the nursing home.

"I'm so proud of you." She went on about the good he was doing for the community. "Don't look so embarrassed. A mother can brag about her children if she wants to. Now tell me about you and Maddie."

This news wasn't so good. He told her about the marathon and Maddie deciding to stay in San Diego. She asked about Mr. Ingram and who was caring for him in her absence, vowing to resume her church visits to keep an eye on him. She rubbed Chevy's arm. "Are you okay?"

"I couldn't make her come home. I tried."

"Then it's over between you?" She didn't wait for his answer. She moved to the stove to check on the bubbling pots. "You two were perfect for each other. She blossomed, and you opened up to the world. I hope you know what you're doing."

"What I'm doing?" he asked, a little offended. "I had no say in it. I was going to propose to Maddie in California."

She whipped around, her face shining with delighted surprise. She tempered her enthusiasm before going on. "I didn't know Maddie had so much power over you."

This made him bristle. He loved Maddie, but he was the man in their relationship.

"I mean, she barged into your life and made you fall in love with her, and then she just waltzes right out of it."

"She didn't play me. Maddie loves me. She just wants to experience life."

"And you were so controlling she had to move to the other side of the country to do it."

"I'm not controlling. Maddie has always been responsible for her parents. She went to college in Charleston, but had to come home right after graduation. She hadn't been out of the state until I took her to Virginia Beach."

"You gave her a taste of freedom and she turned on you."

"Maddie didn't turn on me," he defended. "Maddie did what she needed to do. I didn't like it at first—I don't like being separated from her now—but I support her decision. I'll always stand behind what Maddie feels she needs to do. Just like she's supported me through this whole thing with Pop. When I asked her out, she didn't hesitate to say yes. She ignored all the rumors and got to know me. I won't turn my back on her, and I resent you being so negative about the situation—like Maddie and I won't get past it."

His mother watched him with curious satisfaction. "She loves you as much as you love her. Don't let her get away."

"You took me right where you wanted to go," Chevy said. "You like Maddie and you want us to be together."

"I love Maddie." Mama turned back to the stove and continued cooking.

Greyson and Sutton arrived first with the rest of the Ballantyne family close behind, including Sierra and Courtney. Mama was in her glory, ushering everyone into the kitchen insisting they set up for a big reunion dinner. While they were distracted with catching up, Chevy pulled his brothers away and found their father in the den.

Pop was sitting in his favorite chair, listening to jazz made hard by the overzealous notes of a trumpet. They filed inside the den, Greyson and Kirkland taking a seat on the sofa. Chevy positioned himself between his brothers and his father where he'd been most of his life, anxious to put an end to the discord tearing their family apart. He set his feet firmly, crossing his arms over his chest.

"How much does Sutton know?" Pop asked without preliminaries.

"Everything." Greyson repeated the story Chevy had given them. "Was it worth hurting Mama to hide Alex's affair?"

"Alex has a way of sucking you into his deception," Kirkland answered as the best authority on the subject. Being Alex's friend had cost him. At its height the friendship threatened his relationship with Sutton, putting a strain on the family as everyone tried to remain neutral in their fight.

"At the time," Pop said, "I didn't think your mother would ever have to know. Sutton has been like a daughter to us. If I could save her the same humil'ation Alex's father caused his wife, I had to try. I didn't know Marbeth knew till you boys told me. She never said a word."

"What has Mama said about it all?" Chevy asked.

"I didn't tell your mother because I didn't want her in the middle. If I had known she was upset…I would have told her a long time ago. We talked. Everything's going to be okay be-tween us."

"Sutton knows everything now, and she's handling it well." A slow smile spread over Greyson's face. "We're trying to have a baby," he announced with great pride.

Pop looked somewhat relieved.

"Why didn't you just tell us this when we asked?" Kirkland wanted to know.

"Because you didn't ask." Pop looked at each in turn. "You started digging into my past. None of you were man enough to come to me and ask about me and Eileen."

They suffered his harsh words without a counterargument because he was right.

"Chevy was the only one willing to come directly to me with this. Even though it was after the fact. All you boys had to do was come to me and ask, but you went behind my back. I thought I had taught you better...I thought we had a better relationship than that."

"Pop." Chevy took a step forward, wedging himself be-tween his father and brothers. "You're right. We should have just come to you. We didn't, and we were wrong. You have to know we were looking out for Mama."

"It's the only reason I'm willing to forgive you."

Ignoring Pop's dislike for expressions of affection, and his uneasiness with it himself, Chevy stepped forward and posi-tioned himself for Pop's embrace. "I'm sorry, Pop."

Slowly, Pop extricated himself from his chair and stood, allowing Chevy to wrap his arms around him.

"Sorry, Pop," Greyson said, joining them.

Kirkland made up the final link. "Me too, Pop. Sorry."

A little while later, the entire family sat outside near the gazebo and had dinner together. There was so much catching up to do. Mama made plans to spoil her granddaughters, whom she had missed terribly. Both Greyson and Kirkland were thankful for the time they would have alone with their wives. Being surrounded by his family made Chevy feel almost whole again—except for the part of his heart Maddie held captive in San Diego.

It was nice to see Pop trying to maintain his stoic exterior when he was overjoyed to have them all together again. Chevy liked hearing his mother laugh as she fussed over providing the perfect meal for her family. Her roses were in full bloom, the fragrance bringing back childhood memories and conjuring up stories of the mischief they used to get into. For once, thanks to Maddie opening his heart, Chevy welcomed the sentimentality.

As nightfall came, they lounged in the backyard, their full bellies helping to make the mood more serene. Chevy watched the dynamics of the couples around him. The Ballantyne men were big into displays of affection—something that would have surprised Chevy years ago when they were into excess instead of true love. Sierra was at his side, forever his sidekick. Courtney toddled over and joined them. Chevy lay out on the grass, resting on his elbows as he watched the interactions around him. He wanted this—he needed this— and it was time he had it.

"I need your help," he announced after gathering his family around. "What I want you to do is radical, but I need you to do it without too many questions. Everyone has to be involved to make this work—from Courtney to Pop."

His family responded with unconditional agreement. Whatever he needed, they would do. They were a family, and the Ballantyne family stuck together through it all.

Chapter 28

San Diego

San Diego was made up of sunny days. Day after day, the sun shone with the only reprieve being the occasional rain shower. And Maddie was sick of it. Chevy had made her appreciate the magnificence of the seasons—the changing leaves creating new and unique scenery each year, and the beauty of a fresh snowfall. She ran down the beach, remembering her walks through the woods with Chevy as Placido and Porter pulled them along.

She missed the slow quiet living of Hannaford Valley. The cost of living here was much higher than Hannaford so she could only afford a building crammed between two others, making noise an unbearable factor of daily living. The city actually had a noise ordinance—as if people didn't know the value of serene evenings surrounded by family. The constant barking of dogs, buzzing of construction machinery, and roaring of big trucks was deafening. The only break she received was when she visited Richard's upscale neighborhood, or running along the beach. She headed home, the scenery becoming less rich as she jogged along.

Richard was out on a date, which meant she would have to suffer the heat made unbearable by the lack of air-conditioning. She took a long shower and slipped into a lightweight nightgown. She made a salad California style with lots of nuts and cranberries. She thought of the wonderful meals Chevy had cooked for her. California cuisine was good, but couldn't compare to the loving touch Chevy added.

Maddie lay across her bed in front of the window fan watching the television at her feet. A full stomach and vigorous exercise combined to help her drift off to sleep. It didn't take long for images of Chevy to assault her subconscious. He smiled in her dreams. They were always outside, running and playing like kids. The scenes never came to completion, something waking her before he could lower her to his bed and make love to her.

"Answer the door!" one of her neighbors shouted, rousing her. They must be tired of the noise pollution too.

Maddie stumbled out of bed, half asleep, to answer the obnoxious pounding at her door. She didn't know whether to be angry with Richard for his rude awakening, or be fearful something was wrong because his greeting was so uncharacteristic. She shook herself awake as she unlocked the door, prepared to handle each situation.

Maddie's eyes went wide. Chevy was standing at her door, his mouth set into a fretful scowl. He looked good, a welcome remembrance of home. He was dressed in dark jeans and a tight black T-shirt that stretched across the bulk of his chest muscles. White sneakers had replaced his boots, but the black Stetson remained.

She wasn't sure she could believe her eyes. She had been sleeping, dreaming of him.

"I've come to bring you home." He removed his hat, striking her speechless with the severity of his golden brown eyes.

She loved him more than she believed possible. She missed him, but didn't understand how much her body and mind needed him until he appeared at her door. Her heart pumped uncontrollably, making her head swim and her knees weak.

"I rented a car so if I have to hog-tie you to bring you back, I can—no airport security to interrupt my flow."

Maddie opened her mouth, but no words came.

"It's time to come back to me, Mandisa," Chevy added, and everything went black.

When Maddie came to she was in her bed. Chevy cradled her head in his lap, pressing a cold cloth to her forehead. It took a second for her vision to come into clear focus. She reached up and held his chin in her palm. "Is it you?"

He smiled, displaying a perfect row of white teeth behind lips designed for hours of kissing. "It's me, Mandisa."

"I love you."

"I love you, too. You fainted."

"When I saw you," she added with a smile. "I shouldn't have left you."

"You did what you needed to do. Now it's time to come home."

For the first time since leaving home, she admitted the truth. "I don't like it here—not without you."

He pressed the cloth to the back of her neck. "It'll make things go much smoother."

"What things?"

"Taking you home. Everyone's waiting."

"When you take me home, will you take me back?"

He gave a curt shake of his head. "I never let you go."

She tried to sit up, but he pressed her back down into his lap. "I don't want you passing out on me again."

She wrapped her arms around his waist, burying her face in his stomach. He released the knot of hair at the back of her neck and massaged her scalp. She melted, relishing his touch.

"How quickly can you pack?" he asked.

"Very."

"Pack tonight, tie up loose ends in the morning, and then we're out of here."

She wanted to know about her father. She asked about his family, and if everything had been settled with his father. He laid her back on her pillow while he told her about mysteries that began when they were kids and infiltrated their adult lives. The ending was happy, and everyone had gained a greater appreciation of family bonds.

He left the bed to crank up the fan. "It's hot."

The heat had risen for Maddie too, but it had nothing to do with the temperature outside.

He moved to the tiny kitchen and brought her a glass of ice water. He poured one for himself and rejoined her on the bed. "Are you sure you're okay? Do you need to go to the hospital?"

"I'm fine. The heat, and the shock of seeing you at the door." She sat up slowly, sliding over to make room for him in the bed.

Chevy fit his large frame in the bed, raising his knees to accommodate the length of his legs. He stared at the television, sipping at his water to mask his uneasiness. She wondered if they would be able to pick up where they had left off, or if they would have to begin the dating ritual again.

His presence filled her with heady desire. She watched him, paying attention to the small details—the way his chest rose when he took in a breath, the lazy blinking of his long lashes, the pucker of his mouth as he gulped down the last of his water. She reached out and grabbed a loose curl at his shoulder. He turned to her, his eyes asking a hundred questions. She answered by snuggling up next to him, placing her palm firmly against his chest and pressing her mouth to his.

When their lips touched, Chevy grasped her arms—a thirsty man being given a glass of water—and pinned her to the bed beneath him. In the madness, Chevy's clothes were removed and Maddie's nightgown was discarded.

She kissed him long and hard, showing him how much he had been missed. All this time, everything she was looking for was right in Hannaford Valley. She coaxed him to unlock his heart and trust her again.

He'd come ready for their reunion, and prepared his towering erection to seek her heat. He suspended himself on one arm as he positioned himself at her slick folds. He rocked his hips, fitting himself inside, teaching her to accommodate his size again. Her body remembered with unbridled fondness, stretching to take every inch he offered. She whispered lifelong promises in his ear as he slipped inside. She bent her knees and lifted herself to meet his advancements. She pressed until the wiry hair framing his penis scratched her burgeoning mound.

Chevy took on her weight in the palms of his hands, bringing her bottom up into each of his thrusts. He pumped hard, and she responded with wild lunges of her hips. She moaned as her body tightened around him, encouraging him to repeat the strokes that brought her to the edge. His body became rigid, signaling his imminent climax. They came together, both shouting about the glorious feeling they received when the person they loved gave them an orgasm.

"Take it to the Motel 6 down the street," Maddie's next door neighbor shouted, pounding on the wall.

Chevy collapsed on the bed, dragging Maddie onto his chest, and the bedrail snapped. The man downstairs banged on the ceiling, and they erupted in laughter.

Maddie awoke in the middle of the night with Chevy's lips on her lower back. He used his tongue to tickle the dimple at the bottom of her spine. His fingers trailed the crease of her bottom, lingering over unexplored caverns before traveling lower and dipping into a pool of wetness. There were no outside noises this late at night, only the sound of the rotating fan blades and Chevy's kisses on her spine. The perspiration covering their nude bodies made them sticky, and there was an erotic sound every time he pulled away, separating them.

"Are you awake?" he whispered into the darkness.

"Yes." She folded her arms underneath her forehead.

"Go up on all fours."

She smiled, remembering some of the sensual tricks he had showed her. Teaching her there were hundreds ways of making love, and none would be boring with him. She moved to her hands and knees, dropping her head to watch his shadow as he positioned himself beneath her.

At this vantage point, Chevy's mouth was in perfect alignment for his oral exploration. With sure hands, he parted her and with a confident tongue, he lapped at her taut bud. The first flick of his tongue threatened to flatten her, but his shoulder came up, nudging her back into position. He continued his unrelenting pursuit. Quick, darting strikes with his tongue threatened to destroy her sanity. She was shimmying her hips, and making animalistic noises sure to wake her neighbors. She fought off the rising climax, wanting it to last much longer. Chevy undermined her authority over her own body, by pushing one long finger inside her. He added a firm pressure to the pucker between her crease, and the sensations skyrocketed, radiating out from her core, saturating her body in ecstasy.

Chevy didn't let her rest. He moved inside her until the early hours of the morning, ignoring the neighbors' warning that they would call the police. He turned her body inside out with pleasure, making up for the time they'd been apart. He made love to her, telling her how beautiful she was and how much he had missed her. He smiled mischievously when she claimed to have had enough, and showed her new tricks he could do to make her scream. He begged and he demanded—he gave and he took. When finally his manhood sided with her and refused to go on, he wrapped her in his arms and went to sleep, promising more in the morning.

"I have something to show you." Chevy appeared under the archway of the kitchen, fresh from bed, still nude.

"I wonder what," Maddie said, turning from the stove. She was dressed and anxious to tie up loose ends so she could go home. "Can we eat breakfast first?"

"You're insatiable, woman." He went into her only closet and came out with his suitcase. Sometime during the night he had retrieved it from the car. Most of the night was a sexy haze, and Maddie didn't remember him leaving the apartment. He dug through the bag, finding a small leather case. After pulling on his underwear, he joined her at the table consuming the small kitchen.

"I have to keep my strength up." He winked at her before shoveling eggs into his mouth.

"What's in the bag?"

"Insatiable and impatient." He went into the bag and pulled out an envelope from Photomart. He handed it to her as he explained. "There were some things I needed to do, too. Being apart from you gave me more time to think than I'll ever need again, so don't ever leave me. I've been so devoted to defending animals and the environment, I wasn't seeing the forest for the trees."

Maddie groaned at the corny analogy.

"I'm not a poet," he reminded her. "Watching you with your father helped me realize there are people out there not able to fight for themselves. The seniors in Hannaford Valley don't have adequate, affordable housing. Doc Carter can only do so much, and with most living on limited incomes, they can't get the medical care they need." He nodded toward the envelope she was holding. "Take a look."

Excitedly, Maddie tore open the envelope. Inside were photos of the old nursing home with construction equipment surrounding it. She flipped through the pictures to see Chevy standing with the mayor and Todd during a ribbon-cutting ceremony. In the background was a sign reading BALLANTYNE RETIREMENT VILLAGE.

"What did you do?" she asked, astonished by how much he had accomplished while she floundered, trying to find herself in the world.

"The nursing home is being completely refurbished to provide better living conditions. We broke ground on the retirement village earlier this month. There will be individual assisted-living housing, a new apartment building, and a senior activity center. Kirkland put me together with a company who has a great plan. There's going to be a walking garden modeled after the botanical garden in Charleston.

"Todd has agreed to oversee the medical center. No one will be turned away because of inability to pay. The clinic is going to operate on grants and individual donations. Housing will be based on income level. Greyson has called on all his old corporate friends to help. My mother is starting a special volunteer program at the church focused on helping older adults in the community."

"This is wonderful. If something like this had been available for my father—"

"If not for you, *this* wouldn't be happening. I witnessed what you were struggling to do. People who have the means to help have to help in any way we can."

Maddie left her chair and sat in Chevy's lap, offering him a kiss. "You are the best—most wonderful…" The tears threatened. She buried her face in the crook of his neck until the emotional wave passed. "I love you, Chevy."

Chevy had everything planned. Once they settled her business, and she stopped by Richard's to thank him and say good-bye, they were on the freeway, heading cross-country to Hannaford Valley, West Virginia, where Maddie belonged. She would miss Richard, but he had gotten his promotion and would be traveling across the country building business. She would see him again.

"California is just too big for me," she told Chevy as they motored down the highway.

"We're going to get this out of your system."

"What do you mean?"

"We're going home the long way. We're stopping to see every tourist attraction we can. The next time you feel the need to see the world, it'll be a planned vacation with a guaranteed return date."

Chevy hadn't exaggerated. They crossed twenty-five hundred miles over the next two weeks. Chevy gave her the adventure of a lifetime, as they visited Phoenix, Santa Fe, Texas, Oklahoma City, Missouri, Illinois, Indiana, and Kentucky. They drove during the day, stopping to visit interesting tourist attractions. They checked into a hotel in the evening when Maddie reached over and stroked Chevy's thigh. She saw parts of the country she would never forget while building memories that would stay with her until she was old and gray.

"We'll be home by early afternoon," Chevy announced as he held her in his arms.

She pulled the sheet up to cover their naked bodies. "I'll be happy to get home and see my father, but I'm sad this trip has to end. It'll feel strange sleeping in separate houses after being together every night for two weeks."

"We need to talk about that."

"I don't like the tone of your voice." She lifted her head to look down at him.

"What tone?"

"Tentative."

She placed her hand on his chest. His heart strummed beneath her fingers. He held her around the waist while stretching to the leather bag on the nightstand. He placed the bag on his stomach as he searched for what he needed.

"Chevy, I don't think I can go again. You're wearing my body out."

He laughed, overflowing with male pride and vanity over his skills. "Calm yourself." He pulled out a ring box, familiar to her from their last day together at the marathon. "I want you to marry me, Mandisa."

A slow smile spread across her face as her heart warmed. "Aren't you going to get down on one knee?"

"You blew that. I'm not asking anymore. I'm *telling* you we're getting married."

"Really?" This was reminiscent of their conversation at the Purple Party about her Vanity impersonation.

"Yes, really. I'm prepared to do this shotgun wedding style. When we get back, we're getting married."

"When we get back?"

"As soon as."

"I have to discuss this with my father, and I have to plan, and—"

"I've already asked your father permission." At least he had done something the traditional way. "The planning has been taken out of your hands, too." He pushed her hair over her shoulder. "This is going to happen. The only control you have over the situation is *how* it's going to happen. You can walk down the aisle in a pretty dress with flowers, or I can throw you over my shoulder and haul you down the aisle kicking and screaming. I'm prepared either way."

She gave him her best pout. "Well, I guess I have no say-so."

"Not really."

"Oh!" She socked him in the arm.

"Ow." He rubbed his shoulder. "You messed it up the last time. Don't blame me."

She gave him the evil eye.

"Damn." He threw back the sheets and rounded the bed.

She scooted to the edge of the bed, hopping with excitement.

Chevy went down on his knees, placing the ring box on the floor next to him, and taking her hands in his. He looked up at her with earnest, loving eyes. "Mandisa, I love you. I want to spend the rest of my life with you. I want you to have my kids. I want—"

"Too canned," she interrupted.

He growled, took a deep breath, and spoke from his heart, his eyes softening with every word. "Mandisa, I love you. When I think about my future, I see us growing old together with a bunch of kids around us. I want to roll over every night for the rest of my life and find you lying next to me. I can't imagine making love with anyone else." He paused. "I can't exist without you in my life, because the truth is I almost died when you left me."

"Chevy—"

"Mandisa, will you marry me?"

"Chevy, I thought about you every day while I was in San Diego. Nothing makes sense without you. I want to marry you more than anything in the world."

He reached for the ring box, flipped the lid, and slid the most perfect ring Maddie had ever seen onto her finger. The diamond and platinum ring completed their circle, giving their relationship the ultimate conclusion—a new beginning.

Chapter 29

When Maddie arrived in Hannaford Valley the next day, she was surprised to find how serious Chevy had been about getting married immediately. They drove directly to the mayor's house to obtain the license. Chevy explained there was no waiting period and blood test requirements, so they could be married right after signing the license.

"Where are we going? I have to see my father before we run off and get married!"

"You're not getting out of my sight, Mandisa." He glanced at her, enjoying her nervous energy.

"Where are you taking me, Chevy Ballantyne?"

"To my cabin. Relax."

When they arrived at his cabin, she relaxed with warm memories of the times they had shared there.

"Who do all these cars belong to?"

He cut the engine and turned to her. "Don't freak out."

"What's going on? What did you do?"

"We're going to get married."

"Yes." She touched the band on her finger.

"Right now."

"What?"

"My family is here. Your father is here. I gave them specific instructions on what to do before I drove to California. They've had three weeks to get it all together. Sutton and Maddie picked your wedding dress. My mother planned the reception. My father hired the reverend and arranged for us to get the license this morning."

"I can't just go inside and get married. I have to make arrangements for my father."

"Did I forget to tell you about that?" His coy smile was endearing, but Maddie was still reeling from the reality of being a married woman within the hour. "Your father is moving in here with us until I can finish building the *father-in-law* suite I'm adding off the living room."

She craned her neck to see evidence of construction. Chevy was always doing something to perfect the cabin, so she hadn't noticed the lumber covered in a black tarp next to the house.

"And the wedding won't be inside. It's out back in a clearing near the woods where we walked in the winter."

"Chevy—"

"You said you would marry me. I made you promise this morning when you were digging your nails into my back. Are you backing out on me now?"

"No, but—"

He leaned across the seat and pressed his mouth against hers, ravishing her with a kiss that left her speechless. "Mandisa?"

"You're amazing."

Minutes later, Maddie was walking down the aisle, laughing as Toby Keith sang "What Goes On in Mexico Stays in Mexico." With her father's permission, Greyson escorted her down the aisle—one arm wrapped around hers, and a shotgun nestled in his other arm. Chevy's antics set the tone for the wedding, and although it was wrapped in romance, there were plenty of smiles and lots of laughs. She kissed her dad hello before Todd pushed his wheelchair in line with the chairs. Greyson handed her off to Chevy, who stood tall and proud in an ivory tuxedo.

They stood underneath an archway made of fresh roses as the reverend read their vows. Everyone important to Maddie was there. Her aunt sat next to her father, wiping tears with a white handkerchief. All of the Ballantynes were there, and Sierra sang a tear-jerking rendition of Maddie's favorite hymn. When they said, "I do," Chevy hauled her close, bending her backward with the force of his kiss. They kicked off the reception with the newlyweds dancing to Prince's "Adore."

"How did I do?" Chevy asked.

"It's beautiful. Everything is wonderful." She crooked her finger and had him bring his ear to her lips. "Although I'm feeling more in the mood for 'Do Me, Baby.'"

Chevy threw his head back and roared with laughter. "I think you'll love the honeymoon."

Chapter 30

The Ballantyne saga, ten years later

Chevy gave his mother her first blood Ballantyne grand-child—and then he gave her four more. Chevy Jr. arrived after Chevy and Maddie spent two years traveling. During their honeymoon on the Nile, Chevy realized he enjoyed seeing the world as much as his wife did. It had been Maddie who told him it was time to settle down at home and start their family.

A year after Chevy Jr. arrived came Owen. When Derek came two years after that, Maddie began to worry she was re-peating Mama's history—having a houseful of rambunctious boys. She became a full-time mother, giving up her job at the library. A year later, as soon as Derek was out of diapers, Lind-sey was born. While celebrating their seventh wedding anni-versary, they decided four children weren't enough and Chantal was conceived.

With five kids, Maddie's father, and two old dogs, they de-cided their family was big enough. They had to leave the cabin after Owen was born, moving into a house especially built to accommodate a growing family. They still slipped away to the cabin to be alone together. They remained near the rest of their family in Hannaford Valley, surrounded by mountains, fresh air, and wonderful neighbors.

At eighteen, with a golden voice and gorgeous face, Sierra was giving Greyson fits. The boys were hanging around, but Sierra's focus was on her singing career. The latest was that she was going to compete in a big televised contest in Charleston. If she won, she'd get a recording contract with a major label. She had already appeared in five commercials, and had offers for more. It took all of Sutton's patience to calm Greyson's nerves. Maddie had no idea how Sutton was handling three kids, a husband, and a flourishing family law practice.

Cassidy and Maddie ran in fifteen more marathons after the San Diego race. They both had one medal for finishing first before they retired and settled down to care for their families. Cassidy's artwork still graced the covers of romance novels, while Kirkland focused most of his time on the Ballantyne Wilderness Lodge. Courtney was adorable, positioning herself as Sierra's manager. The two were inseparable. They remained in Kirkland's childhood home. They were a cute family, proving age truly did not matter when it came to being in love.

With time, the Ballantynes found a way to extricate themselves from the antics of the Galloway family. Mr. Galloway passed away years ago, and Mother Galloway spent most of her time in Ohio with her illegitimate son, Eddie, and his wife, Carla. Every now and again, Maddie would hear pieces of gossip about how she was faring in the big city.

"Boys, settle down." Chevy's presence was immediately felt when he entered the living room.

Maddie lived for the moment when her husband came

home after a long day of work. She knew he would tell the boys to straighten up, even if they weren't being unruly—he was a hard disciplinarian like his father. After he spoke with the boys, he'd find Lindsey and Chantal in their room and smother them in hugs and kisses. Next he always checked on her father, asking if he needed anything. Over the years, the effects of the stroke had taken their toll and he was now confined to his wheelchair. He told Maddie every day that he had lived a full, rich life and she should not mourn him when he passed.

"Mandisa," Chevy breathed.

She turned away from the stove, opening her arms to receive him. "How was your day?"

He made her melt with one of his kisses. Over the years, the potency of Chevy's kisses had increased, making her a lifetime addict. "I missed you," Chevy answered when he pulled away. "How did it go around here?"

"Good."

"I got a call from Junior's teacher again." He shook his head. "He's growing up to be a real knucklehead."

"None of my children are knuckleheads, excuse you."

"Well, that *nonknucklehead* is on punishment for a week."

"Chevy—"

He covered her lips with his finger. "You spoil the kids." He replaced his finger with his lips. "You look tired." He traced her hairline near her ear. "Don't cook. Let's order pizza. I'll stay home tomorrow to help you with Dad and Chantal."

And this was why her love for Chevy grew every day. He saw to her needs, and did whatever he could do to make things better for her.

He took a seat at the kitchen table, and she joined him with the phone book.

"We should divide the kids up between Mama and Greyson and go out of town for a long weekend. Dad can stay with Kirkland until we get back." He took the phone book and began flipping the pages. "What?"

"Don't you 'what' me." She smiled. "What are you up to, Chevy Ballantyne?"

He smiled. "You got me."

She moved into his lap, wrapping her arms around his neck.

"It's been a while since we've been on a trip."

"You wouldn't happen to be saying this because it's our anniversary this weekend."

"Maybe." He nuzzled her neck. "Anywhere you want to go, just tell me. I'll make it happen."

"You've already made me as happy as any woman could ever be."

"What? Are you talking about last night? Because that was nothing. There's a lot more in store."

She swatted at his chest. "You're terrible."

"I was thinking we could add one more to the bunch. You'd hardly notice. What's the difference between five and six?"

"Stop it! No! You aren't serious. Are you?"

He studied her for a long time. "What do you think?"

"I think five is enough."

"Okay, we stop at five."

"We found each other. We have a strong extended family. Our kids are great. We've fulfilled our destiny."

ABOUT THE AUTHOR

Kimberley White is a Detroit native who received her education in the Michigan school system. She is a registered nurse with sixteen years of experience in trauma and critical care, and is currently pursuing her master's in nursing. She uses her nursing experience in her writing to address topics such as domestic violence, hypertension, and sexual harassment in an entertaining and informative manner.